The Cardiff Lockdown Murders

Stephen Puleston

ABOUT THE AUTHOR

Stephen Puleston was born and educated in Anglesey, North Wales. He graduated in theology before training as a lawyer. The Cardiff Lockdown Murders is his fourth novel in the Inspector Marco series

www.stephenpuleston.co.uk
Facebook:stephenpulestoncrimewriter

OTHER NOVELS

Inspector Drake Mysteries

Brass in Pocket
Worse than Dead
Against the Tide
Dead on your Feet
A Time to Kill
Written in Blood
Nowhere to Hide
A Cold Dark Heart
Prequel Novella– Ebook only - Devil's Kitchen

Inspector Marco Novels

Speechless
Another Good Killing
Somebody Told Me
Prequel Novella– Ebook only -Dead Smart

Copyright © Puleston Publishing Limited
All rights reserved.

ISBN: 9798329964165

In memory of my mother
Gwenno Puleston

Chapter 1

In normal times I would have balked at the instructions from Superintendent Cornock to attend the Cardiff Domestic Violence Taskforce forum by complaining that a detective inspector should be focusing on more important matters. But the coronavirus pandemic had changed everything. I had spent months getting to grips with a new kind of policing – shoplifting was down, burglaries didn't happen and it had become a running joke in the Southern Division of the Wales Police Service that our regular burglars must have feared the virus more than the prospect of being caught. Interviews were conducted in rooms kitted out with screens and video links for non-serious matters. Bottles of hand sanitising gel seemed to occupy every spare surface around Queen Street police station, and my desk drawer was full of standard-issue WPS face masks.

One weekend I'd been seconded to work with the roads policing unit, checking on vehicles driving over the Severn Bridge from England into Wales. Reminding people that the regulations about travelling away from home were different in Wales. This was met with utter incredulity, but threatening to issue fines soon sent the visitors heading back over the border.

Sitting in my room I could hear the gentle throbbing from the air-conditioning units of the shops and offices of the city centre. Cardiff was gradually getting back to normal with restaurants reopening, and shoppers returning to the arcades and malls. But one thing that hadn't remained the same during the recent pandemic was the level of domestic violence. The press reports highlighting the impact such crimes had on families and communities had been dwarfed by messages to stay at home and the alarming numbers of deaths from the virus.

The briefing memorandum that Superintendent Cornock had sent me was sitting on a corner of my desk. Long overdue appraisals and case reviews from two other inspectors in Southern Division were taking my time but I kept glancing over at the documentation, knowing I needed to read it in more detail before my meeting later that morning.

Lydia Flint rapped her knuckles on the door to my office. 'Coffee, boss?'

I nodded my agreement and followed her through into the small kitchen. Lydia was always deferential, but she had a steely determination. Her long auburn hair had been cut short, and it gave her wide mouth and full lips more prominence. She flicked on the electric kettle and heaped coffee into two mugs.

'Have you read that briefing memorandum?'

'Top of my list.'

She pulled a face as though my attempt at humour was unwelcome.

'Domestic violence is a scourge on society. Did you know that New Zealand has the highest level of domestic violence anywhere in the world? The police are called to an incident once every four minutes. Hard to believe, isn't it?'

Lydia poured the hot water and added milk to both steaming drinks. It was the time of day when I could have reached for a cigarette. If I was to stick to my rule of only five per day, I'd have to pace the next four carefully.

I headed back to my office, coffee mug in hand. 'Once I finish the reports on my desk I'll get around to it.'

'You need to *read* it, sir.'

Lydia had a way of emphasising certain words and 'sir' at the end of her last comment implied that I should know better than to be flippant about paperwork and strategic meetings. So, when I got back to my room, I deposited my drink on a coaster and reached for Superintendent Cornock's memorandum.

An inspector from the serious crime team, who normally attended these forum events, had been transferred to West Wales at short notice. I hoped that my presence would be temporary, and I had suggested to Cornock it would be much better if he found an officer more suited to the politics of committees: false, insincere smiles and dubious handshakes. 'I didn't know you had so much self-awareness,' Cornock had replied, giving me an uncertain frown.

I had rolled my eyes, shrugged my shoulders.

Getting to know myself had come at a heavy price. I was dry now but when I had stared down into the bottom of an emptied glass the damage I was causing to myself and my family had been the last thing on my mind.

Lydia answering the telephone in the open plan office that doubled as an Incident Room interrupted my rumination and I turned my attention back to the memorandum. The first part was an internal document distributed to various senior officers of the Wales Police Service. The name of a chief superintendent headed the list and I knew he was a determined individual dedicated to his career. The full forum meeting with the rest of the 'stakeholders' was going to be in a few days' time, and the names of two prominent politicians were the only ones I recognised.

The statistics were sobering. The cost to the Welsh economy from domestic violence was measured in the millions. The impact on families and children in particular was impossible to calculate. Witnessing violence against a mother could have long term implications on a young child's mind. It was the repeated assaults by the same man against the same woman, often the mother of several of his children, that made me realise how deep-seated the problem actually was.

It reminded me of the frustration I had felt as a young uniformed officer called regularly to homes where men had assaulted their wives or partners. A sickening familiarity to the excuses for their behaviour compounded the feeling of helplessness. The bruised face of a woman standing in the hallway of her home as she cowered behind a muscle-toned man challenging me to do something had stayed with me for a long time. After a standoff I'd left when the older officer with me had tugged at my sleeve, defusing the tense situation, but not calming my rising anger.

I turned back to the reports and read a dizzying array of statistics about repeat offenders and how the root cause had to be tackled before it reached the point at which criminal offences took place. Lydia's earlier mild reprimand focused my attention on finishing the report in good time. I even committed to memory some of the statistics, hoping I'd have an opportunity to regurgitate them and impress my colleagues.

Before leaving I visited the bathroom. Staring into the mirror after washing my hands I decided I needed a haircut – strands of my unruly hair were brushing my collar. I'd chosen a powder blue button-down shirt and my herringbone jacket complemented the dark grey chinos. The chief superintendent would be in full uniform that morning, so I drew a comb through my hair and adjusted my shirt, making certain it sat neatly at my waistband.

Back in my office I grabbed the memorandum and made for the conference room in good time for the meeting.

Conversation drifted from the open door and I could hear the booming voice of Chief Superintendent Harper. Inside I helped myself to some water. I couldn't stand the stale coffee served in the flasks with a push-button top.

'John,' Harper said. 'Superintendent Cornock told me you volunteered to represent the WPS contingent on the Cardiff Domestic Violence Taskforce forum.'

There wasn't a trace of irony in his voice or on his face.

'I hope I can be of help.'

'Let me introduce you to the other members of the team.'

There were two detective sergeants who'd been part of a team I had run on a murder investigation several years previously. Three young detective constables were introduced in turn and I nodded politely excusing myself for not being good with names. They each smiled courteously.

Alison Swan was the last to be introduced and she gave me a warm smile and, although her upper lip was a little thin and her eyes were set slightly apart, she had an intense warmth. She held my gaze a fraction longer than she needed to.

'Detective Constable Swan was recently transferred from Eastern Division,' Harper announced. 'She was on the specialist domestic violence team in Newport. After the spike in domestic violence during the pandemic we'll need all the specialist expertise we can get.'

'That's very kind of you, sir,' Alison replied.

Harper busied himself with calling the meeting to order getting us all to sit down around the table. I glanced over at Alison. She gave me another warm smile. Perhaps representing the WPS on the forum wasn't going to be such a bad idea after all.

Harper's voice filled the room as he galloped through the various minutes from the previous meeting before announcing the reason for my presence. I nodded gravely.

I had been listening to Harper for a few minutes when the mobile in my jacket pocket began to vibrate. I debated whether to ignore it and carry on listening. Harper had a reputation for not welcoming interruptions. I let the vibrations run to their end, only for them to restart immediately. Surreptitiously I pulled the handset from my pocket and read the message.

Inspector Marco. Please respond. Attendance required at murder scene.

I scrambled to my feet mumbling apologies to Harper as I left.

Chapter 2

I pounded down the stairs towards my office as I tried to maintain a conversation with operational support. 'Give me all the details you've got.'

'I'll send you what I can, Inspector,' the irritated voice announced.

'Do you have the names of the officers present at the scene and have the CSI team been notified?'

The line went dead and I cursed under my breath. Making for my room I called over to Lydia, 'Get your coat.' My mobile bleeped with the postcode and an address in an industrial estate to the west of the city. 'There's a body.'

Lydia was ready when I returned, shrugging on my jacket.

After negotiating the narrow corridors, we reached the stairwell and took the stairs to the car park. Queen Street police station was an old building and, by now, unsuitable for modern policing but it was in the middle of Cardiff and redevelopment proposals had fizzled out long ago. Pushing open the door I pointed the remote at my Mondeo, deactivating the alarm. We dashed over and within seconds I was accelerating around Callaghan Square and then down the A4160 west towards Leckwith.

Overhearing Lydia's one-sided conversations was frustrating as she tried to pin down more details about the circumstances of the scene. And being delayed at traffic lights only ramped up the tension. The first few hours after the discovery of a body were always the most valuable. It gave us the best opportunity of gathering evidence and then making an arrest. I broke the speed limits and flashed my lights often enough to make clear my urgency as I hammered the car through the suburbs of the city.

It took longer than expected to drive down Penarth Road and, when a dustbin lorry came to a halt, blocking the road ahead of us, I cursed and shouted. Blasting the horn had no effect on the men dragging wheelie bins to the rear of the vehicle. I hoped the officers at the scene were doing their best to preserve the evidence and make certain it wasn't contaminated.

Once we were clear of the obstruction I pressed on until Lydia raised a hand pointing to a junction. 'It's down that road, boss.'

I indicated right and slowed. After a couple of hundred metres Lydia looked to her left down another junction and spotted a police car parked across the road. I braked and after reversing drove the short distance before parking. There was no sign of a scientific support vehicle or the CSI team.

We left the car and found the entrance of a builders' merchant. We pushed our warrant cards at the two young police officers who looked visibly pleased to see us.

'He's behind that wheelie bin,' one of the officers said tipping his head over my shoulder.

I turned and saw another officer standing quite still, feet wide apart, near where his colleague had gesticulated.

'Who found the body?' I said.

'One of the staff at the office. She noticed the bin had been moved from its position the night before and thought it was a bit odd.'

'We'll need to talk to her in due course.'

I turned to Lydia. 'Let's take a look.'

The body of a man in his mid-forties had been dumped behind the wheelie bin on top of fragments of pallets and odd bits of timber. I wasn't going to do anything to disturb the crime scene – preserving evidence was the realm of the CSI team – but I would need to know the identity of the dead man soon enough. There could be a family worried about his absence.

There were no pools of blood around the place. My initial impressions suggested the body had been dumped after being killed elsewhere. And, if that were the case, it would make our job that much harder.

The sound of a vehicle parking nearby took my

attention. I straightened and realised the scientific support vehicle had arrived. Alvine Dix emerged and strode over towards me. Working with her was always a challenge but she was the most experienced crime scene manager in Cardiff, probably the world, if you believed her self-confidence.

'So, what have you got, Marco?'

'And good morning to you too, Alvine.'

'No time for pleasantries. Let's get on with it.'

I nodded towards the wheelie bin. 'The staff from the builders' merchant discovered a body. I can't see any blood, but he looks badly beaten.'

'I hope you haven't been contaminating the scene,' Alvine narrowed her eyes. It was designed to send a shiver of fear through any reasonable person, but I'd seen it so many times I was accustomed to it.

'You know me better than that.'

'Don't give me any of your bullshit.'

'We'll need an identification as soon as.'

Alvine ignored me and gesticulated for the two crime scene investigators hauling equipment from the van to get started. She paced over towards the bin barking instructions to the two CSIs in her slipstream.

'Charming as usual,' Lydia said in a hushed tone.

'You know what she's like – it's nothing personal. Let's go and talk to the person who found the body.'

Inside, the manager led us to a room near the reception where a woman, her face the colour of stale bread, sat sipping water by a table. She gave us a blank, lifeless sort of look as we entered.

'This is Valerie,' her boss said. 'She found the body this morning.'

I sat on one of the chairs by the table and Lydia did likewise before explaining to Valerie that we hoped she could help us with our inquiry. She shared an incredulous glance between Lydia and me clearly unable to comprehend what had happened.

'I don't know. I don't know,' was all she said.

After a few minutes it was clear Valerie had seen nothing of significance and she kept repeating that she had never seen a dead body before. The other members of staff were equally unhelpful, and we left telling Valerie another officer would take a detailed statement in due course – if they could get anything useful from her.

By now the pathologist was busy at work. Alvine Dix stood a few yards away staring at him intently. She'd probably given him a lecture about contaminating the crime scene despite his one-piece plastic suit and years of experience.

I knew Paddy McVeigh well enough to know he wouldn't be fazed by Alvine Dix. After finishing, he moved away from the corpse, nodded to Alvine, said nothing, and walked over to Lydia and me.

'Good morning, John.' Paddy still had the warm Irish accent of his childhood. 'Your man was beaten repeatedly or possibly even run over by a car.'

'Any idea how long he's been dead?'

'I'll have a better idea at the post-mortem, but I'd guess at least eight to ten hours.'

Alvine shouted over, 'We've got his identification.' She held up a plastic evidence pouch with a driving licence and a wallet. I joined her and read the name of Frank Armsby and an address in Whitchurch in the north of the city. 'Now if you don't mind, everyone else can bugger off and leave this place to me and my team. And that includes all the staff at the builders' merchant.'

The manager moaned about the damage to the business that forcing the premises to close would have, but I told him he had to follow Alvine's instructions to the letter. I warned him the crime scene investigators would be at the site for the rest of the day. Hopefully there'd be some preliminary results by the evening and the post-mortem tomorrow would provide useful evidence too.

Half an hour later we pulled up to the pavement outside Armsby's home. It looked like any other semi in Cardiff. The front garden had been paved over. Tufts of grass and weeds pushed their way along the cracks of the surface. An old wooden fence lined the drive that led to a garage at the rear. The house had UPVC windows and a burgundy-coloured door. Lydia took a call from operational support confirming that Armsby hadn't been reported missing.

If there was a Mrs Armsby she was going to get one hell of a shock when we arrived on her doorstep. Lydia held up the plastic pocket Alvine had given us with the key recovered from Armsby's jacket.

'I wonder if he's got any family?' I stepped towards the door. 'Only one way to find out.'

The bell that rang inside sounded ordinary, the sort any suburban semi-detached property would use. No response. No sound of a radio playing in the kitchen or television in the sitting room. Lydia then used the key and the door squeaked open.

'Hello, this is the Wales Police Service. Is anybody at home?' I called out.

Nobody responded.

We entered the house and I poked my head into the sitting room at the front, its venetian blinds tightly closed. Two leather sofas, a large television and an expensive-looking surround sound system filled the space. No picture or prints hanging on the wall and no cupboards with books or family knick-knacks.

At the rear a conservatory had been added which led out onto the garden. It doubled as a dining room, with a seating area to take advantage of the sunshine in the glazed area. Lydia peeked inside a cupboard filled with a selection of drinks bottles.

The kitchen was equally functional. The usual kettle and toaster, and a coffee machine, and alongside it a metal stand with a stack of different coloured pods.

'It is very ordinary,' Lydia said after closing a cupboard door that had exposed packets of cereal, dried fruit and tins of beans.

'It looks like he lives on his own.'

On the first floor we found Frank Armsby's study, converted from one of the bedrooms at the rear. Two enormous screens dominated a bespoke desk that filled one side of the room. Stationery was organised neatly underneath one end of the desk alongside a printer and the computer.

I called operational support and arranged for a team to remove Armsby's computer. Even if it was locked with a password the technical boffins could access anything without too much difficulty. And once Armsby's mobile phone had been dusted and checked by the CSI team the history of his calls could be checked too.

'He was an accountant, boss,' Lydia announced, reading from a file of papers.

My mobile rang and I noticed Superintendent Cornock's number. 'I understand you've identified the victim as a Frank Armsby. Get back here. There's something you should know.'

Chapter 3

After rubbing a generous dollop of sanitising gel over my hands from the dispenser I kept in the car we headed back to Queen Street. En route we stopped at Mario's for lunch with Lydia. This did not mean a sit-down, three course affair with pleasant conversation and convivial company. And it was already three o'clock in the afternoon, so we stood at the takeaway bar and ordered a sandwich each with a can of soft drink before returning to the office. One of my mother's favourite television programmes featured the Sicilian detective Montalbano. She could listen to it in her native Italian and it always surprised me how he could take hours for lunch and still catch the bad guys. And in Sicily they had the Mafia to contend with.

I sat at a desk adjacent to Lydia, who had returned from the kitchen with two plates and I watched her carefully opening the sandwich pack. Mine was a soggy chicken variety and I gathered my thoughts about the priorities in hand. I found myself tugging at the packaging, knowing that if I yanked too forcefully the filling would go all over the desk.

'I'll get a board organised, boss,' Lydia said.

I took my first mouthful of sandwich and realised how hungry I felt.

I nodded and reached for my phone.

Paddy McVeigh answered after one ring. 'Make sure you're here first thing in the morning. I'll be starting the post-mortem early. I'm going to London in the afternoon.'

Then I called Alvine Dix. 'What do you want Marco?' Her voice contained enough venom to worry a rattlesnake. 'Don't you know I'm busy.'

'I've got a meeting with Superintendent Cornock. He'll want to know what progress you've made.' It sounded plausible enough and I could relay to my superior officer exactly what was happening at the murder scene.

It didn't seem to have much effect on Alvine. 'I'm still

here, as are the rest of the team and we're going to be here for another couple of hours. Don't disturb me again. I'll ring you when I've got anything to report.' She finished the call abruptly and I turned my attention back to my lunch.

Lydia piped up. 'Operational support have been in touch telling me they've got a team at Armsby's house now. They should have his computer and all the other personal possessions back here by early evening.'

There was no nine-to-five in a murder investigation. The demands on time meant working long into the evening and weekends. I wondered what we would learn about the life of Frank Armsby. I snapped open the can of soft drink and washed down the last mouthful of sandwich.

'You'd better get some preliminary stuff done on Armsby – police national computer check, finances et cetera. And requisition his mobile phone data.'

Lydia scribbled on her notepad as I left the Incident Room and made my way through the corridors of Queen Street until I stood outside Superintendent Cornock's room, gathering my thoughts. I buttoned my jacket and knocked on his door.

He shouted a greeting and I entered. He stood sprinkling powdered food over the surface of the fish tank and I was convinced there was a new, colourful addition to the inhabitants swimming inside. Cornock never missed an opportunity to remind me how peaceful a fish tank could be. I'd seen him staring at it whenever he'd had difficult decisions to make. He waved me to a visitor chair and I sat down.

'Frank Armsby,' Cornock announced as though he were introducing a guest speaker at a Rotary club dinner. He fidgeted with the papers on his desk before continuing. 'He has been the subject of two previous rape prosecutions, and he was facing another investigation at the moment.'

I raised my eyebrows. Armsby would definitely not have made it to a Rotary club dinner.

Having to deal with different superior officers was part and parcel of everyday policing and, apart from a brief period when Cornock took time off to handle a family crisis, I had never answered to another superintendent. It meant I knew how far to push my occasional indiscretions and how much he would indulge me.

'Both reached the stage of court appearances. The judge dismissed the first case on the basis that there was inadequate evidence and the second resulted in an acquittal before the jury.'

Cornock looked up from the papers, sharing with me his disquiet. He continued. 'This latest case was at an early stage. The Crown Prosecution Service were involved in reviewing all the evidence.'

'And what happened?'

Cornock nodded. 'The CPS didn't want to run the risk of another trial involving Armsby failing.'

A decision to prosecute would have been made on the balance of the evidence – was there a realistic prospect of the case succeeding? And was it in the public interest for the prosecution to proceed? Both previous prosecutions should not have influenced the prosecutor, but common sense meant the CPS would be hyper-careful.

'Has the victim been told?'

'She was notified in the last two days.' Cornock kept his voice serious. 'She wasn't pleased.'

'I'll need her name and contact details.'

'Be very careful, John,' Cornock said. 'Take Lydia with you when you go and see her.'

'Yes, sir.'

Cornock glanced at his watch. 'And you need to speak to the officer that dealt with the case originally.' Cornock tapped the file of papers on his desk. 'I've got the original files for you to read.'

Back in my office I dropped the files onto my desk and

caught up with Lydia. A civilian team was erecting a board and one of the support staff and an intelligence officer I knew from previous cases were talking to Lydia. We exchanged pleasantries. I gazed over at the board where everything about Armsby's life would soon be mapped out: his family, friends, finances and what he ate for breakfast. Somebody had reason enough to kill him and we had to find the evidence and then the killer.

Once the team had left I sat with Lydia in my room as night drew in and the lights of my office seemed to glow more brightly. 'Armsby had faced two previous charges of rape and neither prosecution was successful – one was dismissed by the judge and in the other the jury acquitted him.'

Lydia raised her eyebrows. 'An upstanding member of the community.'

'There's more. He had recently been investigated for another sexual assault charge. The CPS decided not to press charges.' Now I tapped the papers on my desk.

Lydia whistled under her breath. 'And the victim...?' She jerked her head at the file.

I nodded. 'A Judy Campbell – we'll need to speak to her.'

'And the other two victims?'

I shuffled through the files Cornock had given me and, keeping the recent case pushed the others to Lydia. 'I suggest you read through all the papers. We'll have to treat them as persons of interest.'

'Apparently rape prosecutions are down dramatically in the past year. The CPS very often decide not to bring charges.'

The chances of a conviction could be low too. It was a poor reflection of modern society that we hadn't been able to find a better way to successfully deal with complaints of sexual assault.

Lydia sounded exasperated. 'And it's reckoned the

number of reported sexual assaults is a fraction of the offences that actually happen.'

'Do we know any more about Armsby's background?'

'He ran an accountancy business from an office in Whitchurch.'

'Family?'

'Divorced a few years ago with teenage children. His ex-wife lives in Radyr.'

'We'll need to speak to her.'

'I'll organise a time after the post-mortem tomorrow.' Lydia lifted the file from the desk and got up. 'I've checked the area near the scene for any CCTV and the builders' merchant was a blind spot.'

'Hopefully the post-mortem will give us more details.'

I read through the papers relating to the recent investigation into Armsby. By the end I shared the frustration that emanated from every page and sentence of the reports. The officers were convinced Armsby was guilty, but there was no guarantee of conviction in any criminal case. Juries could be fickle and easily swayed by eloquent advocates but even I could see there was enough evidence to justify a prosecution. It would give the victim her day in court, but by robbing her of that opportunity the CPS had removed her prospect of justice.

Visiting Judy Campbell would be top of the list tomorrow.

It was late when I got home. The answering machine announced that a message waited for me. I listened to my mother's voice telling me that she needed to speak to me and that she had already spoken with Jackie, my ex, about organising for our son, Dean, to spend October week with her and Papà at their caravan in Tenby. And that I should plan to join them, suggesting that it would do everyone good to leave Cardiff after the prolonged lockdown of the pandemic. Her plans to take Dean to Lucca over the summer had been postponed and my mother had been disappointed, especially as some elderly relatives were in poor health and my mother feared they might not live long enough to see Dean again.

The second message was from Rob, one of my regular footballing mates. Live games had resumed in empty stadiums, so we'd started watching the games in each other's homes with our boys. His son was the same age as Dean and this week it was Rob's turn to host. We wore scarfs and bought pies to eat at half-time, but it wasn't the same as sitting in the stadium, of course. Calling Mamma would wait until tomorrow, but I rang Rob and spent time making small talk, discussing the latest Bluebirds' signings.

By ten-thirty I'd been channel hopping for half an hour until I found the late evening news from Wales. It carried an update on a local spike in coronavirus incidents in Newport but nothing about the discovery of Frank Armsby's body.

I had no doubt that by tomorrow the press would be in touch.

Chapter 4

Staring out of my apartment window the following morning as I was finishing breakfast – chewing on a piece of toast, drinking an Americano – I wondered if it would be another twelve hours before I'd be back here. In the middle of any investigation my home felt like a place where I slept, showered and drank coffee before leaving for the day. It might as well have been a hotel room. So I paused, meandering through into the sitting room where I flicked on the television and found the news channel and a news report about the US presidential election.

I finished the coffee, found my car keys, pulled on a coat and left the apartment. After unlocking the Mondeo, I found an Elvis CD in the glove compartment. 'Lonesome Tonight' filled the cabin as I negotiated my way into the traffic. I drove north through the city, skirting round the castle and the civic buildings before heading right towards the University Hospital and the mortuary.

The sprawling site had been extended and developed piecemeal over the years, so finding a parking slot could be a nightmare. I spent ten minutes driving around, leaning forward gazing through the windscreen having my hopes of an empty space dashed when the rear lights of a small car were revealed. In the end I gave up and parked on a yellow line, sticking an *On Police Business/Heddlu Swyddogol* notice on the dashboard.

I scribbled my name at the bottom of the health and safety forms the assistant produced, then I found my way through into the bowels of the building. Paddy McVeigh always used the same mortuary and I could hear classical music drifting down the corridor.

'Good morning, John,' Paddy said, waving me over after I'd pushed open the door. 'It's one of Wagner's more accessible pieces don't you think?'

'Of course.'

A mortuary assistant entered through another door

pushing the trolley with Frank Armsby on it, covered in a white cloth that draped over the sides.

'Frank Armsby.' Paddy read from his tablet. 'He's in his early forties with no underlying health conditions and was reasonably healthy.'

Once the trolley was in the right position Paddy got to work. He pulled back the sheet covering the corpse with a dramatic gesture. I could never get accustomed to the rituals of a post-mortem. It amazed me that any doctor would want to spend his life amongst dead people.

Armsby's clothes were dusty and dirty. The prospect they held some vital clue, possibly even DNA we might be able to use to identify a suspect made the post-mortem an essential part of our investigation. It might also give the family closure, or certainly help in the grieving process. But something about the little we had discovered about Armsby's background and his family suggested that I wouldn't be offering sympathy and condolences to a heartbroken widow that afternoon.

Paddy recorded in detail the steps he was taking. Minute fragments of stone and chippings were removed and catalogued carefully. The CSIs had already emptied his pockets, but Paddy examined each again. After the clothes had all been removed and neatly packaged in evidence bags Paddy looked over at me a glint of excitement in his eyes as though he were warning me of what was to follow.

He took time examining the head and neck and shoulders pulling the skin to examine each blemish. The bruising around the torso looked ugly and extensive. Where there should have been the upright outline of Armsby's rib cage there was now a flat crumpled area. He stood back for a moment and turned to me. 'I haven't seen injuries like this for some time.'

'Do you have any idea what caused them?'

'Let me finish the post-mortem first.'

He continued his examination of Armsby's upper body

including the hands, wrists and upper arms. He examined the dead man's fingers in turn, taking scrapings from the nails of each.

He reached for the scalpel and drew it along the chest and abdomen, creating a Y-shaped incision extending from both shoulders to the navel. He opened the rib cage using stainless steel bolt cutters, then removed the heart and lungs, dictating the details of each step he was taking. He carefully examined the organs at an adjacent bench, opening each using what looked like a razor-sharp butter knife.

By the end I could feel my breakfast rumbling in my stomach, so I made excuses and left. I found Paddy's office and I eased open a window, pulled a cigarette from the packet in my jacket pocket and fired my Zippo into life. Smoking wasn't permitted inside a building, but I was almost outside and there was nobody to complain.

I threw the butt end into the gravel path outside as Paddy came in.

'Smoking is bad for you.'

'Post-mortems have this effect on me.'

Paddy slumped into the office chair by his desk. He took a mouthful of water from the bottle he bought with him. 'He was battered. Really fucking battered.'

I'd never heard the pathologist so exasperated.

'You'd better explain that in more detail.'

'He died from multiorgan failure. His heart was damaged, probably from one of the broken ribs, and the sac containing it, the pericardium, was full of blood. It only takes a little blood in the wrong place to stop the old clockwork from pumping. I'll do a more detailed analysis on his heart and lungs and other vital organs to see if there were any underlying conditions, and I'll send samples for routine toxicology.'

'So how was he battered?'

Paddy blew out a mouthful of air. 'Car accidents are usually the main cause of that sort of catastrophic injury to the body. They were more common years ago when cars didn't have airbags and the braking systems weren't as effective as they are now. It's remarkable how people can survive car accidents these days.'

'He wasn't involved in a car accident though. He was found dumped behind some bins.'

Paddy noticed the irritation in my voice. 'I know, John. I'm using that to give you context. My conclusion is that he was probably run over by a vehicle of some sort. One of his legs has been broken and the other crushed. But it's the injury to his torso that's significant. His rib cage and the vital human organs aren't designed to take that sort of punishment.'

I shuddered. Various scenarios that might have led to Armsby's death crowded into my mind. Was he meeting somebody? Did he know the driver?

'And before you ask,' Paddy said. 'I'll do everything I can to see if there is any forensic evidence on the body to link back to a particular vehicle. We might get lucky and find some paint fragments.'

'Send me the report as soon as you can.'

Paddy nodded. 'Are you watching the game on Saturday, John?'

I knew Paddy was a fan of the Cardiff Blues rugby team, rather than Cardiff City – the 'Bluebirds' – football side. 'Sure thing. A friend has a son the same age as Dean. So we watch it at home and make a fuss of them.'

'I'll be glad when this pandemic is over, and things can get back to normal.'

'Sure thing, Paddy.'

Normal for Paddy meant filling his hollow legs with beer and taking a taxi home when he couldn't walk straight. Drinking orange juice in a crowded bar with a bunch of football supporters either drowning their sorrows or celebrating a victory was not my idea of a social event any longer. Years ago, perhaps, but now I enjoyed spending quality time with Dean.

After collecting Lydia from Queen Street, we travelled north-west towards Radyr and the sprawling new developments at the edge of the city. Expansion was proceeding at a frenetic pace and the extension to the suburb would have schools and doctors' surgeries and play areas but for now it was like a construction site. Lydia told me that Frank Armsby's former wife had been very clear about the time for us to see her as she had arranged for her parents to be present. And we were early so we spent half an hour sitting in a café.

'How did you get on with the post-mortem?' Lydia said.

'Paddy reckons he was knocked down by a car that ran over him several times.'

Lydia grimaced. 'That would suggest he was meeting somebody. Perhaps somebody he knew.'

A waitress bought Lydia's latte and my Americano. I tore open the packaging of one of those fancy caramel biscuits. Lydia continued, stirring sugar slowly into her drink. 'Forensics should have finished with the computer removed from Armsby's house by later this morning and I've been promised the results of his mobile phone today.'

'Excellent. Let's hope the family can give us more details. Might be something in his background. And we need to get the uniformed lads visiting all the industrial units near the builders' merchant where we found his body.'

'If he was knocked down by a car then somebody must have moved him.'

I nodded.

Lydia added. 'And why move the body into the builders' merchant's car park?'

I had learned that criminals rarely think logically. Sometimes there was no reasonable explanation. I shrugged. 'Let's wait to see the forensics report.'

I paid for our drinks and we headed back to the car.

Finding Kim Armsby's new home turned out to be a challenge. The satnav didn't recognise the postcode and Lydia's direction took us down a narrow track until it abruptly stopped. I gazed through a gap and spotted the development, which meant doubling back to a roundabout where we had taken a wrong turning a few minutes earlier. The new detached properties were huddled over each other, and when we pulled up outside Kim's property, I noticed a Mercedes C class and an Audi saloon, both reasonably new and sparklingly clean.

We reached the top of the paved drive, but I didn't need to knock, as the front door was opened by a tall thin man in his early seventies with a mop of silver-grey hair. His skin was healthy, his eyes clear and his clothes looked expensive. The dog collar made guessing his occupation unnecessary. He pushed out a hand. 'William Lambert, how do you do. I'm Kim's father.'

I flashed my warrant card; Lydia didn't bother once Lambert had ignored mine. 'Detective Inspector John Marco and this is Detective Sergeant Lydia Flint.'

'Do come in,' he sounded cheerful, businesslike.

He led us through into a sitting room. It was well-decorated, the sofas and furnishing sumptuous. Pictures of a boy and girl populated a glass display cabinet. A large oil canvas of a landscape scene had pride of place over the mantelpiece.

Lambert drew a hand in the air pointing towards the two women sitting on a sofa. 'This is Detective Inspector Marco and Detective Sergeant Flint. My daughter Kim, Inspector, and my wife Helen.' Lambert pointed to the empty sofa nearby and I sat down next to Lydia. Staring over at both women I realised neither looked terribly upset.

Instinct and training cut in, so I offered condolences. 'I am sorry for your loss.'

Kim was the first to reply. 'You needn't be.'

She glared at me while her mother looked on slightly embarrassed. There was nothing uncomfortable in the uncompromising look her father gave me. 'Frank and Kim divorced several years ago. He was a difficult person.'

Helen winced. 'My husband is being charitable, too charitable. Frank Armsby was an odious individual who caused Kim nothing but grief.'

Lydia pitched in. 'How long have you been divorced?'

The feminine touch did the trick: Kim barely missed a beat as she shared her history. 'He was charming and seductive at the start of our relationship and he could be good fun and great company. But once we were married, he changed almost overnight. He became manipulative and abusive. He wanted to control everything I did, when I went out, what friends I went with and how I spent my money. I had to open a separate bank account secretly at one stage.'

William Lambert had the voice accustomed to dominating a situation. 'And he even tried to persuade me to unravel a family trust so that he could benefit financially.'

Kim continued. 'It was when the children started school that I couldn't stand it any longer.'

She paused and I took the chance to interrupt her. 'Was he physically abusive towards you?'

Her lips quivered and she stared down at her feet. William Lambert replied on her behalf. 'Kim put up with a lot of abuse over the years and as you probably know violent husbands can be experts at controlling their wives and hiding any evidence of physical injury.'

'Did it affect the children?'

William Lambert again. 'They're both at a boarding school in England that has strong connections to the Anglican Church. We thought it best in the circumstances. We felt that they would benefit by being away from Cardiff. A family trust is responsible for payment of all the fees.'

Before seeing Kim Armsby and her parents I had worried about how I would raise the question of the two previous court cases against her former husband. I guessed Kim and her parents would have been glad, even overjoyed had he been sent to prison. 'Were you aware Frank had been prosecuted twice for serious sexual offences?'

By the lack of response, I had my answer.

'He had recently been investigated for a third time. But the Crown Prosecution Service decided not to bring charges.'

William Lambert filled the void after my last statement. 'I daresay you'll be considering the victims of Armsby's atrocious crimes as possible suspects. No man deserves to be killed, Inspector, but you will excuse us if the grief you might expect from our family is absent.'

After the reaction from Kim and her parents my next question seemed trite, almost pointless. 'Do you know of anybody who would want to kill him?'

Kim shook her head listlessly. We thanked the family and left.

'What did you make of that, boss?' Lydia said once were back in the car.

'I thought vicars were supposed to forgive and forget.'

Lydia turned towards me. 'Surely you don't think they could be involved?'

Nothing about William Lambert or his wife or Kim Armsby suggested they had killed Frank Armsby, although all three were perfectly content he was dead. My mobile bleeped with a message as I switched on the engine. I turned to Lydia. 'The uniformed lads have found Armsby's car.'

Chapter 5

Habit made me switch on the satnav, which directed us back towards the middle of the city and the disembodied voice filled the cabin with instructions to retrace our steps back to Penarth Road. I indicated right and passed a scrap metal merchant before taking a left by a kitchen warehouse. We were a few hundred metres from the builders' merchants where Armsby's body had been discovered. The road petered out into a piece of waste ground and covering the entrance was a marked police car. Alongside a skip full of builder's waste were piles of wooden pallets and a navy BMW 3 Series.

I parked and we joined the young uniformed officer who informed us the crime scene investigators were on their way. I peered inside the car. A grey fleece lay abandoned on the rear seat. A bottle of water stood upright in the centre console.

'Anything?' Lydia said.

'Why did he park it here?'

I gazed over and in the distance I could see a gap in the fence that marked the perimeter of the waste ground. 'Let's go and take a look.'

We traipsed over the gravel surface and stopped at the opening I had spotted earlier. Beyond it was the road that led down to the builders' merchant where we'd found Armsby's body.

'After parking the car he must have walked over and through this gap and then down towards the builders merchants,' I said.

'Unless the car was moved by someone else.'

I didn't reply directly. 'He was meeting somebody. We need to find out who called him the night he was killed.'

'Are we going to wait for the CSI team to arrive?' Lydia paused. 'The operational support team are at Armsby's offices and we're already late.'

I gave the scene one final scan. Who had lured Armsby

here? And why had he parked his car on waste ground? I turned and said to Lydia, 'Let's go.'

Armsby & Co occupied a nondescript building on a side street off Whitchurch High Street. It was the end property of a terrace that included a quaint old-fashioned teashop, a charity shop supporting a local animal rescue centre and an artisan bakery. An officer attached to operational support was sitting behind a desk where a receptionist would have greeted customers. He nodded. 'The staff are in the office at the back.'

The building was deceptively long, and an extension reached out at the rear.

I pushed open the door of a room with a sign that said 'Conference Room' and found another officer sitting round the table with two individuals. A woman in her fifties with very short hair and severe looking glasses, her make-up smudged by tears, looked up at me. The second was an intense looking man in his late thirties who avoided any eye contact. He wore a white shirt discoloured by age and frequent washing. None of the customary handshakes with either of course.

'This is Alan Thomas who worked as a bookkeeper for Armsby and Barbara Webster who was the receptionist.' The officer announced.

'I'm Detective Inspector John Marco and this is Detective Sergeant Lydia Flint. We are in charge of the investigation into Frank Armsby's murder.' I sat down by the table; Lydia did the same.

'Can you tell me anything about Mr Armsby that might help us with our inquiry?'

Thomas and Webster both gave me blank looks.

'Did Mr Armsby have any enemies that you are aware of? Had he received any threats against his life? Somebody who gave you cause to think they might want him dead. Did he have any disgruntled customers?'

Thomas was the first to reply. 'Mr Armsby was an accountant. I never knew anything about his private life. I came in, did my job and went home. I don't know anything about who might have killed him. What's going to happen to this place? What's going to happen to my job?'

'Is there anybody in the past few days or weeks who has had an argument with Mr Armsby?'

Webster and Thomas shared an embarrassed glance. Webster responded. 'That woman came in again last week. The one who made the allegation against him – Judy Campbell. She came in threatening and she was in a hell of a temper. She told him she'd make certain she got even with him and that he wouldn't get away with it.'

Lydia cut across her. 'Did he tell you what she had alleged?'

She shook her head briskly. 'Not all the details. I didn't want to know. It was none of my business, but he did say she made things up about him. Frank, I mean Mr Armsby, was nice. I never had a cross word with him.'

Would she feel the same after a conversation with Kim Armsby and her parents?

'If there's anything else that you remember about Frank Armsby or his customers or clients or friends then please contact me.' I pushed a business card over the table.

I nodded for the officer from operational support to follow us as we left. 'Make sure you get a full list of Armsby's clients.'

He nodded and we left.

Chapter 6

We left the car and traipsed over to the secure entrance at the rear of the building. After I punched in the six-digit security code we took the stairs to the Incident Room on the third floor. Like any city centre police station built in the early decades of the previous century the place was a warren of offices and conference suites refurbished to suit the needs of modern policing. In the morning shades of disinfectant and polish from the activities of the cleaning staff overnight mixed with the odour of damp clothes and tired bodies. By the afternoon the sound of activity in the city centre, taxis idling, warbling buskers and the bustle of shoppers drifted inside. Evening and night shift could bring with it the smell of spices being roasted and fat frying takeaway food.

As we reached the third floor it struck me that if the plans for a new building ever came to fruition, I'd miss the old place.

Lydia draped her coat over the back of her chair and settled at her desk. 'I'll get started on his laptop.'

'And get his mobile from forensics – we need to know his contacts.'

Lydia nodded.

I booted up my computer and read through the emails clogging my inbox. I deleted most without even reading them. If anybody complained I could always offer the spam filter as a convincing excuse. I stopped when I read the email from Paddy McVeigh and downloaded the post-mortem report. Reading the cold, harsh language always reminded me of the brutal reality of the work he undertook. Was multiorgan failure a painful way to die? Pathologist's reports never ventured an opinion about that.

I spent an hour speaking to uniformed officers about the inquiries they'd been making at the business addresses near the builders' merchant. The results of a Google search on the monitor of my computer gave me a bird's eye view of Penarth Road and the businesses that lined the route from

The Cardiff Lockdown Murders

Cardiff to the town that gave the road its name. They were the sort of premises every town in Wales would have – builders' merchant, a tile warehouse, timber yard.

A sergeant leading one of the teams summarised the position. 'Everyone we've spoken to has heard about the murder. But at night the area is deserted. There are a couple of premises with CCTV cameras and I've requisitioned the footage.'

We needed to track Frank Armsby's movements from the middle of Cardiff and build a picture of his final few hours.

The killer had chosen this location specifically because it didn't have CCTV cameras and there were few people around late at night. A public appeal might jog memories, unearth a snippet of information, something buried deep in a person's memory that might give us a thread. So I called Superintendent Cornock. He listened carefully and, after I'd finished, he said, 'I agree, speak to someone from public relations.'

A conversation with a civilian in the PR department gave me the email address and once I had drafted the barest outline I attached it to a message asking it be given priority for immediate release. I didn't have to wait too long for my document to be returned, amended and polished and revamped with all the usual keywords and clichés. Grudgingly I realised why we had a public relations department.

The early evening news would carry the piece and Southern Division's dedicated phone line operators would soon be fielding calls. Mining through to find a nugget of important information would take time.

I heard Lydia's voice through the open door. 'Something you need to see, boss.'

In the Incident Room I found a chair and sat down by her side. She was working her way through Armsby's laptop. She also had his mobile phone on the desk alongside it.

'I've been able to establish that Armsby was using an internet dating service.'

'Nothing wrong with that.'

'He had a date the night he was killed.'

'Are you sure?'

'There's overlap between the activity on the internet dating site on his laptop and his mobile. I can see messages going back and forth between him and a woman called Caitlin. I don't have a surname at the moment.'

'Is there a photograph?'

Lydia nodded. She scrolled through the website, eventually double-clicking on the image of a smiling woman in her forties pitching her head slightly towards the camera clearly trying to get her best image recorded. Was I looking at one of the last people to have seen Frank Armsby alive? Or, more importantly, was I looking at his killer?

'And there are messages between both of them on WhatsApp. They were going to meet at a restaurant and bistro in the middle of town. It was his suggestion.'

'What do we know about Caitlin?'

'She's forty, works in finance, home in the Bay. Likes science fiction films.'

'We need to contact her.'

'I'll message her through this internet dating page. If she doesn't respond we'll need to get a warrant for disclosure of her details.'

'I'll speak to the restaurant.'

It took me a few seconds to find the number for La Lanterna and even less to dial it and ask for the manager. He was called Sam and after explaining what I needed he confirmed they kept a record of the names of all the bookings. Luckily, they had CCTV too. I wanted to punch the air. I settled for breathlessly telling him to expect me within the hour. I grabbed my coat off the back of my chair and joined Lydia.

'The restaurant has got CCTV,' I said. 'Get your coat.

Let's go.'

Lydia scrambled to her feet and followed me down the stairwell to reception. It was no more than a ten-minute walk to La Lanterna. I'd seen the adverts for the place but, more importantly, my mother hadn't mentioned it and unless a restaurant had her seal of approval, particularly an Italian one, it would have a doubtful pedigree. I pushed open the front door. Extravagant bunting and the Italian flag adorned the entrance hall. A waiter came over, a keen, hopeful look on his face. Since the pandemic a lot of restaurants in the city had closed and the ones that had survived were fighting over every customer. I raised a hand, showed him my warrant card and said, 'The manager's expecting me.'

He scuttled off into the bowels of the restaurant and I picked up a menu card. The cynic in me reckoned the restaurants had increased their prices in the past few months. I suppose it was only to be expected. A small, thin man with a well-developed paunch came over and introduced himself as Sam who I'd spoken to earlier. The accent was more Bargoed than Bologna.

'I'm Detective Inspector Marco and this is Detective Sergeant Flint.' We both flashed our warrant cards. 'We are investigating the murder of Frank Armsby and we believe that he may have eaten here two nights ago. Have you found the CCTV footage from that evening?'

'No problem, follow me.' He led us through a corridor into his office. The monitor screen was divided into four images, presumably from the four cameras set up to cover different parts of the building. Sam sat down and announced. 'After you called, I accessed the footage you wanted to see. I also found the reservation confirmation. Armsby booked a table for two people for seven pm.'

A couple of clicks and the screen came to life.

I stared down and watched the activity as the restaurant opened and customers arrived. Sam fast-forwarded to six forty-five and fiddled with the controls so that only the footage from the camera near the entrance lobby was shown. At six fifty Frank Armsby arrived, wearing the same suit and shirt I'd seen the previous morning.

Armsby disappeared from the footage as Sam explained he had been taken to his table. A few minutes later the screen filled with the image of a woman. One of the members of staff smiled and joked with her and pointed towards the main section of the restaurant before leading her inside. Sam switched the footage to a camera showing Armsby and Caitlin smiling broadly at each other.

'I'll need a copy of all this footage.'

Sam nodded.

I gave him a business card with my email address and he promised to forward the footage on to us. Now we had focus to our investigation. We knew exactly where Armsby had been on the night he was killed and who he was with.

Back in the Incident Room Lydia clicked into her computer and checked the monitor for a reply from the mysterious Caitlin. She turned to me and shook her head.

'Tomorrow, make an application for a warrant. We need to talk to this woman.'

The following morning, I chose my second-best pair of brown brogues, the ones with the two-tone shine to match my dark chinos. The socks were an extravagant stripy pair Jackie had arranged for Dean to give me one birthday. My white shirt was neatly ironed and tucked carefully into my trouser waistband. I was meeting officers from the team that had investigated Judy Campbell's recent complaint against Frank Armsby. Alison Swan's name was mentioned as one of the officers, so I was determined to make a good impression.

I drove up from my apartment in the Bay past the tinplate works and, after skirting the imposing walls of HMP Cardiff, I parked at Queen Street and met Lydia who was clutching a coffee in a fancy recyclable takeaway container.

Coffee never tasted the same somehow in the plastic mugs that cafés offer. I prefer to sit down and take time to enjoy an Americano.

'Morning, boss,' Lydia said.

I acknowledged the greeting and we wound our way to the Incident Room where Lydia booted up her computer.

The reports from the dedicated public helpline had arrived overnight and I spent time scanning through them trying to identify if there was anything of value. Helpfully, several of the callers had been on Penarth Road the evening Armsby was killed. They needed to be interviewed by the uniformed lads and it struck me that I should be asking Superintendent Cornock to allocate further resources to assist Lydia and me.

Two witness had allegedly spoken with Armsby when he had stopped them to ask for directions. Another had seen him bundled into a white transit van and the registration number he gave belonged to a taxi in Newcastle upon Tyne – he was dismissed as another time waster. It was much as I'd expected but all the threads would need to be followed up.

I'd been planning to spend the first couple of hours that morning reviewing the documentation from the office of Armsby & Co as well as chasing Alvine Dix for a forensic report. So I wasted no time and called her.

'Good morning, Alvine.'

'You sound bright-eyed and bushy-tailed.'

'I'm looking forward to a full day's work and a detailed comprehensive report from the crime scene manager.'

'Bugger off, Marco. You can be a smarmy git, you know that don't you?'

'And there was I thinking you would succumb to my charms.'

'No chance of that. I know what Italian men are like.'

The image of Alvine and a swarthy Italian lothario came to mind. It made the most unlikely, almost comical, pairing.

'Have you been able to finalise the forensic report?'

'You should have it later this afternoon. I've had to send off some of the samples of his clothes for further detailed analysis.'

'How long will that take?'

Alvine gave one of her long deep sighs. 'It'll take as long as it takes.'

I finished the call and turned my attention to the paperwork removed from Frank Armsby's office. I scrutinised the list of his customers, mostly small businesses, pubs and clubs, the occasional builder and anonymous-sounding limited companies. Lydia stood by my doorway a few minutes before ten o'clock tapping her watch reminding me about our meeting.

Formally dismissing Judy Campbell from my investigation wasn't something I was prepared to do just yet. But she was the only person of interest with enough of a motive to want Frank Armsby dead. I doubted my meeting with the team that dealt with her complaint would be that helpful but I was due to attend the forum on Friday so it might make me better informed. And seeing the officers again would give me the opportunity of speaking to Alison Swan.

Lydia led the way as we trooped through Queen Street exchanging greetings with other officers before we arrived at the conference room. Sergeant Irene Price was a severe-looking woman in her early fifties. She was a humourless individual who'd spent her entire career on the various teams dealing with sexual offences and domestic violence. If opposites attract, Mr Price was probably a stand-up comedian in a gay bar.

'Good morning, John.' Even though I was her superior officer she ignored my rank. Privileges of advanced age, I thought. 'I understand you're going to be representing the serious crime team at the forum on Friday and that you're in charge of Frank Armsby's murder inquiry.' She turned to

Alison Swan sitting by her side. 'This is Detective Constable Swan.' I smiled at Alison and reached out a hand.

'We've met.'

'Good morning, Inspector.' Alison smiled back.

After an hour listening to Price, I was no better informed about the rape allegation against Armsby, but I knew an awful lot about investigating rape allegations and the inadequacies of the Crown Prosecution Service's lawyers who reviewed the cases. It made Price quite indignant. 'So you see, John, we're fighting a losing battle. Real, gold-plated evidence is in short supply and unless the culprit coughs, prosecutions can be awkward.' Then she sighed. 'I'm looking forward to retirement.'

'You've done your thirty years?' I said.

'Thirty-five, and I'm off to Spain the minute I retire.'

'How much digging around did you do into Armsby's background?' Lydia said obviously hoping their work could save us some time.

Price dragged out a reply. 'He is an accountant in the suburbs. He does people's tax returns and balance sheets and profit and loss accounts. And by night he is a sexual predator. That's all I needed to know about him, and I wanted the Crown Prosecution Service to back me up.' She added under her breath, 'Bastards.'

Alison made her first contribution. 'Men like Armsby are emboldened by decisions not to prosecute them or by juries acquitting them. I was convinced he became more confident, more brazen after the first case where the judge dismissed the prosecution. The jury should have convicted him on the second case, but he had enough money to be able to pay for the best lawyers who wheedled a worm of doubt into the jury's mind.'

'We shall need to interview Judy Campbell.'

'Her mental health is fragile at the moment. And the decision not to prosecute Armsby hasn't helped.'

It reminded me of Cornock warning me to be careful,

but protocols meant I had to speak to Campbell. 'Even so we'll need to talk to her.'

Alison nodded. 'It would be best if I contact her first and arrange a time. Is there any evidence to implicate her?'

'No, but Superintendent Cornock will expect me to interview her even if it's to eliminate her from the inquiry.'

'I'll get back to you, Inspector.'

'I've got the files of the two failed prosecutions, but some background on both would be helpful,' I said. Price gave Alison a brief nod. 'Constable Swan here can liaise with you about both inquiries.'

Alison gave me another warm smile.

I let my imagination wander as I returned to my office. I wondered what sort of liaising I could actually get organised with Alison Swan. A message reaching my mobile brought me back down to earth.

'Meet me Lefties. One hour'

Chapter 7

When Alex Leftrowski left his native Russia, he had no grand plans to be opening a bar in Cardiff and develop it into a popular watering hole. He arrived in the city penniless but resourceful and within a few years had opened the eponymously titled Lefties. I had spent many an hour after work propping up the bar or sitting at the tables discussing the finer points of the Cardiff City football team's defence and attack strategies. Since those days I had moved on from a five-pint-a-night habit as Lefties had moved on to offering a more sophisticated ambience. An enormous Italian coffee machine had pride of place on a counter and the cappuccino and espresso cups carried a discreet branding advertising Alex's creation. He had even added a modest tapas selection to the early evening menu.

I yanked the door open and spotted Alex busy replenishing the chilled cabinets, waiting for his regular lunchtime trade. I pumped the sanitiser on the bar and rubbed the gel into my hands – it had become a regular routine wherever I went.

He gave me a warm smile. 'John Marco. It is good to see you.'

'Alex. You're all right?' It was the sort of question that didn't really need an answer.

'I am good. Business is good, after all that disruption with the virus, things are better now. Things will be better in future.'

I doubted whether the owners of the bars and clubs that had closed permanently in Cardiff in the past few months would agree with him. Alex kept his overheads manageable and his lifestyle modest, making it easier to survive.

'And how are the boys?' I always enquired after his sons.

He snapped open the top of a bottle of orange juice and poured it into half pint glass before topping it up with lemonade. 'They drive my wife mad.' He shrugged.

'Teenagers, what can you do?'

He waved a hand away when I offered to pay.

I sat down in a discreet corner and took the first mouthful of my drink. Reaching for my mobile phone I decided to check my emails but didn't get the chance, as the man who had requested to meet me sauntered into the bar. Terry had been a regular informant for me for many years. A source of reliable, useful information and the two-way relationship worked well. Every detective needed their 'Terry'. He wasn't warm and cuddly, but he had an engaging personality and a finger on the pulse of every major organised crime group and criminal activity in the city. Usually I contacted Terry so his request to meet was intriguing.

He stood nervously as Alex pulled him a pint of Brains. When a customer entered, he twitched a glance at them. He took a long slug of his drink before walking over towards my seat.

'How are you doing, Terry?'

He wiped a hand over his mouth. 'Marco.' He acknowledged simply.

'What's this is about? I'm a bit busy.'

'I know, I know. You're in charge of the Frank Armsby investigation.' It was a mixture of a question and a statement. My involvement hadn't been made public but people like Terry had ways of finding things out about current police investigations.

'What if I am?'

He took another mouthful and cast another searching glance around the bar. Nobody paid us any attention.

'You need to know something.'

Terry was like a ham actor in one of those crime dramas on the television where they dragged out the dramatic pauses. 'Get on with it, Terry.'

'You're probably going to find this out soon enough, so I wanted to tell you myself. I met Frank Armsby a couple of days before he was killed.' He emptied the glass to below half.

'Okay,' I added slowly. 'You'll need to give me more details about why this is relevant. And why were you meeting Frank Armsby? He was an accountant.'

'I had a business meeting with him.'

I couldn't help myself. 'Come off it, Terry.'

He gave me an offended look before finishing his drink. He dipped his head at the empty glass, and I gesticulated a request to Alex to pour Terry a refill.

'I don't like this place no more. It's gone downhill since it became all fancy with them coffee machines and snacks.'

'It's tapas, Terry. Have you ever been to Spain?'

He nodded. 'I went to Majorca a couple years ago. Don't remember much about it. I was shit-faced most of the time.'

When his second pint arrived, Terry took a mouthful and eased back in his chair as though the alcohol had a magical medicinal effect.

'All I can tell you, Marco, is that I went to see Frank Armsby on behalf of somebody I was doing business with. I can't give you any more details because it's confidential.' He tapped the side of his nose with his forefinger. 'But I can tell you that Frank Armsby isn't the mild-mannered accountant fixing people's tax returns.'

I doubted Terry was alluding to the abortive prosecutions and the recent inquiries.

Terry added, 'Do you remember Jim White?'

White had managed a nightclub owned by Frankie Prince, a well-connected Cardiff criminal who had been gunned down in a shootout with some Polish gangsters.

'Of course I remember him.'

'Well, he's kept himself well under the radar.' Terry lowered his voice. 'He operates out of an office in Newport, down by the docks. He runs launderettes, pubs and even some fancy cafés and bars. But it's all about laundering cash.'

'And who is this person you're doing business with?'

'Like I said, Marco, that's confidential.'

'But why are you coming to me with this information?'

'I don't want you pinning anything on me. Armsby was killed down Penarth Road. I've never been down there. I don't know where the fuck it is.'

'Come on, Terry. If I have reason to think you're connected, then you're going to have to help with my inquiries down at Queen Street. How would your business associate like that?'

'I spoke to Armsby for fifteen minutes. In his office. What are you going to do –interview all his clients and ask them?' He mimicked an official sounding voice. '*Excuse me old chap. Did you kill Mr Armsby?*' He gave me a challenging glare.

'That's not going to fly, and you know it, Terry.' I leaned over towards him. 'I've known you a long time. So you'd better tell me exactly what is going on. Do you really want me to broadcast that you're a person of interest in Frank Armsby's death?'

Terry hissed, 'You wouldn't do that.'

I sidled out of the bench seat as though I was making to leave.

'Sit down, there's no need to be like that,' Terry whispered as he skimmed a worried look over the most recent customers to enter the bar.

As I retook my seat opposite Terry, I cast a glance over at Alex who raised a hand in a gesture inviting me to order more drinks, but I shook my head. Terry and I were done.

'I've got a murder inquiry and you're wasting my time.'

Terry gulped down more of his drink. 'Armsby was working for Jim White. He was working a scam with White to launder money through dodgy companies. Armsby would turn a blind eye, but White got wind of a rumour that Armsby was going to double-cross him.'

He paused and dragged the back of his hand over his mouth. Then his eyes took on a dark hard glaze.

White had an axe to grind with Armsby, but I knew he wouldn't do the dirty work himself and that someone else would have to be involved.

'I need names, Terry.'

Terry shook his head slowly.

'Get back to me when you've got more detail. In the meantime, I'm going back to Queen Street where I'm going to add your name as a person of interest.'

I left Terry gazing down at the bottom inch of his beer. I didn't look back and nodded to Alex as I passed the bar, heading for the exit.

Chapter 8

Mulling over my discussion with Terry dominated my thoughts on the way back to Queen Street. Adding his name as a person of interest would only draw attention to his status as an informant. And his recent meeting with Armsby barely justified his inclusion on the Incident Room board, even though it suited me fine that Terry would think so.

'Caitlin Prior has made contact,' Lydia said, getting to her feet as I entered the Incident Room. 'She'll be calling in during her lunch hour.'

'Excellent.' Frank Armsby's image peered down at me from the board, together with a printed list of the prosecutions and the names of the victims involved.

'I've established the identities of the other two complainants,' Lydia said reading my mind as I was staring at the names of the two women. 'How did you get on with your meeting?'

'Apparently Armsby was linked to a man called Jim White who worked with a gangster called Frankie Prince a while back. Prince got himself involved with some serious East European mafia types and he was killed in a bloody shoot out in Cyncoed. Apparently, Jim White has businesses that are laundering money on a big scale.'

'How does that help us? Shouldn't we be telling the economic crime unit?'

'I want to identify all the clients Armsby saw in the few days before he died.'

Lydia sounded a cautionary note. 'Unless the CSIs come up with direct forensic evidence, we're going to have to rely on tracking mobiles and CCTV cameras.'

She was right, of course. But I couldn't ignore the possible link to an organised crime group. 'Do we have the CCTV from the restaurant?'

'Came through this morning, boss. And I've put together a list of CCTV cameras that might have caught Frank Armsby driving down Penarth Road.'

'Good.'

The telephone on Lydia's desk rang and after she took the call she nodded briskly thanking the receptionist. 'Caitlin Prior has arrived.'

Lydia followed me down to the ground floor and into the conference room where Prior was waiting. A bottle of water stood before her on the table and after the introductions we sat down. Prior had a delicate 'v' shape on her upper lip as though a careful artist had taken his thumb and gently formed the parting. Her lipstick was a vibrant red and she wore a dark top of a pinstriped material. Her eyes were filled with defiance and determination. A black-and-white photograph would have complimented the perfect proportions of her face.

'Hello Miss Prior. We are investigating the murder of Frank Armsby. Can you tell us everything you know about him and the night he was killed?'

'I can't believe it.' Her bottom lip quivered. 'The message you sent me was the first I'd heard about it. I don't really look at the news. It's all so tragic. The poor man.'

'How well did you know Mr Armsby?'

'That was our second date. We went to a restaurant in the Bay on the first. We were getting on so well. He took an interest in my work.'

'What do you do for a living?'

'I'm a supervisor in a call centre. We specialise in financial services – selling insurance policies. It's all very boring but I've been there a long time and I enjoy it.'

'What did you and Frank talk about?'

'Small talk, I can't remember.' Her voice faltered.

'Did he seem distracted in any way on the night you met, as though there was something on his mind?'

'I didn't notice anything.'

'Did he mention that he was going anywhere after seeing you?'

She reached for a handkerchief from her bag and wiped

away a tear.

'I've never been involved with anything like this before.' She blew her nose delicately.

'When did you leave the restaurant?' Her answer confirmed the time we knew already – at least her recollection was reasonably reliable. 'And where did you go afterwards?'

She looked a bit baffled. 'I went home.'

'Did Frank Armsby make any reference to where he might be going after you left?'

'No. This whole thing is so upsetting. Will I have to give evidence at a Coroner's Court?'

'That'll be a matter for the coroner to decide. In the meantime, we'll contact you if we need any more details.'

We escorted Caitlin back to reception and watched as she left Queen Street.

I turned to Lydia. 'Something wasn't right there. She was overdoing all the emotion.'

'Maybe she was upset.'

'After a second date? And why ask about the Coroner's Court? It sounded as though she was familiar with the process involved.'

Back in the Incident Room, I was about to make for my room when Lydia asked, 'Do we add her to the board as a person of interest?'

I nodded. 'For now. She was the last person to see Frank Armsby alive.'

An email reached my inbox from Superintendent Cornock asking for an update first thing in the next morning. So I settled into making progress with the inquiry. The report from Alvine Dix arrived. She couldn't conclude whether Armsby had been killed near the builders' merchant or at some other location. Minuscule fragments of dust and chippings had been removed from his clothes, but the forensic analysis would take several days and her preliminary conclusion was that he had probably been killed a short distance away from the builders' merchant and his body dumped in the car park.

It didn't answer the question of why Frank Armsby visited the industrial estate in the first place. The crime scene investigators hadn't found anything else near the body.

I clicked into the CCTV footage from the restaurant and reminded myself of the timeline involved. Armsby had arrived a few minutes before seven and had left a little after nine-thirty. After discovering his body the following morning, the pathologist's report had suggested he had been dead for approximately six to eight hours. It took the time of death to midnight, give or take: at least twelve hours unaccounted for after he'd left the restaurant.

I stared at the image of Frank Armsby paying for his meal. It would be the last thing he had ever paid for. Then I found the footage Lydia had recovered from the CCTV cameras along the probable route Armsby had taken. I began with the camera nearest the middle of Cardiff and tried to second-guess where Armsby parked his car. I started the footage at nine-forty, assuming Armsby had taken ten minutes to reach his vehicle. I couldn't spot Armsby's BMW and I persevered with watching footage from the other cameras. I drew a blank.

One explanation would be that Armsby had gone home before travelling to Penarth Road, another would be that he had taken a bus or a taxi, and another that Armsby was killed elsewhere and his body and car moved.

It would mean hours of trawling through CCTV footage. And that meant I needed more manpower – something else to add to the list to discuss with Superintendent Cornock.

I requisitioned a background search on Caitlin Prior before wading my way through financial checks on Frank Armsby. The results were unremarkable. He had a modest mortgage on the house in Whitchurch and owned the office building outright. No unusual patterns in his spending.

By the end of the afternoon I'd heard Lydia speaking on the telephone a couple of times and she came into my office notepad in hand. 'Got a minute boss?' I pointed at the visitor chairs in front of my desk.

'I've tracked down and spoken to Armsby's two previous victims. One of them moved to Norwich soon after the case was dismissed by the judge. She told me she hadn't been back to Cardiff since then. She seemed pleased with the news of Armsby's death.'

'There's quite a group of them.'

Lydia ignored my comment. 'The second woman lives near Bridgend. She admitted being pleased when she heard about his death on the evening news. Then she immediately offered an alibi that she been with her boyfriend bowling and eating pizza the night he was killed.'

'So our only person of interest at the moment is Judy Campbell.' I let the sentence hang in the air. 'And we've got Terry's suggestion Armsby was linked to organised crime and a woman Armsby was on a date with the evening he died is playing to the gallery.'

'Not much to go on.'

Then I recalled that I still hadn't heard from the forensics lab with details of the examination of Armsby's BMW 3 Series. I lifted the handset of my phone and dialled Alvine's number, but it rang for a long time until an unfamiliar voice answered. After establishing that Alvine had left early, ostensibly to go for a walking weekend in the Brecon Beacons, I asked a colleague for a progress report.

'Sorry, Inspector Marco. That should be done by early next week.'

'Next week!'

'You know how it is, we're shorthanded.'

I felt like shouting – how do you explain that to the grieving family? But there wasn't one, so I didn't bother.

Arriving home, I found a lasagne in the freezer and whilst it microwaved I called my mother to confirm the arrangements for our lunch the following day. She would be bookended by a meeting with Cornock and my first trip to the Cardiff Domestic Violence Taskforce forum. In between I'd be doing more digging into the life of Frank Armsby.

I couldn't settle that evening. I should have been watching some thriller on the television but I decided to leave the apartment and drive down to Penarth Road. I wanted to experience exactly where Frank Armsby had been killed at the same time of day as he had been there. Night had drawn in by the time I pulled my Mondeo into a layby and I got out, dragging the lapels of my coat up to my neck. The sweater over my shirt kept me warm as an autumnal wind chilled my skin. Streetlights illuminated the road and the traffic wasn't heavy. A bus trundled northward into the city and the occasional taxi buzzed passed. I tramped down to the junction for the builders' merchant. I stopped and stood peering up the road, trying to work out why Frank Armsby had been here. I scanned the surrounding buildings hoping there were CCTV cameras that had been missed.

I was disappointed. I walked across the road and then into the junction and up towards the builders' merchant. It got significantly darker as the frequency of the streetlights diminished. An occasional weak floodlight bathed the outside of industrial buildings more as a deterrent against an ambitious burglar than a safety device.

A white light bleeped on the underside of a red security box screwed high on the front elevation of the builders' merchant. Passing the entrance and away from the last streetlight, I paused on the pavement's kerb edge. One thing was clear to me. It was the perfect place to murder a man by knocking him over with a car. Out of sight and more than enough space for a vehicle to gather enough speed to ensure the outcome of a collision between a vehicle and a body was beyond doubt.

Chapter 9

Staring into the mirror in the hallway by the door of my flat I noticed my sombre grey suit needed to be pressed. And cleaned. In fact, I couldn't remember when it had last been to the dry cleaners but the wrinkles on the trousers were well established and the jacket had a comfortable battered appearance. I drew a brush through my hair before passing a hand over my shoulders, removing any flecks of fluff. I doubted Superintendent Cornock would notice but my mother, who I was meeting for lunch, certainly would. And I hoped my suit would impress the members of the forum that afternoon. I had already smoked the first cigarette of the day at breakfast in my pyjamas, knowing my mother would smell tobacco on my clothes, so the second of the day would have to wait until after I'd seen her.

I reached Queen Street persuading myself the powder blue shirt paired with my suit gave me an executive air. Lydia soon brought me down to earth. She scanned me, turned up her nose ever so faintly. 'There have been lots of phone calls following the appeal for witnesses. But I think most of them are time wasters.'

'Any of them we need to interview?'

'I'll go through the list in more detail this morning.'

'And you'd better start on the CCTV footage from the cameras along Penarth Road. I couldn't find anything immediately after Armsby had left the restaurant, which suggests he either went home or took a different route.'

Lydia nodded. The board in the Incident Room appeared cluttered. I surveyed the details, fixing in my mind enough to convey to Superintendent Cornock that we were making meaningful progress.

It was mid-morning when I trundled through the corridors of Queen Street to my superior officer's room. After rapping my knuckles on his door, I waited until he shouted an instruction for me to enter. He'd recently had a haircut by the look of the neat short back and sides. He wore one of his regular grey suits, white shirt and a navy tie with red stripes.

'Good morning, John.'

'Morning, sir.' I sat in one of the visitor chairs.

'You'd better bring me up to date.'

'Paddy reckons Frank Armsby was knocked down by a vehicle that then proceeded to drive over him.'

Cornock winced. 'Ouch.'

'Cause of death was multiorgan failure.'

'Any idea why he was on the industrial estate in Penarth Road?'

'We haven't been able to establish that, sir. We've spoken to a woman who was with him for dinner on the night he died. We cannot trace his movements after he left her. Lydia is working on the CCTV footage from various cameras covering Penarth Road, but our preliminary assessment seems to be that he either went home first or took another route.'

'Any forensics?'

'None yet, sir. But Alvine is waiting for results from the lab on samples she recovered from his clothes.'

'What about Armsby's history – he's not exactly a model of an upstanding citizen.'

'Talking to his former wife and her family was depressing enough.'

'And there were two other cases?'

'Lydia has spoken to one woman who now lives in Norwich. She hasn't been back to Cardiff since the original assault several years ago.'

'Check it out just in case.'

I nodded. 'And the second woman lives in Bridgend and immediately offered a detailed alibi when Lydia spoke to her. I'll organise an officer to go and talk to her. Which brings me to the resources we need, sir.'

Cornock sat back in his chair. I had seen the look on his face many times: frustration and annoyance. It would have been easy to take it personally, but I knew it wasn't directed at me. When he replied his voice sounded tired. 'I'll see what I can do.'

'I've also had some intelligence that suggests Armsby was involved with organised crime groups – he was an accountant who offered services that didn't ask too many questions.'

'So, it could be a revenge killing. Jesus, the last thing we want is a couple of the OCG's taking lumps out of each other. The last few months have been strange. Times like these, John, makes policing very challenging.'

I arrived early for my lunch with Mamma. In fact, I made a point of being prompt. It avoided the critical glare, a raised eyebrow and, being from a family with strong Italian connections and traditions, I wouldn't have dreamt of disappointing her.

The maître d' gave her a warm smile when she arrived. Most of the Italians in Cardiff and the rest of South Wales come from a few villages in the north of Italy but Mamma was from Lucca and it gave her a more exotic pedigree. She came over to my table and kissed me on the cheek although she dwelt a second longer than she needed to – checking if she could smell tobacco on my clothes.

'You're looking thin, John.'

I never ate enough for my mother.

'Are you eating properly?'

I didn't need to reply as the waiter appeared at our table inviting drinks orders. We both settled for San Pellegrino, no ice, no lemon.

'How's Papà?' I said, picking up the menu.

'He's well. He is busy. It has been a very bad time. But now the business has picked up and the café has reopened. The new manager is making a go of the place.'

Papà's ice cream business had been able to survive the lockdown and he'd been good with his staff, but it would take a couple of years to get back to the success it had once enjoyed.

We ordered cannelloni and a green salad. Mamma told me about some distant relatives who would be coming to stay in the New Year and how busy she was helping my father but I knew it was all a softening up exercise for drilling down into my relationship with Jackie, my ex, and our son, Dean.

We had almost finished our meal when Mamma asked, 'Have you spoken to Jackie?'

It was open-ended enough and I was tempted to ask, "about what?", but thought the better of it, so settled for a simple noncommittal reply. 'I'm seeing Dean on Saturday, work permitting, and I spoke to Jackie about the arrangements a couple of days ago.'

It satisfied her because she nodded approvingly. 'I've invited Jackie to come down for October week with Dean.'

I stopped mid-mouthful and peered over the table. 'You could have asked me first.'

She dismissed my reservations with a roll of her head.

'I would have liked to have been consulted. I thought it was going to be Dean and me with you and Papà.'

'But Jackie is Dean's mother.'

'I know...'

'And it's good that you two are getting on so well.'

'Mamma, you're—'

'What?'

I finished the last piece of pasta and gathered my thoughts. But Mamma continued. 'And you and Jackie can have some time together.'

She made no secret of the fact that she hoped Jackie and I would reconcile and that we could provide a home for Dean. I wasn't certain she realised exactly how my relationship with Jackie had developed. We had both treated a recent night of intimacy when we had fallen into each other's arms as a temporary lapse and not as a longing to rekindle some long-extinguished flame.

'It would mean I'd have to sleep on the sofa.' It was a half-hearted and lame response. Mamma raised her eyebrows at me in mock incredulity.

Arguing was futile, so we finished our lunch, she kissed me again, twice on the cheeks, thanked the maître d' for a wonderful lunch and set off for her afternoon shopping. After negotiating the crowds in the St David's Shopping Centre, I wound my way through the back streets towards Queen Street.

I spent an hour reviewing the notes of the minutes of the last meeting of the Cardiff Domestic Violence Taskforce forum that Chief Superintendent Harper had sent me. It had words like 'outcomes' and 'stakeholders' and lots of management-speak to create the impression that progress was being made. I read the statistics about domestic violence within households, which was shocking enough, but the success rate for prosecutions of sexual offences was sobering. Most women who were assaulted never came forward because they were terrified the system would let them down. It disgusted me that rapists could get away with their crimes and that we hadn't been able to build a fairer and better system.

I nudged the car out of the car park at Queen Street and drove east along Newport Road until the satnav bleeped instructions for me to indicate left and then continue for half a mile. Its directions took me to the car park of an anonymous-looking office building. I found the name of the charity hosting the forum meeting and I made my way upstairs to the second floor. Chief Superintendent Harper was already waiting for me in the reception, together with Alison Swan.

'I'm glad to see you're on time, Inspector,' Harper said.

I smiled at Alison, she smiled back.

Seconds later a woman appeared and introduced herself

as the coordinator for the forum. She led us through into an administrative office and announced, 'You all know Chief Superintendent Harper of the Wales Police Service but there are two new officers with him today. Detective Constable Alison Swan and Detective Inspector John Marco of the serious crime unit. We are very pleased that Inspector Marco could join us and that the WPS is taking its participation in this forum so seriously.'

She nodded in my direction. I wasn't certain if she expected me to say anything, so I kept my reply simple. 'Thank you for your welcome.'

She proceeded to go around the room introducing Jack Hughes, an administrative officer, a sheepish-looking man in his mid-thirties with a thin beard and nervous-looking eyes who was introduced as the minute-taker for the meeting. Jenny Sartin was the coordinator of the charity supporting abused women and Penny Larkham was its senior counsellor.

We went through into a conference suite where flasks of coffee and bottles of sparkling water had been set out on a table to one side. In former times, I would have shaken hands but now I exchanged nods of acknowledgement with an officer from Cardiff City Council who led on domestic violence issues, a housing official from another local authority, an officer from the Crown Court and finally a district judge from Cardiff County Court who wore a striking pinstripe suit and a cutaway collar with a severely knotted silk tie. He had a loud booming voice, but it was soon overshadowed by the woman I'd met in reception, and whose name I couldn't remember, calling the meeting to order.

I sat between Alison Swan and Chief Superintendent Harper. Turning my gaze towards each of the speakers in turn I listened intently to their contributions, hoping the chairman wouldn't be asking for my input. Luckily Harper chipped in with comments about how the WPS was giving domestic violence top priority particularly post-pandemic, when certainties about employment and family life had been shaken. Listening to Harper, I realised why he was the chief superintendent and I doubted I would ever have the application for these meetings. I preferred rounding up the bad guys, watching a key turning in a cell door and grinning as a judge handed out long prison sentences.

By the end of the afternoon the room divided into the specific interest groups. Sartin and Larkham defending the abused women with every ounce of their energy while Harper cautioned that the police needed strong evidence to prosecute. The district judge favoured issuing restraining orders as a matter of course and worrying about the consequences later. The housing officials made clear there was an acute shortage of alternative accommodation, which made rehousing the affected women problematic.

Hughes scribbled notes energetically on a pad. I guessed the minutes of the meeting would be finding their way to a long list of email addresses by the beginning of the week. I could quite justifiably argue that my involvement in this forum would be secondary to the inquiry into Armsby's death. And that suited me down to the ground.

Chapter 10

Justifying having an afternoon off during the first few days of a murder inquiry to enjoy the Bluebirds home game against Queens Park Rangers with Dean got me into Queen Street early. There was always something going on, a nightshift taking care of the drunks and brawls in the city centre, the sound of a cleaner vacuuming and telephones ringing incessantly. But at eight-thirty on a Saturday morning it was reasonably quiet. I sat on the edge of a desk listening to the activity in the building and took a moment to peer at the board.

The face of Frank Armsby looked down at me. It was emotionless and anonymous.

To the left was a list of the women he had assaulted. Judy Campbell's name was at the top followed by the two women whose cases had been abortive. Imagining the sort of ordeal one had faced in giving evidence with Armsby in the dock staring at her made me shiver. Our system, with a judge sitting on an elevated podium bewigged and gowned, as well as barristers similarly dressed, must have been intimidating. It reminded me I had to speak to Judy Campbell, so I made a mental note to email Alison to set something up.

Lydia had also attached to the board the image of Caitlin Prior. There was something about her reaction to Armsby's death that appeared forced, unnatural even. Would she be featuring again in the inquiry?

I went through into my office and booted up my computer. I deleted a dozen or so email circulars that didn't need to be read or pondered in any detail: the politics of the workplace didn't interest me. When I saw the email from Alvine Dix entitled 'Report Update' I clicked it open.

The attachment had details of the forensic results from Armsby's BMW 3 Series. I read about the gravel and chippings and particles of sand recovered from the passenger's and driver's foot wells. Fragments of skin had been removed from the cupholder between the driver and passenger seat and Alvine reckoned there was more than enough to extract a reasonable DNA match. She warned me it would be a few days before the full results would be available.

But it was the results of the fingerprinting that took my attention. There were three complete sets and three partials. One belonged to Frank Armsby another to an unidentified individual and the third to Jim White. None of the three partial prints could be traced. I smiled to myself when I relished the prospect of interviewing Jim White. But we had a lot more digging to do before I could have the pleasure of his company across a table in a windowless interview room.

I heard Lydia entering the Incident Room, pulling off her jacket, dumping a bag on the desk. I yelled through and moments later she stood on the threshold of my office, portable plastic coffee mug in hand. 'Morning boss, you're in early.'

I waved her in, and she sat in one of the visitor chairs.

'Alvine Dix has sent me the fingerprint analysis from Armsby's BMW. There are three partials and one full set she can't identify – nothing on record apparently. But there is one complete set of fingerprints from Jim White.'

Lydia raised her eyebrows. She took a sip of her drink.

'If Jim White was with Armsby in his car then I think we need to know why, and when. Terry mentioned Armsby had been working for Jim White. Let's do some more digging into White and his empire.'

'Shouldn't we get the lads from the economic crime unit involved?'

I paused. Maybe I could call Boyd Pearce, my previous detective sergeant, who was working in that department. Chasing white collar criminals offered more regular hours, something his wife and young family appreciated.

'You know what they're like, it will take ages to make any progress. We could be waiting until Christmas for a reply. Let's do some background checks ourselves. It can't be that difficult to do a search at Companies House.'

Lydia shrugged noncommittally. 'He might use nominees as directors so we might never find out the full extent of how many companies he controls.'

'Let's do what we can.'

I started on the list of limited companies that we knew were customers of Frank Armsby's accountancy practice. I tried to identify if any had registered offices in the Newport area. It was painstaking stuff. Gradually I assembled a list of how many of Armsby's clients used his premises as their registered office, guessing it was convenient and anonymous. Other customers had registered offices in a building in the middle of the city. I googled the postcode and clicked on Google Street View. The office block looked as though it was occupied by solicitors or accountants or financial advisers. By the time I'd finished I had the details of ten companies with registered offices or with business premises in the Newport area. A postcode search told me that none were in the docks and my initial enthusiasm that Terry's intelligence was reliable waned. I needed a concrete link to Jim White.

It was mid-morning by the time I sauntered through into the Incident Room and noticed Lydia staring intently at the monitor of her computer.

'It took me a while to find Jim White's personal details,' Lydia said.

I sat on a chair by the desk next to hers as she explained the search results. Jim White was associated with several limited companies and I recognised at least half a dozen of the names. 'A lot of those have their registered offices at Armsby's property.'

'Does it give us enough to speak to Jim White?'

'His fingerprints are inside Armsby's BMW which is more than enough to justify us talking to Jim White.'

I spent what was left of the morning – fortified by coffee – focusing on building a picture of Jim White. I requisitioned a search from the DVLA of details of any vehicle registered in his name and I printed off a copy of his photograph from the PNC search. As I was switching off my computer Lydia bustled through into my room announcing she had an address for Jim White in Newport docks.

I stood up. 'Let's speak to him next week.'

I arrived at Jackie's house promptly and pulled my Mondeo onto the drive. She opened the door as I left the car and greeted me outside the house with a kiss on the cheek that lingered. 'Lovely to see you, John.'

Colour had returned permanently to her cheeks after she moved back from Basingstoke to Cardiff once her relationship with Paul ended. His regular nine-to-five job was one of the things she found attractive but, in the end, it hadn't worked out. She hadn't shared with me the details, but when we spent a night together recently it had rekindled emotions I hadn't wanted to unpack. I had disappointed her in the past and let her down badly, focusing on my career and putting my drinking before her. I knew I had a chance now to make things better with her and Dean.

I followed Jackie into the house and heard the tramping of urgent footsteps upstairs. She cast a glance up the stairwell. 'He's getting ready. He's been looking forward so much. I was worried you might not be able to take him with this new case.'

'How did you know about that?'

'Your mother called.' I should have known the answer. 'She wanted to discuss with me the plans for October half term holiday. I'm not certain I should be coming too. It feels a bit too soon, after....'

I nodded.

'What do you think, John?'

I wanted to tell her that I thought Mamma shouldn't interfere.

'I think it might send the wrong message to Dean.'

She gave me a half-hearted smile of approval as the sound of Dean thumping down the staircase filled the hallway. He was wearing the Bluebirds home kit I had bought for him last month and his hair was neat and tidy, and there was an excited look on his face. 'Dad,' he said, 'were going to be late if we don't go now.'

After giving Jackie a peck on the cheek I left, and Dean jumped into the car and we drove down into the city. This week we were watching the game at Rob's house in Llandaff. He had recently bought a new fifty-five inch television which impressed Dean. For every home game we made a fuss of the boys – copious amounts of their favourite soft drinks, pies at half-time and a generous supply of sweets.

I pulled up at a set of traffic lights and two lads wearing Cardiff City scarfs walked over the road in front of us.

'The Bluebirds have signed a new striker, Dad.'

'What's his name?'

Dean pronounced the name of the German footballer perfectly.

'He scored lots of goals when he played in Germany, but he didn't play well with Bournemouth. That's why they sold him.'

'Let's hope he scores for us.' I pulled away when the lights changed.

Dean had supported Queen's Park Rangers when he lived in Basingstoke, but he'd transferred his allegiance to Cardiff City when he moved here.

'How do you feel about watching QPR?'

'Dad,' he sounded exasperated, 'I support the Bluebirds now.'

I smiled, 'Yes, I know, but...'

'Are we still going to Fat Jack's afterwards?'

The burger restaurant was Dean's favourite. 'Of course.'

'Great!'

We arrived in good time at Rob's house and got settled into his lounge, the surround sound filling the room with the pre-match commentary.

There had been two games between both sides in the previous season. One had been a nil-nil draw and Cardiff had lost the other 2-3. When the whistle blew to start the game, Dean sat forward, gazing at the screen. The first opportunity for Cardiff came from a long throw in but Queens Park Rangers were able to clear the danger and one of their forwards set out on a counter-attack. That was the high point of an otherwise uninteresting first half. Cardiff's manager must have inspired his team with the half-time pep talk because they kicked off like men possessed and had one chance after another until one of the midfield players passed a low ball into the box and the centre forward drilled it into the back of the net. We all jumped in excitement, Dean waving his hands and shouting support for the scorer.

By the end Cardiff scored a second and the winner which encouraged us to believe that our team would secure promotion at last. Dean and Neil, Rob's son analysed each move of the game and it amazed me that they could remember the moves in such detail. We made moves to leave for the burger restaurant, a favourite of Dean's and Neil's, when my telephone rang.

'John Marco,' I said, not recognising the number.

'Operational support, sir. We've got a report of suspected murder. You are to attend. The details and postcode are being emailed to you as we speak.'

The woman finished the call and it left me staring at the mobile, cursing my career choice and feeling wretched that I was letting Dean down again.

'Problem?' Rob said.

'Something urgent.'

'I can take Dean back to Jackie's.'

I turned to Dean who was looking up at me perplexed and confused. 'I'm really sorry, Dean. I've had an urgent message about a case.'

'Is it a murder?' Neil said, his young voice full of excitement.

I ignored him. 'We'll go to Fat Jack's next time. Promise.'

'At least we won,' Dean said.

I straightened and turned to Rob. 'I'd better call Jackie.'

Chapter 11

The lights of two marked police cars bathed the houses of the Edwardian terrace in an eerie white glow. The radio inside one beeped and the voice of an officer answering a call drifted onto the street. Another officer stood by the doorway scanning the road. This was a quiet neighbourhood, to the west of Roath Park, an area of desirable and well-appointed homes. As I parked at the end of the terrace, I noticed Lydia's car drawing up behind me. We met on the pavement.

'I thought you watching the game today?' Lydia said.

'It had just finished.'

'Who is the victim?'

'Raymond Carey.'

An officer who left one of the vehicles recognised me. 'He's in the dining room at the back, Inspector.'

He pushed two pairs of latex gloves over towards us and we snapped them on.

'Do you know anything about him?'

'A friend discovered him when he called to collect him. They were going out for a meal.'

We took the narrow path and then three slate steps towards the front door. The officer there stood to one side. 'It's a bit of a mess. And there's another officer by the back door.'

I nodded and entered. Black and white tiles lined the ground floor hallway and the walls and ceilings were painted a rich dark blue. Freshly cut flowers stood in a vase on a round, highly polished antique table. The barest smell of furniture polish hung in the air. A carpet with a tight weave covered the staircase, it looked immaculate, as though it had recently been laid.

A glance into the sitting room showed the tidy, well-organised appearance continuing. I hesitated before pushing open the door to the room I assumed to be the dining room. A fireplace dominated one external wall, its mantelpiece grand and of the same period as the house. Above it was an enormous mirror with the words 'see you later' scrawled in what looked like bright red lipstick.

It was the figure lying on a table that demanded our attention. I stood for a moment; Lydia gasped. The man's arms were stretched out either side of him and each wrist was bound with a rope attached to the table, keeping the body secure. A similar arrangement secured his legs.

His eyes stared lifelessly upwards as though the terror that possessed them in the seconds and minutes before he died had been too much to bear. The face and hair looked healthy and his corpulent body was completely naked.

But what really took my attention was the mutilation of the genitalia. The killer had used a knife in a frenzied attack. It made me feel sick.

I skirted round the table, giving it a wide berth whilst Lydia stood rigid, rooted to the spot. She was scanning the room, taking in every detail as her eyes dwelt on the mirror above the mantelpiece.

There was blood, lots of it, which made me think the wounds were sustained ante-mortem. A piece of rough cloth stuffed into Carey's mouth had spared his neighbours from listening to his screams. But it was the single bullet wound to his chest that probably killed him. I wondered if I could avoid attending the post-mortem. The prospect of listening to Paddy McVeigh explaining how the injuries had been inflicted would be more than my stomach could tolerate.

It was only then that I turned my attention to the rest of the room. Furniture had been pushed to the edges, a pile of clothes deposited in one corner. Raymond Carey had met a brutal end. Was the assailant known to him? There was a very specific signature to the killer's handiwork. Killing someone in an enclosed room like this meant that even a careful, cold-blooded killer would leave a trace. After all, every murder has a motive and every killer leaves a trace.

My mind accelerated through the various protocols.

House-to-house inquiries would need to be completed, the post-mortem undertaken and a full forensic report.

A voice I didn't expect to hear engaged the officer standing by the front door. 'And who the hell is the duty inspector?'

Lydia gave me a surprised look.

'Detective Inspector Marco,' Alvine raised her voice.

'In here, Alvine.'

She entered already wearing a white forensic suit. Instantly, she recoiled, a look of horror crossing her face for a second. 'Christ almighty. Someone's been busy.' Then she looked over at me. 'This is a crime scene so you two can bugger off. And I hope you find the local Hannibal Lecter pretty bloody quick.'

We left Alvine barking instructions at the CSIs on her team. Once they'd finished, we could come back and get a clear picture of Raymond Carey's life. For now, we needed to speak to the person who found the body.

We exited the house, dodging round the investigators scurrying inside with bags of equipment. I stood for a moment with the officer we had spoken to originally and he gave me the contact details for a David Plowman. 'We've had a lot of the neighbours talking to us. All very concerned and terrified about what happened. And there's been journalists sniffing around.'

'Tell the reporters to go to hell.'

The officer gave me a sardonic look.

I continued. 'And tell the locals that officers conducting house-to-house inquiries will call tomorrow morning. In the meantime, if they have any immediate and urgent concerns to call 999.'

Back in the car I punched Plowman's postcode into the satnav and it told me the journey to one of the northern suburbs of Cardiff would take fifteen minutes. Traffic lights and herds of taxis delayed my journey and after twenty minutes I pulled up at the pavement outside Plowman's semi-detached property. Lydia parked a little distance away.

'Who is it?' Plowman yelled from behind the locked door.

'Detective Inspector John Marco and Detective Sergeant Lydia Flint of the Wales Police Service. May we come in?'

'Have you got some identification?' His voice sounded shrill.

'Mr Plowman, you can inspect our warrant cards.'

'Put them up against the window. I'm not taking any chances.' Now his voice began to break.

He drew back the curtain of a downstairs sitting room and peered at the cards we pushed towards the glass.

A few seconds later two chains fell to one side and the Yale lock was opened.

Plowman let us in and urgently cast a glance up and down the street before relocking the door. A suitcase stood in the hallway by a coat stand. 'Are you going away Mr Plowman?'

He stood stock still, with bulging eyes and the inability to blink that only terror could create. He blubbered a reply. 'I'm not staying here. Have you seen what happened to Ray? I'm getting out of Cardiff as soon as I can.'

'Where are you going?'

'As far away as possible. I'm going to drive. Maybe Scotland or Ireland or I'll take a ferry to France.'

Lydia struck a sincere tone. 'Do you have somewhere we can sit down quietly to talk.'

I doubted that anything was going to calm David Plowman.

He led us through into a sitting room where the curtains had been drawn. It was a functional sort of room that didn't have the obvious wealth of Carey's home. Recessed spotlights in the ceiling flooded the room with a stark white light.

'Can you tell me about your relationship with Mr

Carey?' I said.

Plowman took a deep breath. 'We've been seeing each other for eighteen months.'

'Were you living together?'

'We both valued our independence although we did talk about it.'

'So what time did you arrive this evening?'

'We had a table booked at some fancy pub bistro he likes going to. I mean liked...' His voice faltered again. 'I called for him about six. I parked outside as I always do and let myself in.' He paused and swallowed as he shared a glance between Lydia and me. 'I called out and there was no response. I didn't know what to think, I....'

'Did you notice anything unusual?' Lydia said. 'Anybody on the street outside?'

Plowman looked confused. 'I didn't notice anything. I mean I wasn't looking for anybody. Why would I do that?'

Trying to put him at ease I added. 'It is very important Mr Plowman if you can remember anything that might assist us.'

He gave us another blank look before some shouting from outside unnerved him and he gave the curtains and then the door into the hallway a sharp look. 'I can't think, I mean I don't know what to think.'

'Did Raymond ever share with you that he was feeling afraid?'

Another brisk shake of the head. 'He worked in a bank. We were ordinary, straightforward. I don't know why anybody would want to do this to him. It's all a big mistake.'

The body on the table and the extent of the injuries suggested that was far from the truth. Carey had been targeted. One thing I knew for certain was that we needed to interview Plowman again once the initial shock had dissipated. 'We'll need to speak to you again tomorrow morning.'

'Tomorrow? I mean I was—'

'We'll need you to stay in Cardiff. I suggest you book into a hotel tonight if you feel safer doing that.'

'Hotel?'

'And we shall also need to take your fingerprints so that we can eliminate you from our inquiry.'

I don't think Plowman understood, from the baffled look on his face.

I didn't want to intimidate Plowman, but I kept my voice serious. 'We'll need all your contact details – mobile number and email address and an officer will make contact in the morning.'

Chapter 12

I slept badly, images of Ray Carey's body swimming around in my dreams. Even though I'd been doing this job a long time it was impossible to ignore the sight of blood and gore. Sometimes it kept me from sleeping and other times it woke me early. Often it made me want to visit the pub and feel the comforting taste of alcohol on my tongue. Not even the most hardened of detectives I'd met as a rookie constable were immune to the impact that death and human depravity could cause.

I left the flat and drove down to one of the greasy spoon cafés I favoured in the Bay. After ordering a bacon sandwich and a double shot Americano I took one of the red top Sunday newspapers from the counter back to a table and found the sports pages. Reading the analysis of the game brought a smile to my face when a journalist concluded that Cardiff would be strong enough to earn a place in the play-off finals of the championship that season. For a fraction of a second I daydreamed about watching Premier League football at the Cardiff City Stadium and how excited Dean would be at that prospect.

Fortified by thick slices of white bread and fatty bacon and a full-strength coffee, I paid and left. It wasn't raining nor too cold, the sort of miserable autumn weather that lingers. Within half an hour I was parking on a side street near Raymond Carey's home, watching a mobile incident room being lifted into place at the kerb. I nodded a greeting to the operational support officers directing traffic.

Two crime scene investigators stood on the pavement at the bottom of the path leading up to the property, one smoking a cigarette. I joined them and dipped into my jacket pocket, tempted to light up by the smoke drifting into my nostrils.

'First of the day,' I announced, pleased with myself that I hadn't indulged before leaving the flat or after having breakfast.

The Cardiff Lockdown Murders

'We've almost finished,' the CSI who wasn't smoking said.

The other one flicked the butt end into the street. 'Hell of a mess in there.'

'Anything I should know about?'

'Lots of fingerprints, fabric samples. Alvine will send you a report no doubt.'

'Have you been here all night?'

It prompted both men to yawn in unison.

'Marco.' Alvine raised her voice and I looked towards the house and saw her standing on the threshold. I tossed the remains of the cigarette under the tyre of an adjacent car and strode up the path.

'Morning, Alvine.'

'We've almost finished.'

'So what do you reckon?'

Alvine turned her back and gestured for me to follow her into the house. She took two steps into the dining room. The table was in the same place but the body had been removed, awaiting Paddy McVeigh's detailed attention the following morning. 'Somehow he was overpowered. My guess is he was probably knocked unconscious and then stripped before being tied to the table.' She fluttered a hand in the air. 'Then... the killer... the pathologist can give you a better opinion, but I think it must have been one hell of a sharp knife as the cuts were long and deep.'

'Is there any evidence I need to know about immediately?'

'There are lots of fingerprints. Partials and full sets I'll run through the system later this morning.'

'You should get some sleep.'

'Job doesn't get done if you're in bed.'

Alvine's dedication to her career was the stuff of legend in the Southern Division of the Wales Police Service. I knew she enjoyed walking the hills in her spare time, but knew nothing about her private life, which had been the subject of rumour and gossip over the years. Anyone putting up with her brusque, abrupt nature would need the patience of a saint.

'And we collected lots of skin and fabric samples.' She looked over at me. 'Do you have any idea who would have done this?' There was vulnerability to her voice. 'Because you need to find him, Marco. You need to find this bastard.'

I kept her eye contact direct before replying. 'I know, Alvine. I know.'

She left the property and I took time to walk around the house. A team from operational support would arrive soon to remove Carey's personal possessions. Until then it would give me an opportunity to try and tune into his world. Carey lived alone, as did Frank Armsby. They had died violent deaths, but the brutality of Carey's was sickening. The modus operandi for both deaths wasn't similar but that didn't rule out the same killer.

Two sofas upholstered in matching chintzy patterns filled the sitting room. Extravagant swags and tails hung from the pink curtains pulled to either side of the bay window. There were no personal knick-knacks in the display cabinet in one corner, but shelves built alongside the fireplace contained a collection of cranberry glass and blue china. The dining room was clear now although a faint smudge of red lipstick had been left on the mirror. Was there any significance to the words? I paused for a moment to think. Was the killer telling us something or leaving a sign, or perhaps it just offered some macabre catharsis for the killer?

At the top of the stairs a landing led down into a bathroom with navy tiles on the floor and white wall tiles from floor-to-ceiling. I turned and looked in the other direction towards the bedrooms. At the far end of the landing was the master bedroom. It was neat and tidy. I eased open a massive, mirrored built-in wardrobe door and surveyed Carey's clothes. I ran a hand along the lapels of a couple of suits – they felt expensive and well-tailored.

A second bedroom was sparsely furnished – a single functional bed and a simple wardrobe. It didn't look as though Carey had regular guests to stay. The final bedroom had been converted into a study. A bookcase lined one wall and scanning the contents suggested he organised books by topic. A section on history had volumes about the Eighth Army's campaign in North Africa during the Second World War and half a dozen about Winston Churchill. A thick Italian dictionary stood between several tomes on learning the language. The ubiquitous Ian Rankin and Val McDermid dominated the crime fiction section. Carey was tidy, even to the point of being obsessive about the positioning of the books at the edge of each shelf.

The sound of movement downstairs and voices from the operational support department meant that the computer and possessions on the desk in the study would soon be back at Queen Street. Idly I opened some of the drawers and found some personal correspondence and stationery. Back on the ground floor I retraced my steps towards the mobile incident room where a uniformed sergeant was fielding enquiries from two middle-aged women. I avoided his pleading look and stepped back onto the pavement, fishing my mobile from a pocket, and messaged Lydia. Her reply was brief – *Still with Plowman. Call later.* I turned and watched as the two women sauntered back up the road discussing in hushed tones, no doubt, the inadequacies of the Wales Police Service.

'I've got two householders that need to speak to you.' A name badge on the sergeant's sweater said Thomas. I hadn't come across him before.

'Have any of the house-to-house inquiries been productive this morning?'

'A lot of the usual time wasters.'

A murder inquiry was rarely that simple or straightforward. Thomas gave me the names and addresses of the householders and the first property was next to Carey's. I pushed open a small gate painted a vibrant black and walked up the path to the front door. The garden was immaculate and the borders clean and weed free. Mrs Richards opened the door. She was a striking, tall woman with imposing round spectacles and a determined look on her face. Her steel grey hair could have made her sixty-five or seventy-five. From her strong chin and slim build, I guessed it was the former.

I pulled my warrant card from my pocket. 'Detective Inspector John Marco, Wales Police Service. I'm leading the investigation into the death of Raymond Carey. The sergeant at the mobile incident room tells me you may have information that might assist.'

'Yes, of course.' The accent was educated, confident and very English. 'Do come in.'

She led me down the hallway into the kitchen where a man of about the same vintage as her sat by a table. A Sunday newspaper and the supplements covered the top. Alongside them were a mug of tea or coffee and a plate of biscuits. 'May I offer you some coffee?' Mrs Richards asked.

The man stood up. 'I'm Alan Richards.' Same accent as his wife but he didn't match her headmistressy tone. 'Take a seat.' He gathered up the newspapers. 'Country is going to the dogs since that coronavirus business. Looks like there could be a recession for years. And there's so much more talk about an independent Wales now in the press I don't know what's going to become of us.' I caught sight of the headline in the paper that announced further substantial job losses in the manufacturing industries of the Midlands. Hoping that things would return to normal was difficult when normality had been changed beyond recognition.

I sat on a chair and Mrs Richards organised my drink preference. 'How well did you know Raymond Carey?'

'He was pleasant enough I suppose. He moved here

about three years ago.' Alan Richards replied looking over at his wife who nodded confirmation that his dates were correct. 'But I can't say we knew him very well.'

'Did you know if he had any family?'

Richards shook his head. 'Sorry. I've seen his boyfriend or partner, whatever you call it, arrive at the house a few times.'

Mrs Richards placed a china mug carefully on a coaster in front of me and found a chair nearer her husband. 'We are quite private people, Inspector. We certainly don't go prying into other people's business. I wouldn't want you thinking that at all.'

I wanted to say – your neighbour has been murdered in his own home, for Christ's sake.

'No, of course not. Were you home last evening?'

Both nodded without saying anything.

'Did you hear anything from next door?'

'We didn't hear a gunshot if that's what you're asking, Inspector,' Mr Richards replied.

Mrs Richards added. 'We had a discussion on Skype with our daughter who lives in New York at five pm and then we were about to organise our evening meal when we heard the commotion and the officers who arrived at about six-thirty.'

'Did you see anybody entering or leaving the house yesterday?'

'Actually,' Mrs Richards sounded tentative, 'it was earlier that afternoon, when I was in one of the bedrooms and I happened to look out and saw someone leaving. The side of his head had been shaved carefully but I couldn't recognise his features because he pulled a hood over his head as he darted for the gate into the road.'

An eyewitness, progress at last. 'That could be very important, Mrs Richards. Can you remember any other details? And can you be more precise about the time?'

Her brow wrinkled. 'I don't think I can.' Her voice was

clear and assertive. 'Although I was in the bedroom at about half past three.'

'Was there anybody else on the street, somebody else who might have seen this person?'

Now she sounded uncertain. 'I'm not sure. I didn't notice anyone.'

After half an hour I had all the details I needed from Mrs Richards. I thanked them for their assistance and left. Uniformed officers were leaving some of the other adjacent properties and I met them on the pavement. None of the other homeowners had seen or heard anything. It amazed me that the sound of a gunshot had not been noticed by any of Carey's neighbours.

I spent another hour reassuring worried householders, although one occupant, a tall angry man who looked down at me, announced that Carey's lifestyle would earn him eternal damnation. I was glad to be back at Queen Street and when I arrived Lydia was slurping a mug of coffee. It made me realise I was overdue a caffeine injection as well as my second cigarette of the day. I settled for a drink and heaped a teaspoon and a half of instant coffee into a mug while waiting for the kettle to boil. I sat in one of the spare chairs next to Lydia.

'I've never seen anyone so terrified.' She didn't have to explain she was referring to David Plowman. 'He hardly slept all night, apparently, and he was as white as a sheet when I saw him this morning.'

'We'd better do some background checks into David Plowman.'

'Do you think he could be involved?' Lydia proceeded to answer her own question. 'He'd have to be an amazing actor to put on and continue the degree of emotional intensity we saw last night and this morning.'

'People can be clever. Killers can be remarkably resourceful.'

Lydia didn't look convinced.

I had almost finished my drink when Superintendent Cornock entered the Incident Room. Lydia scrambled to her feet. He waved at her to sit down and then he glanced at the board and perched himself on the edge of the desk.

'The whole world and his dog are asking about the murder of Raymond Carey. I've had all the main news outlets making contact, asking for details. Thank Christ that nobody has got wind of the ritualistic nature of the injuries – yet. And I want it to stay that way.'

'Yes, sir.' We both said in unison.

'Is there any immediate link between Raymond Carey and Frank Armsby?'

'At this stage it looks like the circumstances of both deaths are different,' I replied.

Cornock nodded briskly. 'I know, but that doesn't rule out the same killer.' I guessed he was pondering if a second team would be needed. But it was still early in the investigation, too early to make assumptions. I knew Cornock well enough to know that he would wait until he could be certain.

'The post-mortem is going to be conducted tomorrow and hopefully the house-to-house inquiries will help. I've already spoken with one witness who saw someone leaving Carey's house that afternoon.'

'Excellent.' Cornock got to his feet. 'Carey was killed in a residential area so somebody must have seen something. Keep me posted.' He breezed out of the Incident Room and Lydia and I got back to the priorities in hand.

By the end of the afternoon we had a picture of Carey on the board together with images of the dining room and the intimate photographs of Carey's body from the crime scene. The little we knew about Carey had been bullet-pointed as a list under his name. More information would be added in due course. I was about to decide we couldn't make much more progress that afternoon when the telephone on my office desk rang. I hurried through to answer it. When I picked up the handset all I heard was the dialling tone, and then my mobile rang in my jacket pocket. I didn't recognise the number but I recognised the voice – Boyd Pearce, the detective sergeant I had worked with over a number of investigations. He was now working in the economic crime department. 'I hear you're the SIO on the murder of Raymond Carey – I think we should talk.'

Chapter 13

Paddy McVeigh met me at the mortuary reception area the following morning. 'The locum pathologist who attended at the scene last night rang me first thing. She said she'd never seen anything like it.'

'Have you seen the photographs?'

Paddy nodded. He led me down the corridor towards the mortuary. 'Did you watch the game?'

'Great result.'

'I miss going to the stadium and the craic in the bar afterwards.'

The Irish word was code for a ten-pints-of-lager-night when Paddy's eyes would roll around in his head like the metallic balls on a pinball machine. It was camaraderie I had left behind years ago, although Paddy blithely ignored that I was sober.

Inside the mortuary Carey's body was under a sheet on the post-mortem table. On another table nearby photographs taken from the scene had been laid out in a neat order starting with a wide-angle overview of the room before leading to intimate shots that spared no detail.

When Paddy uncovered off the body, I winced at the sight of the mutilated corpse.

Paddy stared down at the chest before announcing simply. 'I think we can say a bullet was the likely cause of death. It's not the sort of thing a body can survive.'

Paddy picked up Carey's right forearm before scrutinising his wrist. He did the same examination to Carey's right foot and the similar discolouration around his ankle before repeating the process on the other side of the trolley. 'The bruising to the wrists and the ankles suggests he must have thrashed around whilst he was on the table.'

Cutting open the chest and abdomen with a deep 'Y' incision, followed by the sound of ribs cracking before body parts were removed always made me feel squeamish so I was pleased when Paddy started a detailed examination of

Carey's genitals. As he prodded and poked and examined Carey's bits I felt quite numb. He dictated details of the wounds, including the length and depth of the lacerations. Paddy took his time, stepping back occasionally, pondering before dictating more notes. Eventually he turned towards me. 'The injuries are compatible with a very sharp blade having been used repeatedly over his genitalia. There would have been a lot of blood.'

'It was all over the table and the floor nearby.'

Paddy turned back to the corpse. 'And they were inflicted ante-mortem.'

'Jesus. It must have been horrendous.'

Paddy paused. 'The gag in his mouth would have muffled any screams, but he would have suffered.' He glanced over at me. 'I'll need to see the GP records before I can write a final report.'

I was beginning to feel queasy. I didn't want my breakfast to be littering the mortuary floor, so I made excuses and found the smokers' area outside the front door. Smoking the second of the day soothed me. I let the smoke waft through my lungs. I ground the butt into the concrete by my feet and went back inside where Paddy was sitting in his office scanning the monitor on his table. He beckoned me over and I sat on one of the visitor chairs.

'The cause of death was a single bullet wound to the heart.' He sat back in his chair, a deep frown creasing his face. 'Somebody wanted to inflict serious pain and suffering on this man.'

I nodded.

'You need to find this person, John,'

I nodded again.

Before I left the hospital a call from Sergeant Thomas from the mobile incident room asked me to attend.

I parked my Mondeo in one of the side streets nearby and walked over. Two uniformed officers were deep in conversation with four members of the public on the pavement. I threaded my way towards the entrance of the mobile incident room and spotted Thomas inside. 'Inspector Marco this is Francis Levine.' He waved a hand as a formal introduction to the man standing in front of him.

'I saw him,' Levine said in a loud booming voice.

I glanced at Thomas who was having trouble hiding a grin.

'I saw the culprit walking down our street with a shot gun. It was like something out of a John Wayne film. He had this flowing overcoat that reached to his knees.'

I smiled at Levine. 'And when exactly was this?'

'Saturday afternoon of course. The day Raymond Carey was killed. I can describe the man's face in detail and how tall he was. He was very distinctive.'

'I see.'

'I insisted to Sergeant Thomas that I had to see you so that I could give you my eyewitness account. I've already spoken with Assistant Chief Constable Neary who is a personal friend of mine and she mentioned you were the senior investigating officer in charge.'

ACC Neary was keeping very dodgy friends, I concluded. The man's account sounded implausible but for the sake of appearances I sat down with him and jotted down the details. Knowing he enjoyed the attention being involved in the inquiry I added. 'It would be very helpful if I could ask you to spend some time with an artist so that we could get a decent impression of what this man looked like.'

'Of course, I should be delighted to assist.'

'And I shall be sure to tell Assistant Chief Constable Neary that your information has been extremely valuable.' Lying came naturally somehow in dealing with this sad individual. I ushered him out before turning to Thomas.

'Sorry about that, sir,' Thomas said. 'He just wouldn't leave.'

'Have you made any more progress this morning?'

'Not much. I'll send you all the details later today.'

Boyd Pearce was deep in conversation with Lydia as I entered the Incident Room. He had put on weight since I had seen him last. He wore a flash suit and white shirt and sombre tie. The lads of the economic crime unit favoured smart clothes, as though it would make them as canny as the dodgy accountants and rogue businessman they investigated.

'Good morning, sir,' Boyd said. Lydia added a greeting.

'I've just had a detour to talk to a time waster who described the killer walking the streets near Carey's house like Clint Eastwood from one of those spaghetti westerns.'

Boyd and Lydia raised their eyebrows.

'How did you get on with the post-mortem?' Lydia asked.

'Paddy was pretty shocked. The gunshot killed him, but the injuries were inflicted ante-mortem.'

Both officers grimaced.

I stood by the board giving the images a detailed look. By now I was becoming immune to the sight of blood and the horrific wounds. The ghoulish looking 'see you later' had little effect. I didn't want to feel numb. I wanted to be focused and determined. I had a killer to catch.

'It looks like some sort of ritual.' I turned to Lydia. 'Have we heard anything from the forensics team?'

She shook her head.

'Chase them.'

Then I turned to Boyd. 'What did you want to tell me?'

'We are in the middle of the complex investigation involving property fraud. There is a dodgy mortgage broker and a dishonest chartered surveyor running a scam. One of the people involved is Jim White.'

'Really, our old friend Mr White. And is Laura still hanging around with him?'

Laura Prince was the wife of Jim White's old boss and she had switched allegiances to White once she knew Frankie Prince's long-term prospects were diminishing rapidly due to his involvement with the East European mafia. She had been proven right when Frankie Prince had been killed in a hail of gunfire.

'Not exactly the darling couple of Cardiff but they have a comfortable, quiet lifestyle, including a house in Spain, all paid for by White's activities.'

'And how does all this fit into our inquiries?'

'Jim White had a connection with Frank Armsby. Armsby had a reputation for turning a blind eye to companies that laundered cash. Armsby was no more than a sideshow.'

'So what's changed?'

'Raymond Carey,' Boyd said sharing a look between Lydia and me. 'He was Jim White's banker.'

I sat back in my chair. Now we had a link between both men. And that link pointed directly towards Jim White.

'I'll send you a briefing memorandum soon as I can.' Boyd stood up and made to leave. I asked about his family; his wife was expecting their second and the regular hours of the economic crime department suited him perfectly.

'Don't you miss the excitement of working here?' Lydia said.

'Never a dull day in economic crime,' Boyd replied.

Neither Lydia nor I believed him. We watched him leave and I announced, 'I'd better go and talk to the superintendent.'

Cornock was sipping tea from a china cup when I entered his room. He had a plate of fancy Viennese-type biscuits and he offered me one, but I declined. 'My only indulgence of the day, John.'

'I've spoken with Detective Sergeant Boyd Pearce of the economic crime unit. They have a live inquiry into Jim White.'

Cornock gave me a pensive look as I continued. 'Frank Armsby worked as an accountant for Jim White apparently.

White is known for businesses that launder money.'

'And how does this directly impact on the two murder inquiries?'

'Carey was White's bank manager. Apparently, he was quite happy to accommodate White's activities.'

'So you think Jim White is the main focus of your inquiry into both deaths?'

'We need to look into the connection.'

'But I've seen the photographs from the crime scene at Carey's house. There's something ritualistic and barbaric about the whole thing. It's more than a gangland killing.'

'I know, sir. But we cannot rule out both deaths being linked.'

Cornock didn't reply immediately. I could see his mind working. I was justifying how to keep both inquiries under my direct supervision. 'Okay, John, for now you can deal with both inquiries simultaneously. And I've allocated Detective Constable Wyn Nuttall to join your team. Keep me fully informed.'

Pleased, I got up before Cornock could reconsider. He added, as I reached the door, 'And I've arranged for a profiler to attend this week to assist. The nature and type of injuries to Carey's body justify additional psychological assistance. I want to keep an open mind about all the circumstances.'

Having an outsider interfering in my investigation was the last thing I wanted. But I had learned it was wise with Superintendent Cornock to choose my battles carefully. And getting him to agree for me to investigate both deaths felt like a minor victory so I mumbled my agreement and left. I pondered how I could sideline a profiler, and make absolutely certain I was in charge and that nobody was going to really interfere with how I would conduct the case.

Chapter 14

'There's going to be a profiler,' I announced to Lydia as I entered the Incident Room.

She looked up from her papers and raised her eyebrows.

'Superintendent Cornock wants to be ahead of the curve and he thinks the injuries to Carey's body justifies getting a profiler in as soon as possible.'

I yanked a chair from underneath a desk and it squeaked as it crossed the wooden floor. I sat down and looked over at the image of Raymond Carey and Frank Armsby on the board. 'We'd better get a full search done to identify if other force areas have had similar deaths. It could be a copycat killer, after all.'

Circulating the other police forces in the United Kingdom requesting assistance to find a killer with a particular modus operandi sounded all well and good in practice, but I knew that in reality the request might languish in the email inbox of an administrative officer. And that would mean dozens of man-hours – none of which were available, even with the additional resources Superintendent Cornock had promised – chasing for the results.

'Get it done. The Super has also allocated Wyn Nuttall to join us for the rest of the inquiry.'

Lydia nodded. I couldn't tell from the expression on her face whether she was pleased with the prospect of working with Wyn Nuttall again. When he had first been a member of my team, he had been inexperienced and a little naïve, although conscientious.

I marched over towards the board. 'Let's see if we can identify if Armsby knew Carey. If they had clients in common there's a chance they met – those bankers are always having fancy dinners together. I've seen them in the hospitality suites at the Cardiff City Stadium.'

'We'll need details of Carey's diary and his clients.'

I was staring at the board but replying to Lydia. 'See if you can set up a meeting for tomorrow morning. I'm going to chase the forensics report.'

'We need to speak to Judy Campbell, the last woman who complained about Frank Armsby.'

I turned to face Lydia, pleased that it meant another opportunity to call Alison Swan. 'Leave that to me.'

Once back in my office I booted up my computer and trawled through the emails in my inbox. I was deleting so quickly I almost binned an email from Alvine Dix with the report from Carey's property attached. A couple of clicks later it was downloaded and I began reading its contents. A detailed section referred to the various shards and fragments of clothing recovered. Snagged against a tiny piece of exposed timber on the door frame of the kitchen were pieces of material resembling the CSIs' hazmat suits. Preliminary analysis suggested the garment could have been purchased on the internet and that it did not resemble in any way the protective equipment used by the Wales Police Service.

Several full and partial fingerprints had been recovered from the property. What really drew my attention was that one partial set matched a full set from Frank Armsby's car. No danger now of Superintendent Cornock justifying a new team to investigate Carey's death. There was a direct connection between both. I forwarded the email to Lydia, yelling through the open door of my office as I did so that she needed to read the report.

What would the profiler make of both deaths? Armsby had been killed in the dead of night in an industrial estate on the outskirts of Cardiff whereas Carey was mutilated in his own home. How would the profiler explain that?

Speaking to Alvine Dix about the contents of her report often filled out and joined the invisible dots.

'What do you want, Marco? I haven't got time to spare.' Alvine said after she recognised my voice.

'I've had your report.'

'So?'

'So I wanted to talk to you about it.'

'What do you want to talk about – get on with it.'

'Do you have to be somewhere else?'

'Don't be an arse, Marco.'

'You make reference to recovering a portion of fabric that resembled a hazmat suit. Is it similar to the sort of personal protective equipment talked about during the pandemic? I wanted more details.'

'We found it in two places – leading into the dining room and on the door frame into the kitchen. It suggests the killer was "forensically aware".'

'Everyone knows what PPE does but not everyone wears it around the house.'

'Unless you happen to be mutilating a man's body with a long, sharp-bladed knife at the same time and you want to cover your tracks.'

'Is there any way we can identify where the PPE could have been sourced from?'

'I'll do what I can, Marco. But there's no guarantee.'

Then she rang off before I could continue. I needed to prioritise the work that Wyn Nuttall could get on with once he joined the team tomorrow. There were hours and hours of CCTV footage from various cameras around Cardiff that would identify how Armsby's vehicle had reached Penarth Road. The automatic number plate recognition cameras wouldn't be enough by themselves so Wyn Nuttall would have to spend hours in front of screens building a picture of Armsby's final movements. It might even give us details of anybody in the car with him. Before turning to Raymond Carey's laptop, I found my mobile and called Alison Swan.

'I need to interview Judy Campbell. Have you been able to speak to her?'

Alison sounded harassed. 'Look, now isn't a good time.'

I tried to sound casual. 'Perhaps we could meet up later? Maybe have a drink after work if you've got time.'

She didn't pause too long. 'Thanks. I'll message you

once I've finished.'

I smiled to myself. It was exactly what Chief Superintendent Harper and Superintendent Cornock would expect: I was liaising, connecting all the threads in a complicated investigation. It wasn't a date, of course, merely a preliminary conversation between two colleagues.

I spent the rest of the afternoon interrogating Carey's laptop. The emails I discovered were unremarkable and uncontroversial. It surprised me he had subscribed to the same internet dating website as Frank Armsby. There was no suggestion the service was exclusive to heterosexuals and I wondered if Carey was bisexual. A conversation with David Plowman might provide the answer but before blundering into that scenario I spent time identifying if Carey had actually met anyone through his internet dating activity. I had heard before about people using dating websites just to see 'who was available', as though the whole process was like choosing a domestic pet. It suggested his relationship with Plowman wasn't as secure as Plowman had believed.

Terry's comments when I met him at Lefties filtered back into my mind. I'd be speaking to Terry again very soon. If anyone knew where a gun could be sourced in Cardiff it was Terry. And if he didn't, he would know somebody who did. An hour spent reading through Armsby's client list didn't give me any indication of who Terry's mysterious contact was. He would have to tell me sooner or later. Meeting Carey's superiors would provide us with more background. We could begin to put together more of the building blocks to assemble a link between Carey and Armsby.

It was late afternoon when Lydia appeared at my doorway and I ushered her in.

'I've got an arrangement for us to see Carey's supervisor, a Mr Ford, at the bank tomorrow morning, nine o'clock.'

I nodded. 'Good.'

'And I've had a result of a background search on Caitlin Prior, Armsby's date on the night he was killed.'

'Anything interesting?'

'Her background checks out right enough. She lives in the Bay in one of those apartment blocks. She's single and works in one of the big call centres in town.'

When my mobile buzzed with a message from Alison I snatched at it and read the details smiling as I did so.

'Early start in the morning, then,' I said, although Lydia was giving me a perplexed look.

The barmaid at Lefties Lounge nodded towards a table in a corner where Alison was seated. I ordered an orange juice, no ice or lemon, and joined her.

I sat down opposite her, and she gave me a warm smile. 'I'm sorry if I was a bit off earlier,' Alison said. 'It's all a bit hectic at the moment. There's one journalist who's going out of his way to create problems. He's chewing over all the reports and assessments of domestic violence and abuse that took place during the pandemic and comparing the Wales Police Service to all the other forces in the UK.'

She took a long slug of her drink.

'It makes me so angry; he's trying to take advantage of the fact that during the pandemic there were all sorts of restrictions in place. Officers I knew got really poorly with Covid-19 after they'd responded to complaints. They could have died. And all this journalist wants to do is to run articles about how badly we performed.'

'The press? What would you expect?'

'A bit of fairness, surely. Why don't they report about the root cause of this problem – that violent men need to be stopped?'

Her commitment made her all the more attractive.

'Have you spoken to Judy Campbell?'

'She's been through hell.'

It was a simple enough statement that carried a depth of

emotion.

Alison continued. 'I've spoken to her briefly. She is only prepared to discuss things if she can do so in the offices of the DependAssist charity – you know, where the forum meeting took place last week.'

There were no protocols for where I had to meet a potential witness or person of interest, but her request was certainly unusual. 'Does she want someone from the charity to be present?'

'Penny Larkham, the counsellor, has been exceptionally supportive. I don't know how Judy would have come through it without her help.'

'Let's arrange a time, soon as.'

Alison nodded and I turned the conversation away from work and asked about how long she had been with the WPS. We exchanged potted life histories and as she relaxed, she laughed at my jokes, smiled when I told her about my Italian heritage and gave me warm sideways glances with her large eyes and striking blue irises. I drank a second orange juice and organised a sparkling water for Alison. It was later than I had imagined when she excused herself, promising to call me with a time for me to speak to Judy Campbell. Before she left, I decided to chance an invitation for a dinner date.

'I was wondering – if you're not doing anything on Friday night, I could take you to an Italian restaurant I know?'

She stood by the edge the table now and smiled at me broadly. 'That'll be nice, thank you.'

I grinned all the way back to my car and all the way back to my apartment.

Chapter 15

Lydia put a CD into the player of my Mondeo as we left Queen Street the following morning without sharing her choice. When Rossini's *The Barber of Seville* filled the cabin, I nodded my head. It was one of my late grandfather's favourites and when I'd spent time with him on a Sunday, he'd share his love of Italian opera. I loved my *nonno* but I preferred Elvis to Rossini or Puccini.

'*Largo al factotum*,' I announced authoritatively.

'Top of the class, Inspector.' Lydia sounded impressed.

It was still early, and traffic streamed into Cardiff along Newport Road. The satnav directed us through the streets until it announced we had reached our destination, the large business park on the edge of the city. Lydia and I stared out through the windscreen, but we couldn't see the bank's offices. After another few minutes of crawling around in low gear Lydia drew my attention to an inconspicuous sign with the name of the bank and we found a slot in which to park.

The woman on reception – perfect make-up, heavy lashes and sharp uniform – was expecting us. 'You're here to see Mr Ford?'

I nodded and she pointed us towards comfortable chairs by a table decorated with glossy magazines. Moments later a man in his mid-forties bustled in – slim build, a crisp white shirt complemented by a perfectly knotted tie. He gave our warrant cards a cursory glance.

'Please follow me.'

He led us down a corridor before pushing open the door to a conference room. He waved a hand at the immaculately polished table and chairs. He sat down, his face set into a hard frown. 'How can I help?'

'We're investigating the death of Raymond Carey and we need to learn more about his background. It would be helpful if you could provide details of his employment and what he did here.'

'Do you think his death could be linked to his work?'

Incredulity laced his comment.

'We're working on a number of lines of inquiry at the moment.'

I could sense Lydia moving uncomfortably on the chair next to me. Standard platitudes weren't really my modus operandi but I wanted Ford's cooperation. I continued. 'What did Mr Carey do here?'

'He was a senior relationship manager and very experienced. I can't believe that anything connected to his work contributed to his death. After all I'd heard—'

I raised a hand. 'Mr Ford it's part of our job to build a clear picture of Mr Carey and his life.' I tried to sound relaxed, even displaying the palms of my hands in an accommodating gesture. It did the trick.

'Raymond had worked for the bank for over twenty years, man and boy. Although I was his superior, we were broadly contemporaries. Raymond never had much interest in progressing up the career ladder.'

'Were there any difficulties with his customers? Any complaints? People disgruntled with the quality of service he offered or decisions he made?'

'A lot of businesses have failed since the pandemic but unlike the financial crisis in 2008 the banks haven't been blamed. When people stop spending and companies stop buying the whole economy slows down.'

Lydia pitched in. 'So, no hate mail or disgruntled customers?'

'None, I'm afraid.' Ford sounded certain.

I continued. 'And what about his relationships with colleagues in the bank?'

Ford's hard-set features didn't share much emotion.

'Not very much to say.'

I searched for a flicker of emotion in his eyes. Was there a wariness for a moment? He dipped his head. 'There was some controversy a few years ago when there was an issue with certain other employees.'

'Issue?'

Ford threaded the fingers of both hands together. 'It was at a time when Raymond was... coming to terms with... his sexuality.'

Lydia got a serious tone into her voice. 'What sort of issue are we talking about?'

'Two male staff members complained about Raymond. He was working in the regional office in Bristol. It seems he may have misinterpreted things.'

Lydia again, not giving Ford any leeway, 'Things?'

Ford gave her an exasperated look. 'They made a complaint of sexual harassment against Raymond. They went through the usual HR system. He was given a reprimand and soon afterwards he was transferred here.'

'We can get all the details from the personnel file,' I said, not wanting to drag out Ford's uncomfortableness unnecessarily.

'Surely you don't think any of those employees could be responsible?'

'Tell us about the customers Carey looked after?'

'They were a cross section of all sorts of businesses. He could be good at his work. He had an eye for assessing potential.'

'We'll need a list.' It was the possible link to Armsby and Jim White I needed to check out but Ford didn't need to know that and it suited me for him to think all of Carey's customers were of interest.

Ford gave us a strained impatient look. I continued. 'It's routine, I assure you. And we'll need to see his office or workspace.' Ford raised an eyebrow in surprise. I added, 'This morning before we leave, please.'

Ford nodded his head nervously, then he stood up and led us into the bowels of the building.

An hour later we left and walked back to my car. I was clutching Raymond Carey's personnel file and Lydia had all the details of his customers on an external hard drive. Was this going to help us? The ordinariness of his professional working life seemed out of step with the violence meted out to him on the dining table at his home.

'What do you reckon, boss?' Lydia said.

I pointed the key at the Mondeo. I glanced back up at the building. 'We'll need to check out the two employees Ford mentioned. Somehow I cannot imagine a regular nine-to-five banker being a crazed killer.' I yanked open the car door.

'Somebody wanted him dead right enough,' Lydia said, getting into the vehicle.

Wyn Nuttall arrived at the Incident Room as Lydia was about to organise coffee. I knew the detective constable from a previous inquiry and having him join my team added a welcome additional resource. As Lydia headed over to the kitchen, she made a drinking gesture with her hand and Wyn responded with an order for coffee, milk, no sugar.

'Glad to be joining the team again, sir.' Wyn had a warm and cuddly North Wales accent. In normal times he would have reached out a hand, but he kept his arms firmly clamped to his side. It was reassuring to have an officer who had worked with me before joining Lydia and me. Wyn could be thorough and determined so I was pleased Superintendent Cornock had allocated him. He looked over at the board. He had a large head that towered over his neck, giving him an ungainly look.

Lydia returned with the drinks. Wyn pulled up a chair and sat down. I deposited my mug on a desk near the board and looked up at the faces pinned to it.

'Frank Armsby was killed when he was run over, repeatedly,' I turned to look at Wyn who frowned. 'And Carey was killed by a single gunshot, although he had suffered some signs of torture.' I pointed at the photographs of the scene. 'And the killer left a calling card with the words "see you later" in lipstick on the mirror.'

Now disgust filled Wyn's face. 'Are the deaths connected?'

'The modus operandi of both are different but both men used the same internet dating site and both men have connections to a man called Jim White who has form. I want you checking all the available CCTV and ANPR footage to identify Armsby's movements in the hours before he died. And then there are witness statements from the house-to-house inquiries near Carey's home.'

'All the usual stuff then, sir.'

Lydia announced she would work on the lists of Carey's customers and I reminded her to check out any connection with Armsby's clients. A message reached my mobile that Alison had organised for us to speak to Judy Campbell that afternoon and I thought about the possibility of meeting up for lunch. Making progress with the investigation was the priority so enjoying Alison's company would have to wait until Friday.

I wolfed down a sandwich at lunchtime, listening to Lydia, who had identified half a dozen of Carey's customers who were also clients of Armsby & Co. She had pinned to the board the names of the companies. Looking at the names meant very little unless we had evidence to connect them, but it would give us focus to make the connection between both deaths.

'This isn't helping,' Lydia said, finishing a Granny Smith, the core of which she placed carefully into the plastic packaging destined for the bin in the kitchen.

'Let's leave that for now. We've got Judy Campbell to interview.' I read the time on my watch. 'I don't want to be late.'

Chapter 16

Traffic delayed our journey from Queen Street, and I kept glancing at the clock on the dashboard, wondering whether I should call Alison to warn her we might be late. Luckily, I had left enough time and found a parking slot easily enough. Lydia glanced over at the office building where we were seeing Judy Campbell. 'I hope this won't be a waste of time.'

I reached for the door handle. 'Let's talk to Alison Swan and the counselling staff before Judy Campbell arrives.'

We left the car and trooped over to the office. Penny Larkham was in reception with Alison. Formal introductions completed, Larkham led us through into the main part of the building. Jack Hughes, the note-taker from the forum meeting, sat staring at a monitor on his desk in the office when we entered. Hughes scrambled to his feet and organised chairs for us all.

'I thought it would be helpful if you were to get some background first,' Alison said.

We sat down and listened to Penny Larkham. 'We provide professional counselling support for abused women and those subject to domestic violence. As a charity we depend on grants and raising money.' She tipped her head towards Hughes. 'Jack does a lot of the admin support and chasing sources of finance to keep us afloat.' She turned her gaze back to Lydia and me. 'For every woman who complains about a rape or sexual assault or domestic attack there are perhaps ten who don't. This sort of sexual and domestic violence is a scourge on our society. We offer counselling and psychological help. Often victims find it beneficial to talk with somebody completely independent. We're all specially trained.'

As she paused for breath Alison took the opportunity to add. 'Most of the victims are reluctant to speak to the police and they can be distrustful too.'

Larkham continued. 'And with very good reason, knowing the appalling record the Wales Police Service has in pursuing sexual assault allegations.'

She made it sound like a simple statement of fact and not a taunt. I wasn't going to be goaded so I waited for her to continue.

'Judy Campbell is typical of women who feel completely let down by the system. She is an extreme example because Armsby was a serial offender. It was wholly inexcusable for the judge to dismiss the first case against Armsby and the second trial when the jury acquitted him was an absolute disgrace. Same judge again.'

I detected an edge of irritation in Alison's voice when she cut in. 'Penny, perhaps you could explain to the Inspector and Detective Sergeant Flint how you support victims long-term.'

Larkham gave her a brief, hurt look. 'We go out of our way to assist by providing extended facilities to support the women dealing with the trauma such an assault can cause.'

Hughes made his first contribution. 'The scars left by assaults like this can be devastating.' He said it in quiet serious voice while staring at the floor. I noticed the time on my watch, knowing Judy Campbell was expected imminently. Larkham added, 'We have a specific room allocated for interviews with victims of abuse, Inspector. The whole ambience is intended to put them at ease. We've made that room available for your interview this afternoon.'

I wanted to tell her I was only agreeing to this setup because I had no direct evidence implicating Judy Campbell but I had learned from my first attendance at the Cardiff Domestic Violence Taskforce forum that I had to adopt a new more touchy-feely approach. Things might change quickly, though. I smiled at Larkham. 'Of course, I understand. Detective Sergeant Flint and I will be very sympathetic towards Judy Campbell. But I'm sure you can appreciate why we need to interview her.'

Larkham left us when the receptionist notified her that Campbell had arrived. She returned after a few minutes, announcing that Campbell was ready for us. It felt like an audience with the Queen without the footmen and fancy accents.

The room was warm with soft furnishings and comfortable chairs and sofas. Soothing landscapes adorned the wall. Campbell's hair had been straightened aggressively to create a managed bob around her head. Her eye contact was weak.

Lydia and I sat down and I kept my voice low and soft.

'Hello, Judy. We're investigating the murder of Frank Armsby.'

She nodded briskly. She had a prominent nose and when she spoke it made her overbite look pronounced. 'An officer from the team that investigated my complaint telephoned me.' The tone of her voice was cold and neutral.

'I'm sure it must be distressing for you having to go through an investigation that didn't lead to a prosecution.'

Her face became granite-like. 'It was more than that, Inspector. I felt as though I was the one on trial. As though my word wasn't being accepted, as though no one was prepared to believe that he raped me. The system is weighted against women making a complaint. And everything is run by men. After all, how many of the senior officers who reviewed my case are women? And how many of the prosecution lawyers are women?' She answered her own question. 'None involved in my case.'

Lydia picked up the conversation. 'The procedures we have for managing and dealing with sexual assault cases may be broken but at the moment it's the only system we've got.'

Campbell gave Lydia a steely glare. 'Is that supposed to be comforting?'

I decided that debating the niceties of the criminal justice system with Judy Campbell wasn't going to be productive. 'Judy, I can only guess that speaking to us is the last thing you'd want to be doing. But we cannot ignore your connection to Frank Armsby.'

'Connection, is that what you would call it? Has it come down to that, a *connection* or maybe it was an *association*? Or perhaps a *dalliance*, although the night he attacked me certainly didn't feel romantic.'

Judy continued before I could reply, 'At first there was something really engaging about him. He could be charming and witty and generous. I even for a moment considered he might be 'the one'. We had things in common – enjoyed the same films and television programmes. I'm thirty-eight, Inspector, and I'd love to have children and...' She let her gaze drift over my shoulder through the window and out into the street fixing it on something only she could see.

I had to ask her about her whereabouts the evening of the murder. Coming right out and asking her *did you kill Frank Armsby?* was going to be a recipe for a complaint and a severe dressing down by Superintendent Cornock.

Lydia must have read my thoughts; she was getting to know me. 'Judy, I know that this must be extremely difficult but there are protocols and procedures we have to follow. We've spoken to the staff at Frank Armsby's office who told us you'd called there last week.'

Judy brought her gaze and her attention back to the table in front of her. She fidgeted with her hands.

'It was the day after the other officers had told me he wouldn't be prosecuted. I was so mad I couldn't think straight. I wanted to give him a piece of my mind. I wanted his staff to know what he was like.'

Catharsis can be important and beneficial, but I doubted Judy's visit to see Frank Armsby had been either.

'The only thing that has helped are the counselling sessions with Penny. She listened to me for hours and hours. Without her support I don't know what I would have done. I wouldn't have been able to survive.'

I had to ask one final question. I had interviewed

dozens, maybe hundreds, of criminals in the past and you can usually tell in the eyes and in the face and the body language if they are lying. Judy Campbell had made no secret of her distilled hatred for Frank Armsby. I could understand she would feel aggrieved when the system had let her down. The legal process could only be a reflection of the imperfections of us as human beings. Offering that as an explanation to Judy Campbell wasn't going to get me anywhere. So I gathered my thoughts before asking.

'Judy, I don't want you to take this the wrong way, but we need to be able to eliminate you from our inquiries.' I relied on the usual wording. 'So can you please tell us where you were on the evening Armsby was killed?'

She sneered, 'I'm pleased he's dead, Inspector.' She paused. 'No, I'm delighted.'

An uneasy silence hung over the table for a few seconds until she continued. 'I was at home catching up with paperwork and then I watched television. Does that make me a suspect?'

The Cardiff Lockdown Murders

Chapter 17

Wyn Nuttall's navy tie almost disappeared against the shade of his shirt, his pinstripe suit a little too garish for my taste. He got to his feet, an excited look on his face when I entered the Incident Room. Lydia sat at her desk sipping coffee from a tall plastic cup.

'I've been working on the details of Armsby's customers as you wanted, sir,' Wyn said.

Despite my double shot Americano at breakfast I needed more caffeine. I raised a hand and he stopped; mouth open about to say something.

'I need a coffee first.'

The disappointment turned to anticipation as he nodded briskly. I returned from the kitchen clutching a mug with a two-teaspoon instant coffee. In my office I placed the drink on a coaster, hung my herringbone jacket on the coat stand and booted up my computer. A couple of slurps of the hot liquid and checking my emails focused by mind. I yelled at Wyn and Lydia to join me and they entered my room and sat down.

'How did you get on yesterday?' Wyn's initial enthusiasm had turned into inquisitiveness about the outcome of our meeting with Judy Campbell.

'She's certainly got motive enough,' I said.

Lydia nodded her head. 'She was positively pleased he had died.'

I looked over at Wyn. 'Do a search against her mobile records.'

'Sure thing.'

Even if we could establish from triangulation that Judy Campbell's mobile was at her home, it didn't mean she wasn't on Penarth Road knocking down Frank Armsby. Her display of anger and hatred felt natural. She didn't strike me as a person who would turn homicidal.

I glanced at Lydia. 'What did you make of her?'

'Personally, I was convinced that she'd been assaulted

by Frank Armsby. You couldn't fake the sort of emotion she displayed, and I'm amazed the CPS didn't prosecute. But could she be capable of killing Armsby…?' Her voice trailed off.

'Wyn, establish if there any CCTV cameras near to Campbell's home that might have recorded her leaving the house the night Armsby was killed.'

Wyn scribbled on a notepad then he turned his attention to telling us about the work he'd completed on Armsby's customers, producing a sheet of A4 for Lydia and me.

'It hasn't been easy to track down exactly the connections between Armsby and Carey and Jim White. But the details I received from Boyd Pearce and the economic crime team help me find a pattern. I worked back from Armsby's customers and focused on the limited companies.' He pointed to the section on the sheet that had a list of the entities involved. 'I've jotted down which of these businesses bank with Carey and in the final column I've listed how many of the companies have Jim White as the director.'

Wyn looked pleased with himself. 'Some have what I suspect are nominee directors and most of the names have addresses in common and all are linked to Jim White in some way.'

I interrupted. 'If Jim White is connected to all these companies it means he knew Frank Armsby and Raymond Carey. Still doesn't give us any evidence he was responsible for their deaths. And White is the sort of person who could get his hands on a gun.'

'But if White is responsible, why have Carey mutilated?'

'When we find the evidence, we'll find the answer. It's time we had a chat with Jim White.'

Wyn and Lydia stood up and left my office. An email from Superintendent Cornock warned me that Dr Fabrien would be arriving that afternoon. He expected me for a meeting at two pm. I tapped out a brief reply, acknowledging the time but leaving unsaid that I'd be doing everything to make certain Dr Fabrien wouldn't be cluttering up my investigation. Then I thumbed a message to Alison thanking her for arranging for us to see Judy Campbell the previous afternoon and adding that I was looking forward to seeing her on Friday evening. Her reply was instantaneous. *No problem. Looking forward to seeing you again X.* I smiled, stood up and dragged on my jacket before giving my office a cursory look. It looked neat, as neat as I wanted it to be and as neat as a Cardiff detective's should be.

Lydia followed me down to the car park and we made for my Mondeo. I could sense her turning up her nose at the sight of the grit and gravel in the footwell of the passenger side. I thought it gave the car a rather homely feel.

'The superintendent has organised for the profiler to join us this afternoon.'

'It's a bit FBI, isn't it?'

'He thinks the circumstances of Carey's death justify a preliminary input.'

I drove out of the car park and accelerated for the motorway. It was a journey of a few minutes before I took the junction of the M4 towards Newport. The satnav took us down past the Office for National Statistics and then to the Alexandra Docks that dominated a section of the city on a spit of land between the rivers Ebbw and Usk.

We caught sight of the historic transporter bridge, built in an era when tall-masted ships would have sailed up the river. Now it was nothing more than an historical attraction and an enjoyable shortcut.

'So what do you know about Jim White?' Lydia said.

'He was involved with a guy called Frankie Prince. White was the anonymous guy in the background, Prince's fixer and supposedly the manager of a nightclub. But when Prince got entangled with some Eastern European gangsters White could see the writing on the wall and decided to jump ship, taking Frankie's wife, Laura with him.'

'Sounds dangerous, boss.'

'It was for Frankie. After he was killed, Jim White was prosecuted for human trafficking. But he played clever, admitting his involvement immediately so he got maximum credit when the time came for his case to be heard in court. And he gave the economic crime department a lot of useful information about the trafficking of girls into the UK.'

'That can't be a bad thing.'

'That's why he only got an eighteen-month sentence. He was out after five months.'

'And since then he's kept his head down.'

'So it would seem.'

'He probably left jail and dug up all his drug money.'

'Don't sound so cynical.'

'You know what it's like, boss. Nothing ever sticks to these sorts of men. It's like Armsby – Teflon-coated.'

Lydia was right. Professional criminals accepted jail sentences as an occupational hazard. They measured that risk against the outcomes, so they'd have properties registered in the names of nominees, shares in companies owned by friends or distant relatives or even fictitious individuals.

I indicated off the A48 and turned down for the docks area. Dilapidated old buildings scarred the landscape, unsurfaced roads leading to empty plots and warehouses fenced with metal sheets. Tractor units hauling enormous trailers with engine parts pulled past us and I split my attention between the satnav and the road ahead, ensuring I didn't miss the turning.

Slowing, I hadn't realised I was causing traffic delays and a white van behind me blasted his horn before accelerating past, the passenger gesticulating with his arm as it did so. Eventually the satnav took us towards a collection of small workshop units. A car repair business, its front yard littered with old vehicles, occupied one. At the end was a nondescript building and parked almost out of sight I could see an Audi Q5, less than three years old.

'It's over there,' I tipped my head towards the SUV. 'My bet is that the flash Audi belongs to Jim White.'

I pulled into a parking spot and switched off the engine. I had half expected to hear the thud and clash of machinery when I opened the door, but the place was quiet. I looked through a glass partition of a door into an empty workshop. I pulled the handle, but it was locked. I gazed through. No stacks of shelving with bolts or ratchets or workbenches. I turned on my heel and nodded for Lydia to follow me up the stairs to the first floor.

I pushed open the door onto a narrow corridor and the sound of tapping on a keyboard drifted out of the nearest room. Two intrigued faces, one a woman in her thirties the other a pimply teenager, looked up at me from their computer monitor screens when I entered. The woman asked, 'Can I help you?'

'I'm looking for Jim White.'

She dipped her head at the door. 'He's in the office down the corridor. You can't miss it.'

I didn't bother knocking on the door at the rear of the building. White wouldn't be accustomed to the niceties of polite society.

White had put on weight since I had seen him last. A beard of silver-tinged russet hair covered the jowls but it couldn't hide the puffy appearance of his face. He was sipping on a china mug – coffee, judging by the cafetiere on the desk. He turned towards me and a glimmer of recognition creased his eyes.

'John Marco,' he announced simply. The voice still had that suburban middle-class anonymous sound as though it would be at home in a golf club or at a masonic meeting. 'And what brings Cardiff's finest all the way out here to the sunny climes of Newport.'

'This is Detective Sergeant Lydia Flint.' Neither Lydia nor I bothered with warrant cards. 'I'm the senior investigating officer in the enquiry into the murder of Frank Armsby.'

'Frank Armsby. Yes, I know, that was very sad.'

Uninvited, I sat at one of the chairs, gesturing for Lydia to do likewise.

'What can you tell me about your relationship with Mr Armsby?'

'He was an accountant for one of my companies.'

White was on a fishing expedition, wanting to establish how much digging we had already done. 'One of your companies?'

'He did the accounts for a couple of the small businesses I run.'

'And what exactly do you do?'

White frowned. It was my turn to cast the net and White tried to gauge exactly what I knew. Honesty never came naturally to men like White; they were always trying to see how they could second-guess an inquiry. Do their best to outsmart us. 'The Peartree pub that Laura runs has been quite successful, and we've been able to develop a takeaway restaurant. There are couple of small internet businesses that we run from here. But it's all very small-scale.'

'Where were you on the evening that Frank Armsby was killed?'

'What day was that again?'

I reminded White of the date and he feigned puzzlement before turning to his mouse and clicking into the monitor. His eyes darted around the screen until he turned to me and reassuringly said. 'I was playing golf that afternoon. One has to have some relaxation.' He smiled. 'Then I was home with Laura.'

'How well did you know Raymond Carey?' I dispensed with the niceties of reminding White that Carey had been murdered.

For a brief second a heavy cloud filtered across his eyes. 'He was one of those anonymous bankers I'm afraid.

You know what it's like these days, John.'

Using first names was definitely not going to work. 'It's Detective Inspector Marco.'

He gave me another of those really annoying ingratiating grins. 'Times like these, Inspector, there are no bank managers, there are hardly any bank branches. And we're only starting to get over the pandemic crisis. But to answer your question, I think I had spoken with Mr Carey two or three times.'

Before I could say anything further Laura Prince breezed in. She stopped in her tracks when she saw Lydia and me.

'Detective Inspector Marco was just leaving.' White announced.

I gave him a sharp look and settled back into my chair. No one but me decides when I leave a meeting. 'I'm glad you've arrived, Laura. Where were you both on the night that Raymond Carey was killed?'

I searched their faces for a reaction, but I didn't see one, no motion and no tell-tale signs of guilt creasing their faces.

'I really don't think this is necessary, Inspector,' White said.

The reasonableness angle then, I thought.

Laura butted in. 'We were with my family at a christening and birthday party. It lasted all day.'

There was nothing further I needed now so I stood up and Lydia followed me outside.

Sitting in the car I turned to Lydia. 'Something's up. She had an answer for their whereabouts the day Carey was killed without even bothering to ask us for the date.'

'I didn't like either of them. Shame White wasn't locked up for longer.'

I glanced at my watch. 'We should get back to Cardiff in time to meet that profiler.'

Chapter 18

I had time for lunch with Lydia at Mario's, this time sitting on a couple of the stools as we mulled over the interview that morning. The place was bustling although the frantic atmosphere commonplace before the pandemic hadn't returned. Prices had gone up too and Mario had complained things were never going to be the same.

Lydia opted for a salad bowl that had lots of lettuce and other green vegetables. The chicken in my panini tasted rubbery but the sauce was spicy enough. I was chewing a mouthful when Lydia asked, 'Have you ever worked with a profiler, boss?'

I shook my head. I took a sip from a bottle of orange-coloured soft drink that had a very odd taste. 'I don't know what the Super hopes we're going to achieve.'

'It's probably all to do with public relations.'

We finished our meal and hurried back to Queen Street. Wyn Nuttall still had that earnest look on his face I had become accustomed to. I gave him a brief summary of our discussion with Jim White and he nodded seriously as though everything we were telling him was entirely expected and reasonable. 'I'll do some digging into the businesses.'

'And anything from the CCTV cameras that might help us?'

'I haven't finished that yet, sir. But I've tracked down footage near Judy Campbell's home and I should have that later. But the triangulation of her phone confirms she was in the flat the night Armsby was killed.'

I thanked Wyn and left the Incident Room, walking through the corridors of Queen Street wondering if I could leave that evening in good time for one of the regular meetings I attended. I hadn't been for a while, and during the pandemic Zoom meetings weren't quite the same. As I poised a hand to rap a knuckle on Superintendent Cornock's door the sound of gentle conversation emerged from inside. He was cracking a joke, sounding unusually humorous.

Cornock raised his voice when he heard my knock and I pushed the door open. He was standing next to the tropical fish tank with a woman by his side and, for a fraction of a second, I wondered if Dr Fabrien was late.

Cornock looked over at me. 'Detective Inspector Marco, this is Dr Margaret Fabrien.'

Fabrien was about five foot seven, had a narrow face with a pronounced chin, shoulder length hair cut into a neat fringe and wore expensive-looking clothes. The sensuous perfume she wore assaulted my nostrils, flicking switches that hadn't been fingered for a long time.

'Good afternoon, Inspector.' Fabrien had wonderfully translucent green eyes.

'Dr Fabrien,' I managed.

Once Cornock had sat down at his desk he used a formal tone. 'John, let me make clear how we expect Dr Fabrien to contribute. You can then fully brief her about both murders.'

Fabrien sat on the chair next to mine and crossed one perfectly proportioned leg over the other knee, allowing the hem of her skirt to ride up her thighs. Cornock continued. 'Because of the nature of the wounds sustained by Raymond Carey we believe Dr Fabrien's input may help. She's consulted previously with the WPS on the inquiry involving the two dead officers in North Wales.'

Now I heard the French accent. 'That was a very sad case. I worked closely with the senior investigating officer – a Detective Inspector Drake.'

'I remember that case. I met Ian Drake when he came down to Cardiff as part of the investigation.'

Fabrien looked over at Cornock. 'Do you have any suspects?'

'Inspector Marco can fill you in with all the details. The inquiry is at a preliminary stage. After you've finished today you can send us a full report.'

His comments suggested Dr Fabrien wasn't going to be

with us for longer than a day or so. Perhaps Cornock was simply doffing his cap at instructions from an officer higher up the chain of command.

I left Cornock, inviting Fabrien to follow me through the labyrinth of narrow corridors back to the Incident Room. Lydia and Wyn scrambled to their feet as I entered, once they'd noticed Fabrien behind me. Introductions made, I stood by the board intent on outlining a summary when Fabrien cleared her throat. 'I wonder if I may say a few words.' She didn't wait to respond but ploughed on. 'My role here is to support you as police officers. I spoke with Assistant Chief Constable Neary this morning and I appreciate that the inquiry is at an early stage.'

Namedropping ACC Neary would impress Wyn and Lydia. It certainly impressed me. The senior officer she had spoken to was a fierce woman with a determined and resolute approach to policing. She could be tough and uncompromising. Whenever I met ACC Neary herds of elephants had a habit of charging through my body.

'We understand entirely, Dr Fabrien,' I replied.

Fabrien sounded friendly. 'Please call me Margaret.'

I noticed Wyn sharing a glance with Lydia. I ignored it. Margaret extracted an expensive looking notebook from a sumptuous leather briefcase and opened it on the table in front of her, drawing her hand down the spine so the page would lie flat. Then she looked up at me and gave me an imperceptible nod of approval to continue.

'The body of Frank Armsby was found in the car park of a builders' merchant on a small industrial estate on the outskirts of Cardiff. He'd been knocked over by a car and we believe run over several times afterwards.'

A look of disgust and surprise crossed her face. 'It is a rather brutal way...'

'I agree. There are no CCTV cameras in the immediate vicinity and the principal person of interest is a woman Armsby had raped. The Crown Prosecution Service recently decided not to charge him and, understandably, she is livid.'

'Does this man have a history of sexual violence?'

Lydia responded. 'There are two previous failed prosecutions and a recently inquiry where the CPS decided not to prosecute.'

Margaret jotted on her notebook, her handwriting careful and precise. When she looked up she added, 'It does not surprise me. Prosecuting sexual violence is haphazard at best.'

Lydia continued. 'He was divorced from his wife. Both his children are away at school.'

'And the second death?'

I turned to look at the board and pointed to the photograph of Raymond Carey and then to the images of the scene in the dining room. 'He was tied to a table and a single gunshot wound to the chest was responsible for his death. But his genitals had been mutilated ante-mortem. We have circulated all the other forces of the UK requesting details of any similar deaths. After all, it might be a copycat killing.'

Margaret nodded. 'There have been lots of cases of violent assault to genitalia. It usually indicates the killer has some twisted logic. Do you know whether Raymond Carey had any history of being involved with sexual violence of any sort?'

'Nothing is known. We've spoken to his boyfriend, who is very shaken. And one of the links between both deaths is the use by both men of an internet dating site.'

Margaret cut across me. 'So Mr Carey could have been bisexual?' She said it in a manner that made it sound factual, as though she was announcing his hair colour or shirt collar size.

I continued. 'And both men are linked to organised crime.'

Now I noticed Margaret raising her eyebrows and keeping them high. 'So you may be thinking that both deaths are connected to some sort of feud between rival gangsters?'

'Our priority now is establishing the last known movements of Frank Armsby and we're waiting for forensic results from the home of Mr Carey. Gun violence in Cardiff is very rare so tracing the person who acquired the gun is also a priority.'

Margaret closed her notebook, got to her feet and joined me at the board. She gazed at the photographs, unaffected by the horror involved in fixing her attention on the image of the mirror. The red lipsticked letters 'see you later' looked as ominous as they had when I first saw them.

'What do you make of those words?' Margaret asked.

'The killer has left some sort of message. But …'

'But there is no immediate explanation. I shall have to consider that most carefully. And I shall need to read all the documentation and statements, of course.'

'You can use the room next to mine.'

Margaret smiled over at me and I turned to Wyn and Lydia. 'Can you make certain Dr Fabrien has everything she needs.'

Once Margaret had made herself at home, I got back to the Incident Room where Wyn waved me over. 'I've tracked down the CCTV footage near to Judy Campbell's home. She lied to you about not leaving the house that evening.'

I stared over his shoulder, Lydia standing alongside me as we peered at the monitor on his desk. He started the footage at eight-thirty, offering a running commentary as he did so. Judy Campbell owned a five-year-old Ford Focus and he pointed out the number plate as it drove past the camera.

'Have you been able to track its movements?'

'She was certainly driving into town.'

Lydia sounded a note of caution. 'Can we be certain it was her?'

Wyn responded, 'She drew into a services and bought fuel and some groceries at the convenience store so we have a positive identification. But, at the moment, I don't know where she went afterwards. There was a delay, however, before she got back to the flat. The cameras don't record her return until nine-thirty pm.'

'Which is two and half hours before Armsby's death, assuming he was killed at about midnight.'

Lydia clarified, 'The pathologist did say midnight – give or take.'

'Is it possible she left her flat later, taking a different route?'

Wyn again. 'It's possible, but there are no cameras I can check if she took another route.'

I stood back for a moment. 'Where were you going, Judy Campbell?'

'We'll need to speak to her again, boss,' Lydia said.

'Why did she lie to us?' I said. 'And check her mobile phone records to see if she called Frank Armsby the night he died.'

'We've checked it out before, boss,' Lydia said. 'There's no record on Armsby's phone that Judy Campbell made contact with him.'

Wyn nodded. 'It's dead easy to buy one of those pay-as-you-go burner phones.'

'We'll need to talk to her.' I started back for my office but before I reached the door I turned and spoke to Lydia. 'Do we have any link between Judy Campbell and Raymond Carey? Are they connected on the internet? Who does she bank with?'

'I'll get a financial check done on her, sir,' Lydia volunteered.

I nodded at Wyn. 'Check out the dating sites Carey used. Perhaps Judy Campbell used one of them too.'

It was after six pm when Margaret Fabrien tapped a delicate knuckle on the frame of the door of my office and invited herself in. She moved with the sort of elegance and simplicity I'd seen in my relatives in Lucca, as though she had a natural confidence.

'I shall be doing a report, John, but I thought I'd give

you some preliminary thoughts.' She checked the time on her watch. 'My train is at seven. At this stage it is too early to suggest both deaths are connected. I can see why ACC Neary would think my involvement would be justified following Carey's death. Keep an open mind. The intensity of the violence against Carey certainly suggests a deep-seated hatred, whereas Armsby's death could be nothing more than a gangland killing.'

Listening to Margaret got me thinking how attractive a French accent could really be.

'I shall investigate similar cases and include in my report some comments on the lettering on the mirror, but it could be no more than the killer's sick joke.' She stood up. 'Perhaps we shall meet again.'

'I'll look forward to it.'

She smiled, gathered her papers and left.

I arrived at the meeting promptly for eight, wearing a clean shirt under the same herringbone jacket I'd worn that day. Years ago, when I'd been a prisoner to the bottle, keeping up a neat and tidy appearance had been the last thing on my mind. Colleagues would complain about my personal hygiene and comment that I should shave or polish my shoes. I could pretend the opinion of other officers didn't count but my demeanour never endeared me to criminals, so the job suffered. And then my family life fell apart when Jackie took Dean and left.

That had hit me harder than I had realised. After one particular drunken escapade I had returned to Cardiff chastened and embarrassed, ready to change my life.

I looked at myself in the rear-view mirror of the car before leaving and as I locked my Mondeo a sparkling new Range Rover drew up alongside me. The occupant jumped out and greeted me.

'John, how nice to see you.' Judge Richard Patricks had a rich tone to his voice.

'Richard, good evening. I've missed our meetings.'

'So have I. It wasn't the same during the lockdown was it?'

Zoom meetings always seem to be artificial and I could never get the etiquette right for how they were to end. They seemed to last longer than they should have done.

Richard nodded. 'Did you hear about that poor man who was killed by his son during a Zoom meeting.'

'It's much better face-to-face.'

We headed over to the hotel entrance. 'Are you the SIO on the Armsby murder?'

'Yes, still early days. And my team are responsible for the Carey inquiry too.'

In a room behind reception a circle of chairs had been set out. Coffee and tea and bottles of sparkling water sat on a table in one corner.

I sat next to Richard clutching a glass of water and he whispered, 'I was the trial judge on both occasions when Armsby was prosecuted. CPS made a complete hash of both cases. Mind you, the evidence was pretty compelling.'

Judge Richard Patricks could be forthright, and he always liked cases dealt with properly in his courts.

The meeting got going in the usual way and when it was my turn I cleared my throat and said, 'I'm John and I'm an alcoholic.'

Chapter 19

I was the first to arrive at the Incident Room the following morning. It gave me a chance to sit and stare at the faces and details on the board. And think. Margaret's comments from the day before had nurtured a doubt about linking the deaths of Frank Armsby and Ray Carey. The image of Jim White had also been pinned underneath Armsby and I guessed Laura Prince's money and connections probably helped him re-establish his life after leaving prison. I resolved to spend the rest of the morning reviewing everything, going back over every scrap of information, every thread, every lead and every piece of information. I had to find that nugget which would point us in the right direction.

I traipsed over to my office and booted up the computer. I clicked open the email from Margaret Fabrien and read the simple but formal language confirming the conclusion she had summarised yesterday. I played over in my mind what her accent might sound like if she was reading the report aloud. I tapped out a reply, thanking her for her prompt attention and thoroughness. Getting a profiler to advise on a case must have given ACC Neary and Superintendent Cornock a degree of comfort but I wondered how much of it was about covering their backs. It reminded me that we still hadn't heard from the various police forces in the United Kingdom about possible similar mutilations in their areas. So I formally emailed Wyn asking him to chase it up.

At this stage of the inquiry we needed to focus on phone work, CCTV footage and the old-fashioned grind of house-to-house inquiries. Wyn Nuttall and Lydia bustled into the Incident Room and I called over to them as I listened to them scrambling to remove coats and dump coffee mugs on their respective desks.

'Mrs Richards, the eyewitness who lived next door to Raymond Carey, is coming in this morning to help us get an artist's impression organised. Wyn, I want you to take charge of that.' I turned to Lydia. 'I'm not satisfied David Plowman is telling us everything he knows about Carey. There was something about his demeanour when we asked him about his relationship with Carey. There's more he needs to tell us. Get him in here.'

'I'll contact him.'

'Before we see him, I want to go through all of Carey's contacts on the internet dating site he used.'

They turned and left, and I opened my notepad, trying to make sense of where the evidence was taking us. A set of fingerprints had been recovered from Armsby's car identical to a set found at Carey's property. If we found the owner of the fingerprints, we'd probably find our killer.

I never liked loose ends: they always made me think I need to tug at them and see where they lead. And something about Raymond Carey's life niggled. He was in a relationship with David Plowman, who had characterised it as stable and long-term although they weren't living together, and yet Carey was visiting dating websites. Perhaps he had a complicated sex life. At least he had a sex life, I thought wistfully.

Later that morning I heard Wyn leaving the Incident Room and Lydia confirmed that David Plowman would be attending that afternoon. So I refocused on building a picture of Raymond Carey's private life. A murder inquiry gave me and the team every justification to examine every dark and remote corner of a victim's life. It was licensed voyeurism, authorised by the need to bring a killer to justice. Catching and locking up the bad guys was something that always attracted me about police work. Not in a highbrow, intellectual way but more how ordinary decent people needed to be protected against crooks.

I jotted details on my notepad – names and dates and truncated conversations from the previous week. He had met a couple of women for lunch earlier that month – and I managed to speak to one who responded to my email instantaneously. She enjoyed his company, describing him as jovial. How would Plowman react if he knew?

Our meeting with Plowman was for two pm. And I wanted to clear my head, so I called out to Lydia.

'Lunch?'

'My choice?' she said.

'Okay,' I said reluctantly.

We left the station and walked down Queen Street, passing a couple of buskers strumming a lousy version of 'American Pie' outside one of the big shops closed permanently after the lockdown. A vaping stand was doing a roaring trade and I had been tempted before to see whether it would help me kick my five-a-day habit once and for all.

The crowds common in the shopping malls before the pandemic were now a thing of the past. Shopkeepers and companies running department stores were complaining vociferously about the impact on their business.

We crossed over The Hays and then went down into the Morgan Arcade. Crumbs was one of Lydia's regular haunts, perhaps the only one in the middle of Cardiff where she trusted the vegetarian menu. A waitress with tattoos down her forearms smiled at Lydia and pointed to a table in the corner.

'Soup of the day is your favourite,' she said to Lydia who confirmed her order with a smile. Then she turned to me. I hesitated. Normally I'd order a bacon sandwich or a chicken panini. 'I'll have the soup too.'

Lydia poured us a glass of water each from the jug which had a collection of lemon slices floating on top. 'Do you think the profiler is going to help, sir?'

'You know how it is – the top brass wants to feel they've covered all the bases – no stone left unturned.'

Lydia nodded. 'The circumstances of Carey's death suggest someone with a very sick mind.'

'We need to establish where the killer got the gun. London or one of the big cities, at a guess.'

'Even so, boss,' Lydia lowered her voice to a whisper. 'There's nothing to suggest Carey had links with organised crime in London or any of the towns of England with gun problems.'

A waitress brought the soup over in two enormous dishes. Chunks of thick-cut bread were piled onto a plate. I stared at the bowl in front of me – at least it had the benefit of being multicoloured. There were ribbons of green spinach-like material as well as three or four different sized and coloured beans. I struggled to convince myself it would be doing me any good and I hoped my body wouldn't be complaining later that afternoon.

'Healthy eating?' Lydia said as she watched me slather butter over a chunk of bread.

Crumbs was doing a roaring trade in takeaway jacket potatoes and dozens of customers paying us no heed came and went whilst we sat at the table. There were people leading ordinary lives, trying to get back to normal activity after the pandemic shut down.

'I need to talk to Terry again.'

Lydia raised an eyebrow.

'If anyone knows about sourcing a gun in Cardiff he will. Or he can find out.'

'Be careful with Terry, sir.' Lydia managed a formal tone verging on a mild reprimand.

'Times like these, we need all the help we can get.'

When David Plowman sat across from me in the interview room at Queen Street, I could feel my stomach rumbling a complaint. I hoped the effects of the beans wouldn't migrate to something more embarrassing.

'We've done some preliminary work on Raymond's laptop and we discovered he subscribed to an internet dating site.' I looked over at Plowman, waiting for some expression of surprise or disgust laced with theatrical emotion his performance on the evening of Carey's death suggested he might adopt.

'There must be some mistake.' He sounded like a guilty politician caught in a compromising position who was busy digging a much bigger hole for himself.

'My team has been through his computer very carefully. He was in contact with several... women. And there had been various lunch dates.'

Plowman sounded incredulous. 'No, that cannot be right.'

'I have spoken to one of the women, who commented how she had enjoyed his company – she said he was jovial.'

Now Plowman pouted and folded his arms, pulled them tight towards his chest.

'Did Raymond ever have regular visitors to the house? Friends, acquaintances?'

Plowman stared at the table.

'There is an eyewitness who is able to place a man leaving the house on the afternoon he was killed.' Lydia pushed over the table the artist's impression created that morning. 'Do you have any idea who it might be?'

'None at all.' Plowman sounded dismissive, disdainful too.

Now I butted in. 'This could well be the last person to have ever seen Raymond Carey alive.' I moved it a little nearer to Plowman. 'I want you to take a really good look at it. Did Raymond ever mention people from his past? Somebody who might have a reason to want him dead. We really do need to trace this person.' Raising my voice and sounding more belligerent had the desired effect of stirring Plowman to respond.

'I don't know who it is.' Plowman pushed the artist's impression over the table. 'I've never seen him before, and I don't know of anybody that Ray knew who might resemble this person.'

'Did Mr Carey tell you he was meeting somebody that afternoon?'

Plowman glowered over the table. Was he frustrated that he didn't know, that Raymond hadn't told him, hadn't shared with him something about his life that would help us find his killer? I ploughed on, uncertain exactly where the next line of inquiry would take me. 'Did Raymond ever complain about previous partners?'

Plowman straightened in his chair and scolded me, 'I don't know what you mean.'

'Did he have any former boyfriends or girlfriends he complained about. I'm sure you've had relationships that didn't work out, where things ended unhappily.'

'Unhappily? What on earth are your suggesting?'

'The injuries to Raymond's body suggest somebody was making a point of inflicting considerable pain through mutilating his genitalia.'

Plowman shrivelled. Disgust and horror mixing in a tangled expression on his face.

'Mr Plowman, did Raymond have any particular sexual proclivities?'

Plowman narrowed his eyes imploring me to stop.

'If there's anything in Raymond's past that might suggest we should be pursuing a specific line of inquiry then you have a duty to inform us. Now is not the time to be embarrassed or bashful.'

Plowman cleared his throat and gave a meek cough before covering his face with his hands and croaking out in a weak voice, 'He... did have a liking for bondage... but it was never something I....'

'And did he mention any previous partners who he did this with?'

Now he gave me a helpless look, realising he had lost control. 'I'm sorry, Inspector, he didn't discuss anybody.'

Truth could have a physical effect sometimes and he slumped back in his chair. It must have been painful for him sharing intimate details about his partner, but it struck me he was telling the truth. After all, how many of us discuss previous relationships with current lovers?

He leaned back over the table and looked again, more seriously this time, at the artist's impression. 'Who was the eyewitness?'

'One of Raymond's neighbours confirms she saw this person leaving the house that afternoon.'

Plowman picked up the image and stared at it intently then he dropped it onto the table and stood up.

'I need to ask you one more thing. The words "see you later" were written in lipstick on the mirror. Do you have any explanation for that?'

He didn't hesitate or avoid my eye contact. 'None at all, Inspector. Some sort of sick joke, no doubt. I'm going away for a few days. I need to leave this place. I'm going to stay with some friends in Northumberland. I shall be back next week.'

'If you think of anything else then please do not hesitate to contact us.'

We took Plowman to reception and he left the station.

'What did you make of that, boss?' Lydia said as we made our way back to the Incident Room, but she didn't wait for me to reply, 'He was embarrassed about that bondage stuff.'

'He's frightened right enough. I don't think he knew anything about the writing on the mirror, but I can't help feeling that he's still hiding something.'

I pushed open the door to the Incident Room and Wyn jumped to his feet as we entered, a pleased look on his face.

'There's something else you should know, sir. I found some footage of Frank Armsby.'

Lydia and I stood over Wyn's shoulder staring at the monitor as he double clicked the mouse on his desk. Once he'd reached the right section that looked as though it had been filmed from inside a dimly-lit bar he clicked it open. 'I discovered Frank Armsby paid for drinks at one of the hotels at the bottom of Queen Street before he met Caitlin Prior. So

I rang the hotel and asked if they had any CCTV cameras. There's one in the bar area but the lighting was very subdued and the footage isn't clear.'

We watched images of customers milling around the bar, staff pouring glasses of wine, measuring spirits and cracking open mixers.

'This is what you need to see,' Wyn said, hand poised over the mouse. Seconds later he froze the footage on the image of Jim White talking with Frank Armsby.

Lydia whistled under her breath.

'We may need to have another chat with Jim White,' I said.

Chapter 20

'Have you seen the news this morning?' I was finishing my coffee when Superintendent Cornock rang, an edgy desperate sound to his voice.

'I was on my way in, sir.'

'It's all over the bloody newspapers. And one of the radio stations has picked up the details of the Carey crime scene. The PR department is having a collective fit. My office as soon as you're in, John.'

Cornock finished the call. I downed the last of the double espresso, skipping my breakfast toast and made straight for the door of my flat, running a hand through my hair as I glanced into the mirror. My mobile bleeped with a message from Alison as I reached a hand for the front door. *Still okay for tonight? X.* I tapped out a reply. *Of course, looking forward to it X.*

I cast a glance back at my reflection. Did I look tidy enough to be on a date that evening? My mother would have been horrified at the third best jacket I had chosen from the wardrobe, but my chinos were newly cleaned and pressed and my brogues neatly polished.

I trotted downstairs and then jogged over to the car, starting the engine and accelerating out into the morning traffic before heading towards Queen Street police station. It wasn't long before I was punching in the code for the rear entrance and then I took the stairs up to the second floor and Superintendent Cornock's office. The door was ajar and the tone of his voice was quite different from that which I had heard when I'd met Margaret Fabrien. He was angry and somebody was getting the blunt end of his annoyance.

I rapped my knuckles on the door and pushed it open. Cornock saw me and immediately jerked a hand. It wasn't a polite request more of a command and he pointed a finger at the empty chair in front of his desk. One of the junior public relations officers I'd met before sat in the other. Even the tropical fish in the tank swam more excitedly, wagging their fins as they raced around the obstacle course Cornock had assembled.

'The press is going mental, John,' Cornock said. 'Some bloody journalist has got hold of the details about the crime scene in Carey's home. They've been splashed all over the newspapers and later it's going to be covered by that inane talk-show on that ridiculous local radio station.'

I sat down and the PR assistant gave me a feeble smile. I wondered what excuse his boss had made for not pitching up to listen to Cornock's tirade. Cornock slumped into his chair. He blew out a mouthful of air.

The PR assistant ventured a question. 'How would you like us to respond, Superintendent?'

Cornock grunted. 'Tell them all to go to hell.'

The assistant must have thought Cornock was serious 'I don't think that will be possible—'

'Don't be stupid.'

The public relations department had sent someone far too junior to wrestle with Cornock's irritation. He waved a hand towards him. 'I want you to find out who got hold of the story first. I want the name of the journalist. Once we know who he is I'll have some questions for him.'

The man looked genuinely shocked at the implied threat in Cornock's voice. 'Will you be wanting to organise a press conference, Superintendent?'

'For Christ's sake that's all we want. A press conference! You can bugger off back to the PR department and don't come back until you've got the name of the reporter who first broke the story.'

The assistant abruptly stood up and nodded a goodbye to me and pulled the door closed as he left.

Cornock looked over at me. 'I don't know what the world is coming to, John. But I suppose in times like these everything is different. It was easier long ago when we could round up the bad guys, bang their heads together, get a signed confession and then lock them up.'

I did my best to sound diplomatic. 'I wouldn't share that with the PR department, sir.'

Cornock chortled, my attempt at humour clearly successful.

'Seriously, John, have you made any progress?'

My hesitation was enough for Cornock to add. 'That bad eh? Surely there should be somebody who can tell you something about the gun that was used. After all this sort of level of violence is extremely rare.'

'I'm hoping to talk to one of my informants about the possibility they can identify where it had been sourced.'

Normally Superintendent Cornock advised caution about using informants but clearly securing an arrest was paramount in his mind because he said nothing.

'Did you have an opportunity to read the preliminary report from Dr Fabrien?' Cornock said eventually.

'I did. It all seemed very helpful.' I surprised myself with how positive I sounded.

'Really?' Cornock's response wrong-footed me. 'ACC Neary is very keen that the assistance from Dr Fabrien should be greatly valued.'

I made to leave. 'Will you be organising a press conference?'

Cornock dragged his chair towards his desk. 'It looks as though I may have no alternative. Keep me posted, John.'

The pace at which I tramped back to the Incident Room was far less urgent than the speed at which I had covered the distance first thing. As soon as I was back at my desk, I called Terry and confirmed arrangements to meet later. A mid-morning recap with Lydia and Wyn around their desks focused my mind on Jim White, whose image I had removed from the board and placed in the middle of the desk in front of me. 'I'm not going to speak again to Jim White until I know exactly what his movements were on the afternoon and evening Armsby was killed. I need to be able to disprove his lies.' I looked over at Wyn. 'Interrogate all the ANPR cameras for any sightings of his Audi or that flashy sports car Laura drives. And get the DVLA to provide details of all the vehicles registered in his name.'

Wyn nodded.

I paused for a moment looking over at the image of Judy Campbell on the board. 'And we'll need to speak to Judy again. She lied to us. I don't like it when people lie to me.'

I recalled my first discussion with her. She had insisted she wouldn't speak to us unless it was in the safe surroundings the charity offered. And yet she had still lied. Our next discussion would be here, in one of the interview rooms, under caution, tape whirring and a solicitor sitting by her side. Would she find that comforting?

'Let's build a timeline from the CCTV footage and her mobile phone records before we bring her in.'

I spent the rest of the morning cross-referencing statements provided to the uniformed officers who had completed house-to-house inquiries near the home of Raymond Carey and from the businesses and offices on the industrial estate where the body of Frank Armsby had been recovered. But my attention was focused on my meeting with Terry and my date that evening with Alison Swan.

I called the restaurant to confirm the reservation and resolved to make time to get home to shower and change. Alison would understand if I couldn't – she was a police officer, so she knew the sort of demands my job entailed and the irregular hours involved.

It was after two-thirty when I pulled up by the pavement in one of the side streets in Splott near the café which was one of Terry's regular haunts. I locked the car and ambled as nonchalantly as I could, but a group of teenagers kicking a ball stared over at me. Everything about me and my clothes probably screamed 'police officer' but I ducked my head away and avoided their eye contact.

Condensation covering the inside of the window made

it difficult to read clearly the lettering which advertised all-day breakfasts and chef's specials. If frying bacon, eggs and sausages combined with heating up baked beans qualified the owner as a chef then he probably graduated with top marks. A butcher's apron hung from Brian's neck and he gave me the slightest surreptitious nod towards the rear of the café. A second nod told me he'd bring over a coffee and my regular bacon sandwich.

Terry was sitting in a corner table scrolling through his mobile, an enormous mug of tea stewing by the condiment set stacked against the wall. He saw me approaching and straightened. I dragged out a chair and sat down.

'What's this about, Marco?' Terry hissed.

'So, what do you know about Raymond Carey?'

'Fucking pervert.'

Terry put his phone down on the table and took a generous slug of his tea.

'I heard it on the radio this morning.' Terry lowered his head and whispered. 'He had his bollocks carved up.' Then he shivered and looked pleased when Brian arrived and plonked down two plates. 'Nice one, Marco.'

'I need to know who's supplying guns.'

Terry cast an urgent worried look around the other customers in the café. 'Not so fucking loud. Walls have ears.'

'You owe me, Terry.'

'Yeah, yeah. That's what you always say if you want a favour.'

'And what about that extra little cash I organised during the lockdown when your work dried up.' Reminding Terry that I had made his life a little easier never did any harm.

He rolled his eyes in feigned disbelief and tucked into his bacon roll mumbling appreciatively. 'I love these rolls.'

'Guns, Terry. You can find out who the players are. Or else I'll need to look at formally adding you as a person of interest to our inquiry in relation to Frank Armsby.' He stopped eating for a moment. I continued. 'You must have been one of the last people to see him alive. I'm sure the Superintendent would want me to interview you.'

'I'm not having any of that. You know how this works, Marco. That's all a load of shit and you know it.'

Terry was right, the bread really was quite good. And the bacon nice and crisp.

'Carey was mutilated in his own home.' I leaned over the table. 'And then he was shot.' I tapped a finger to my chest. 'It was like something out of *The Sopranos*.'

'What do you expect me to do? Grass up whoever sold the gun?'

'Just get me some intelligence, that's all. We'll do the rest.'

'You're making life difficult, really difficult.'

'I'm sure I can rely on you.'

'Piss off, Marco with all that slimy shit. I'll do what I can and get back to you.'

We finished the rest of our meal in silence. I settled the bill and left.

By seven pm I had showered and shaved, ironed a clean pair of chinos as well as a blue Bengal striped shirt – no tie needed, smart enough without. I dragged on my best jacket as I stared into the mirror by the door from my apartment. I could see that my skin was getting paler and the bags under my eyes heavier. Most people would be planning for two days of unstructured time, enjoying their families but I was likely to spend at least one of those days hunkered down in Queen Street with Lydia and Wyn. Although I had promised Jackie I would call to see Dean over the weekend and perhaps take him out for a couple of hours – go bowling or grab a pizza.

But tonight I had a date with Alison, which brought a smile to my face. I checked around the flat making certain the ironing board had been stored away, the kitchen worktops were neat and tidy, the sink clean – women have a habit of noticing these things. And I'd even changed the bedclothes, just in case.

I took my car up to Canton; these days I didn't need to worry about drinking and driving. I had to worry more about parking. The city seemed to get busier and busier all the time and it meant touring around some of the side streets until I could find a slot.

The maître d of the restaurant treated me like an old friend even though I'd only been there once. It was probably his standard treatment for every customer. I was standing by the bar sipping a San Pellegrino mineral water when Alison arrived.

I turned towards her, unable to hide the pleasure on my face. Her high heels were at least three inches high and her trousers flattered every curve and sinew of her legs. They narrowed to her ankles, but I hadn't noticed when we'd met before how long and curvaceous her legs were. Her blouse was cream and tight-fitting, unbuttoned to reveal enough cleavage to make my imagination race. She didn't need me to tell her, but I did anyway as I kissed her on the cheek. 'You look sensational.'

She took my arm as the maître d led us to our table.

'Can I get you a glass of wine?' I said as she cast a glance at the water I was drinking. 'I don't drink alcohol anymore.'

It was always best to get that explanation into the open as quickly as possible. If I got to know her any better, she'd get a full Marco family history. I reasoned there'd been enough gossip going around Queen Street police station and Southern Division about my antics, so some discreet inquiries and somebody would roll their eyes and tell her all about my previous life.

She turned to the waiter who was standing by the table. 'I'd like a glass of Pinot Grigio please.'

He nodded and, after depositing menus, left.

'Have you been here before?'

'Once, a while back.' Someone told me that the older you get the more baggage you carry around with you and the more you feel you need to over-share on the first date. But it was advice I ignored.

She settled on the pâté: I had some cold meats and a fantastic sourdough.

She laughed at my jokes, I enquired about her career, her family and we talked steadily throughout the evening. My main course of *pollo alla cacciatora* had the meat falling off the bone and she complimented the lasagne. Occasionally her knee rubbed against my leg. I kept it exactly where it was and hoped she'd make contact again. I touched her hand over the table and she gave me warm open smiles.

'My mother says that because I don't drink it means I can eat more pudding.'

Alison giggled. When the waiter arrived, she ordered a panna cotta to my four scoops of ice cream. When I suggested we visit one of the bars in the Bay, near my flat, I hoped that my decision to change the bottom sheet of the bed and freshen the duvet cover might have been sensible.

Once outside, after I'd paid the bill, Alison briefly shivered as the autumn evening chilled her skin. At first, I ignored the mobile ringing and vibrating in my jacket pocket. Alison gave me an inquisitive look as though she were saying – don't you need to answer that? The number of operational support flashed on the screen and I knew in an instant my evening was over. I put the mobile to my ear. 'Detective Inspector Marco, your presence is required at a murder scene.'

Chapter 21

Two vehicles had blocked my car in so I cursed. Helplessly I scanned the surrounding properties, hoping I might spot someone who looked as though they owned them. I didn't have time to waste so I jumped into my Mondeo and manoeuvred it into the street. It meant a ten-point turn and several collisions with the bumper of the vehicle behind and in front. I was on police business and I didn't care, but I was careful enough to take a photograph of the number plates before I left. If there was any damage, operational support could trace the owners.

I had left Alison at the restaurant door after a peck on the cheek and a promise to see her again. I had turned back before breaking into a jog and she had waved as she pinned her mobile to an ear, organising a taxi.

It took me a few seconds to tap into the satnav the postcode for the address in the Bay where the body had been found. The apartment where I was heading probably commanded a premium amongst the properties lining Cardiff Bay.

I blasted the horn at dawdling cars and the occasional taxi pulled onto the side of the road. The towering outline of the Millennium Centre and its lights streaming from the letters carved in the external elevation dominated the skyline. It was a sight I never tired of. It reminded me that Cardiff really was an exciting city. I indicated when instructed to, and cast a glance up at the old Victorian buildings built at the time when the docks were flourishing in the nineteenth century. Immediately to my left a marked police car was parked outside the entrance to the block, its lights flashing.

After parking I trotted over to the door and carded a uniformed constable standing inside. 'Top floor, sir,' he nodded down the hallway. 'There's a lift.'

The lift doors thudded open on the landing of the fourth floor. Instinct made me look for CCTV cameras, but I couldn't spot any and there hadn't been any in the downstairs lobby, although I had noticed the video entrance system. I could hear the chatter from a police radio and spotted an officer standing on the threshold of an open door.

He looked pleased to see me. 'I'm glad you got here so quickly, sir.'

'When are the CSIs expected?'

'They should have been here five minutes ago.' He handed me a pair of latex gloves which I snapped on.

'He's in the main bathroom,' the officer jerked his head at a door to our right.

'Who found the body?'

'His wife. She's with friends in one of the other apartments. I've got her contact details.'

I pushed the bathroom door with the toe of my shoe. It eased open. I looked in and down at the slumped form of a man in his early fifties propped up against a wall as though he had sat down for a rest, his legs thrust out in front of him. But the eyes that stared out blankly and the gaping wound on his head and the blood soaking his white shirt told a different story. Blood smeared the wash basin, an enormous bowl with gold taps, and above it was a mirror with a fancy-looking light. The tiles above the dead man's head were streaked, as was the toilet seat cover and the screen of a shower cubicle big enough for a small dinner party. Somebody had been busy, somebody really had it in for this guy.

I tried to imagine what had happened, first impressions were always important. I hadn't moved an inch. The killer had been here, and as every crime scene manager reminded me, the killer would have left a trace. It was just a matter of finding it.

Andrew Northam was wearing immaculate black brogues. They looked handmade and expensive and new, judging by the lack of wear on the soles. Although his trousers were crumpled and the shirt discoloured they didn't look like the mass-produced Marks & Spencer versions I favoured. The blue colour of the watch face and its heavy metal bracelet suggested a Breitling or an Omega.

Conversations from people approaching down the landing caught my attention so I left the bathroom as Alvine Dix and one of the crime scene investigators appeared at the front door of the apartment.

'John Marco, I might have guessed it would be you. Don't you have anything else to do on a Friday night?'

I spared her the details of my ambitions for the evening. I gave her a brief smile and a quick roll of the eyes suggesting I had no other alternative.

'I hope you haven't touched anything,' Alvine said, fixing me with a piercing stare.

'You always say that, Alvine.'

'And why do you think that is, Inspector?' Her question was rhetorical, so she moved on immediately. So many cases had been compromised by officers contaminating crime scenes that she didn't want to get any of the blame if prosecutions failed because of an officer's incompetence. 'So, what have you got for me?'

I showed her to the door of the bathroom, and she peered in. 'Who is he?'

'Andrew Northam, apparently. His wife found the body early this evening.'

'Imagine coming home to that.'

Alvine took in her surroundings. 'Fancy-looking place isn't?' Then she turned towards the entrance and nodded for one of her investigators to move their boxes of equipment into the apartment.

Carefully, I opened the door into the sitting room. It was an impressive room with large windows from floor to ceiling offering a spectacular view over the Cardiff Bay area. The lights of Penarth twinkled on the cliffside in the distance and restaurants and bars below us would be doing good business. Social distancing measures had only recently been relaxed, although there were regular warnings about the possibility of a second wave of the pandemic. I eased open one of the windows that led out onto a decking area, allowing the cool autumn air to chill my face. I could imagine sitting here on a summer's evening enjoying the view. Andrew Northam certainly wouldn't be doing that anymore.

I stepped inside and slid the door closed. The place had an anonymous, antiseptic feel as though it were only used occasionally. Scatter cushions appeared unruffled, ornaments were placed in precise order, there were no extraneous newspapers or magazines in sight and no personal photographs or shopping lists cluttered the surfaces. Who was he? How had he made his money?

I avoided bumping into two CSIs as I found the kitchen. No stacks of mugs or toaster or bread bin. I eased open the first door which exposed a built-in fridge – empty apart from some orange juice and a bottle of milk. It confirmed my initial impression that this wasn't a flat anyone really lived in. At least they had one of those coffee machines that uses pods. I had never seen the attraction myself, and I preferred my reliable old Gaggia.

I heard Paddy McVeigh's voice in the hallway and went to meet him. 'I was settling into *Game of Thrones*. My son told me I should watch the whole series. He says I haven't lived unless I've watched them all. And now this.'

'Working for the Wales Police Service is much better than *Game of Thrones*.'

Paddy gave me an unconvinced look. 'What have we got?'

Alvine emerged from the sitting room. 'Swanky place isn't it?'

I nodded towards the bathroom as I replied to Paddy, 'He's in there.'

I left Paddy and Alvine and found the narrow staircase up to the first floor and the two bedrooms filling the attic space of the old building. They were spacious and sprawling with built-in cupboards with doors that glided easily just by looking at them. But most were empty apart from some business suits and shirts. There were drawers with ties and cufflinks and new shirts in unopened crisp cellophane wrapping. The smaller, second bedroom had Stieg Larsson and Ian Rankin novels on a bedside cupboard. Large, framed black-and-white photographs of Cardiff hung on the wall, as they had in the first bedroom. Retreating back downstairs it struck me the place could have featured in one of those fancy magazines where rich people boast about their homes.

Paddy had left by the time I returned to the hallway where the original officer said to me, 'Dr McVeigh said that he'll be organising the post-mortem tomorrow morning.'

'I need to speak to Mrs Northam.'

He gave me the details of the neighbour and her mobile number. I took the stairs and found the flat easily enough. I knocked on the door and then spotted the bell, which I pushed a couple of times. Seconds later the door opened and a pasty-looking woman in her fifties peered at me aggressively. I pushed my warrant card towards her. 'Detective Inspector John Marco. I understand Mrs Northam is here.'

She studied my card and the hostility evaporated. 'Of course, of course, Inspector. It's been a dreadful, dreadful evening. Come in. She is in the sitting room.'

The layout of the apartment was quite different from the Northam's above. Architects probably argued with the developer about how to carve up an old building to maximise their return. The sitting room was two-thirds the size of the Northam's and there was no decking nor the views over the centre of Cardiff. A woman with healthy-looking silver-grey hair and a round face running to a little flab looked up at me from the sofa. An Omega hung on her left wrist – was it a match for her dead husband's upstairs?

'This is Angela – Mrs Northam,' the other woman said.

'Can I get you anything, Inspector?'

I shook my head and sat down. 'I'm Detective Inspector John Marco. I shall be leading the investigation. Can you tell me how you found your husband?'

If Mrs Angela Northam had been the first to find her husband's body, then that would automatically make her a person of interest in our inquiry. If she watched enough crime drama on the television she would know what to expect but from the lack of colour on her face and the evidence of tears filling her eyes, second-guessing how we would be running the case was the last thing on her mind.

'He didn't go to work today.' She looked puzzled as though she expected me to mind read. 'He's been working in Cardiff this week.' Now I heard the accent. No trace of Cardiff or South Wales or Wales come to that. This was Home Counties, the product of an expensive education. 'He runs a television production company and most weeks he spends two or three nights here.' She flicked her eyes upwards. 'I mean in the flat.'

'And where do you live?'

'In Carmarthenshire.' She said it as though I should have known, as though she was important enough that it need not be said.

'I've been calling him all day. The office told me he hadn't arrived this morning. They've been trying to reach him all day. Somebody even called at the flat, but he hadn't responded. They'd had to rearrange some important meetings.'

'Where did your husband work?'

She gave me a horrified look as though I had no reason to use the past tense. She quoted the name of a company I'd never heard of. 'I travelled down this evening. I was really worried, terrified.' Her voice broke.

I read the time; it was late. The crime scene investigators would be at the scene for the rest of the night and with the post-mortem organised for the morning I'd need to speak to her again. 'Would you be able to stay here tonight?'

She nodded. Her friend interjected. 'Of course she will. We'll look after her.'

'I am very sorry for your loss. We'll contact you again tomorrow to take a more detailed statement.'

A few minutes later I found myself standing on the pavement outside the building. The dull thud of human activity drifted over from the Bay. I pulled the lapels of my jacket up to my face. A message reached my mobile from Superintendent Cornock – *Call me*. I didn't reply immediately, nor did I return to my car. I walked down to the Bay thinking that I needed to mix with real live human beings, enjoying themselves, relaxing after a busy week. I strolled around the Bay clearing my mind, realising that the weekend would be like any other working day. Then I called Superintendent Cornock.

Chapter 22

Lydia slid into the bench seat opposite me in the café near the mortuary where we'd eaten before. She put a latte down on the table alongside my second Americano of the morning. I hadn't risked eating anything before leaving the flat and I didn't intend to do so in the café either. Post-mortems were rarely conducive to a settled stomach.

'Morning, boss.'

I nodded and Lydia continued. 'Who is the victim?'

'A man called Andrew Northam.'

Lydia had mentioned yesterday that she was planning to visit a food festival in Hay on Wye that day with her boyfriend, a computer engineer, a recent development in her life. 'I could have done the post-mortem and spoken to the family without you.'

She sounded resigned. 'Maybe I can go tomorrow. Pete didn't complain, he had a lot of work to do anyway.'

I hadn't met Peter yet – families always had second place in the life of a police officer, mentioned in passing, tolerated.

I gave Lydia a summary of the circumstances. She stared over at me intently absorbing all the details. At the end she asked the question every detective wanted to know the answer to, 'What did you make of his wife?'

'She was distraught. We'll talk to her again later – it'll be easier to get a better picture of her and Northam today.'

'Superintendent Cornock wanted us to report immediately any suggestion of a link with Frank Armsby or Raymond Carey. Any words daubed on mirror?'

'Nothing like that.'

Lydia quaffed the dregs of her drink and I did the same.

At the mortuary Paddy kicked off with personal chit-chat. 'I want to get this finished quickly. The Blues are playing at home this afternoon and I don't want to miss the game.'

'And we'll be knee deep into this murder inquiry.

Making certain we keep the streets of Cardiff safe.'

'No peace for the wicked,' Paddy added, nodding for the assistant to remove the sheet covering Northam's body.

Lydia had stood a little distance behind me and she moved even further back when Paddy got to work. The sound of each rib in turn snapping under the weight of the cutters elicited a few sharp coughs from her. As Paddy dictated his findings as he examined the various organs I glanced over at Lydia who had a hand pushed to her mouth. She gave a brief reassuring shake of her head telling me that she was in control.

The speed at which Paddy worked gave me the distinct impression he had come to a conclusion about the cause of death before starting. He paused. 'He's been badly beaten – could be a wooden club, baseball bat but after the first couple of blows he was probably unconscious.'

'How long has he been dead?'

Paddy pondered a reply. 'At least twelve hours when we found the body because rigor had almost completely disappeared. So that would take you to early Friday morning – maybe even Thursday night. I can be more certain once we've done some tests.'

'Anything else?'

'Like a note from the killer confessing to killing him stuffed into his shirt pocket?'

'Very funny.'

'He was healthy, all his vital organs were in reasonable condition. Is it connected to the death of Armsby and Carey?'

Shrugging seemed a copout. 'It's too early to say.' But if they were then we had a seriously sick individual to catch.

'I'll send you the report.' Paddy fiddled with his mobile and orchestral music blasted out from two small speakers in the corner of the mortuary. Outside we made for the car and I reached for my mobile. I called Angela Northam's number but it went straight to voicemail, so I rang the landline for her neighbour. She answered it after two rings. 'May I speak to Mrs Northam?'

'I'm afraid she's gone back to her home in Carmarthenshire.'

It meant a two hour round trip and, with Superintendent Cornock needing an update later, I anticipated another long day. 'Do you have the address?' I didn't have the details, having expected to see Mrs Northam in Cardiff. Plas Mawr sounded grand and in the car I punched in the postcode. Lydia didn't look surprised when I announced. 'We've got a trip to Carmarthenshire.'

The journey to the end of the M4 passed quickly but traffic slowed once we were on the A48 heading west after the Pont Abraham roundabout. More trucks and vans than I expected for a Saturday morning delayed our progress. After the roundabouts and the bypass around Carmarthen the dual carriageway became a two lane road. The satnav bleeped for us to take a junction northward before the town of St Clears and the roads narrowed as the countryside widened around us. Lydia had been playing with her mobile since Carmarthen and had announced that Plas Mawr was an historic gentleman's residence with substantial outbuildings set in over seventy acres of land.

The satnav kept giving us instructions about the sections of our journey and where to turn until eventually we pulled up by a stone-built lodge. An ancient metal gate hung from rusty hinges, its white paint badly needing a fresh coat. I turned the car into the drive and at the end of an avenue of trees and shrubs a property emerged.

There was a Land Rover Discovery and two BMWs parked on a section of ochre and golden gravel. I pulled up alongside them and we walked over to the front door. It was painted a glistening black and was slightly ajar, allowing us to hear the muted tones of conversations. I shouted a greeting and a response encouraged me to enter and Lydia followed me inside. A woman appeared from a doorway and gave us questioning looks. 'Can I help you? I was expecting Francine.'

In tandem Lydia and I pulled out our warrant cards. 'I'm Detective Inspector John Marco of the Wales Police Service and this is Detective Sergeant Lydia Flint. We'd like to speak to Mrs Northam.'

'Of course, of course. Come through. She's only just got back.'

Angela Northam gave me a confused look as though I was the last person she expected to see. She gave Lydia a blank look. 'This is Detective Sergeant Flint,' I said.

Angela nodded. I turned to the woman I'd met in the hallway and the two others sitting on the sofa alongside her. 'We need to speak to Mrs Northam privately.'

For a fraction of a second nobody moved. Then the realisation cut in and they scrambled to their feet and scurried out of the room.

'I needed to get away from Cardiff.' Angela said. 'I should have told you, I suppose.'

Scolding Angela Northam was futile, so I sat opposite her on the sofa, Lydia joining me. 'We'd like to ask a few more questions about your husband.'

Angela reached for a tissue from the box on an enormous square coffee table in front of her. There were glossy books on climbing and one featuring the hundred things to do in Wales before you die. How many had Northam completed?

'Does anyone else have a key to the flat?'

She shook her head.

'Is there a cleaner? Or family members?'

Another shake of the head. 'The children are both in London. They're travelling back today.'

She made it sound like a holiday trip.

'Has your husband complained recently about anything – has anybody been making threats against him?'

'How can you say that?' Her voice quivered.

The only conclusion from the post-mortem was that somebody had wanted Andrew Northam dead very badly.

'Does your husband have any financial problems?'

She raised her eyebrows in disbelief. In circumstances like these things were rarely what they seemed and despite the high-end vehicles parked in the drive, the house and seventy acres and the flat in the Bay, something wasn't right with the Northam family.

'The business was doing well. He'd recently won a big contract to do some outside broadcast for an American TV network. We were even thinking of buying a house in the south of France. It's always been our ambition – a holiday home and somewhere we can spend more time when we retire.'

'Does he have business partners?'

'Andrew is the majority shareholder but there are three others involved too.'

Lydia had her notebook open on her knee. 'We'll need the name and address of the business.'

Angela duly obliged and provided all the details which Lydia jotted down. 'Andrew has a study here.'

I took the opportunity to add, 'We'll need to go through his personal things before we leave.'

My request was met with another incredulous look.

Lydia continued, 'When was the last time that you spoke to your husband?'

Angela's mouth fell open, then she reached for the mobile on the coffee table. 'We would message regularly during the day – WhatsApp usually.' She stared at the screen. 'I spoke to him Thursday lunchtime. And I sent him a couple of messages that afternoon but he told me he was working late and that he'd call me on Friday morning. When he didn't, I called the office but they hadn't seen him. By Friday lunchtime I was beside myself with worry.'

'Are there any close friends he would have been in contact with on Thursday evening?' I asked.

'I can't possibly think. I mean we have lots of friends... I suppose I can ask people we know in Cardiff.'

'That'll be our job, Mrs Northam,' I said. 'What would be helpful however is if you can provide us with the names of those he might have spoken to.'

We spent an hour interrogating Mrs Northam about her husband's possible contacts. Lydia assembled a detailed list of friends and business associates he might have contacted. Mrs Northam's attention waned so I decided to ask her to show us her late husband's study. She left us alone inside after giving the room a wistful glance. We spent time checking the cupboards, desk drawers and filing cabinets but operational support would need to remove everything to add to the laptop removed from the apartment in Cardiff. There was nothing to suggest who might want Northam dead. His personal or professional life would hold the clue – perhaps both overlapped and I suspected we'd find out once we knew who hated him enough.

We thanked Mrs Northam and left Plas Mawr to drive back to Cardiff. The journey passed quickly, and I pulled into the car park at Queen Street and looked up at the building, wondering how Superintendent Cornock would react.

Superintendent Cornock was pacing around the Incident Room when I strode in. Wyn sat by his desk looking terrified.

'You won't believe this,' Cornock said. 'Northam was prosecuted for an alleged sexual assault.'

Northam was our third victim and the second to have faced prosecution for sexual assault. Was it more than a coincidence? 'What happened?'

'Case was transferred to Bristol for some reason and the case never got beyond a preliminary hearing before the judge. It was dismissed. I've got the papers from the original prosecution of Andrew Northam.' Cornock nodded to a pile

The Cardiff Lockdown Murders

of papers on the desk near Wyn. 'I've read the pathologist's conclusions and I've spoken to Alvine Dix. I've told everyone the forensic report and any additional analysis needs to be completed as soon as possible.'

Cornock wandered over to the board. 'And you can add Northam's image.'

I paused for a moment. Having Cornock stalking around the Incident Room wasn't usual and I got the distinct impression he was on edge.

He continued, 'ACC Neary has been on the phone. She wants to emphasise how important it is that all the necessary resources are used to identify Northam's killer. His business has received grants from the Welsh Government to produce television dramas and he was expert at glad-handing politicians and the movers and shakers of the Welsh establishment.'

It sounded as though what Cornock was really saying was that someone wanted the culprit apprehended then safely convicted, locked up and the key thrown away.

'Are there any similarities with the modus operandi or circumstances of Northam's death to the killing of Armsby and Carey?' Cornock put his hands on his hips as though he was defying us to challenge him by confirming there were.

'Armsby and Northam were both charged with sexual offences but that's about the extent of any similarity. Both murder scenes are completely different.'

Cornock nodded encouragingly. 'We need to keep a lid on this.'

'The press are certain to get wind of it, sir,' Lydia said reflecting what everyone in the room really knew.

Cornock glanced over to the board.

'It might be better to make a brief statement,' I said, 'rather than allowing the press to chase us for details.'

Cornock still stared at the faces on the board looking for inspiration. 'Dammit. I know you're right, John. I'll talk to the PR department – they can put something together for tomorrow morning.'

Once Cornock had left Wyn piped up. 'I've found something, sir. Northam was using the same internet dating site Armsby had used. And there are messages about meeting up with somebody on the night he was killed.'

Lydia reacted first. 'What's wrong with all these men?'

Wyn and I shared a dull glance.

'You'd better track her down,' I said. 'And build a detailed picture of his activity on the dating app. People in common with Armsby and Carey. This could be crucial.'

As I made for my office Wyn raised his voice. 'I've organised operational support for first thing Monday morning.'

It was a reminder that Judy Campbell could expect an invitation for her to assist with our inquiries in the more formal setting of an interview room at Queen Street. And explain exactly why she had lied to us. At the same time the forensic team would be taking her car apart. 'Thanks.'

Back in my office I booted up my computer and as I waited for it to flicker into life I tapped out a message to Alison. *Sorry about last night. New M inquiry. Perhaps we could try again next week?* The monitor came to life and I clicked into my emails and scanned my inbox. Alison replied quickly *I heard about the case. Hope you're OK. Next week would be lovely. Look forward to it. X.* The kiss made me smile and the chance of a proper date lifted my spirits.

I found the preliminary forensic report attached to an email from Alvine. Frustration made me shake my head as I read there were no fingerprints and little evidence to provide DNA pointing directly to a killer. Paddy's report suggested a violent confrontation in the bathroom of the property. It made me wonder why Northam had been killed there? Had he retreated into the room for safety? I sat back for a moment thinking what a person would do if they'd been surprised by someone entering the flat suddenly producing a club or a baseball bat.

The rest of the day was spent reading the reviews of the house-to-house inquiries and reading the papers from Northam's prosecution. I was accustomed to the formal language of a CPS file, but I couldn't help but feel the victim had been let down. Another case where an abusive man had escaped justice.

Cornock must have rattled the cage of someone at public relations because a draft statement reached my inbox by early evening as I was planning to leave. I read the contents twice before emailing my agreement to the text. I didn't reply to any of the other emails filling my inbox. I closed the computer and went home, hoping I could relax for a couple of hours.

There was a ready meal in the freezer and a bag of salad and some wrinkly tomatoes in the fridge. I sat watching a documentary on television not concentrating on anything that was said – my mind blank, my body tired. After I finished eating my mobile rang and I recognised Jackie's number.

'Hi, Jackie,'

'I know you're busy, John, but your mother spoke to me about the half term holiday arrangements. And I wanted to discuss things with you before I gave her a proper reply.'

'Can we do this another time?' I stifled an enormous yawn.

'There never seems to be another time.' She left the statement hanging in the air for a few brief seconds hoping I'd fill the vacuum. She continued. 'It's just that since the last time when...' She couldn't bring herself to say the words that we spent the night together. 'We haven't been able to talk and your mother thinks the holiday in Tenby might...' Be a way for us to get back together? I almost added.

'Mamma only wants the best for both of us and for Dean.'

'I think it might be a bit too soon. I don't want Dean thinking...'

Another yawn gripped my jaw. 'Can we talk about this again. I really need to get some sleep.'

'Next week perhaps?'

'Of course.'

She rang off. I left the dishes on the coffee table and trudged off to bed.

Chapter 23

Sunday mornings were quiet around the blocks of flats in the Bay. Most people would be sleeping in or watching television or frying bacon for breakfast. I pointed the remote at my Mondeo and its locks bleeped open. A couple of youngsters cycled past, all kitted up like participants in the Tour de France.

I collected Lydia from outside Queen Street, and she gave me directions for Northam's offices.

'I've been thinking, boss,' Lydia said. 'If Armsby and Northam both faced criminal charges for rape then both inquiries have a common link.'

'Let's wait until we're further ahead before we make any decisions.'

Lydia continued, thinking out loud, 'But where does that take us with Carey? Maybe there are two killers at work.'

I pulled into the car park at the offices of Banjax TV. It should have been deserted but it was occupied by half a dozen vehicles, all expensive looking saloons, Mercedes and BMWs, some less than two years old, one with a personalised number plate.

Soap operas weren't really my thing but Doctor Who and Holby City were produced in studios in Cardiff. The pandemic must have had an impact – after all, it would be difficult to film a scene where the actors would have to socially distance. There had been lots of repeats during the months of the lockdown so companies like Banjax TV were playing catch-up with the backlog of production and recordings.

A tall, thin woman prowled around reception chewing a nail. From her gaunt appearance I guessed it had been her only square meal for the past few days.

'Inspector Marco?' she said, peering at me intently. Her eyes were set a little too far back, giving her a ghostly appearance. She glared at Lydia.

'This is Detective Sergeant Lydia Flint.'

'Thank Christ, you've arrived.' The accent was a younger version of Angela Northam. Cultured and urbane, just as you'd expect from an employee of a television production company. I imagined her floating around a reception with A-list celebrities, casually sipping on a glass of champagne, exchanging small talk and laughing politely. 'This is shocking, shocking, come with me.'

She led us through into the bowels of the building. At the far end was a conference room and through the glass panel of the door a dozen or more people milled around inside.

Intense stares connected with Lydia and me as we followed the thin, nameless woman. She announced. 'This is Detective Inspector Marco and...' Lydia helped out. 'Detective Sergeant Lydia Flint.'

'Of course, of course.' the woman said beating herself up verbally for the inadequacies of her memory.

'We're all desperately sad.' The booming voice came from a man in his sixties who sounded as though he was auditioning for a part in King Lear. 'If there's anything at all that we can do to help.'

Talking to each of the assembled audience in turn would take me hours. I glanced at Lydia who gave the briefest twitch of her lips that suggested she felt the same frustration that somehow, we were here to be part of their collective grief.

'We need to talk to Mr Northam's personal assistant to establish his movements in the hours before his death.'

'That's me.' The nameless woman announced. She accompanied it with a limp smile. 'Kirsten Baldwin.'

A woman's voice piped up, 'How is Angela, it must be absolutely terrible for her?'

Several heads nodded in unison. I heard the words 'shocking' and 'desperately sad' with more mumbling agreement. I batted away the occasional enquiry about whether we had made any progress. Real-world policing was going to be completely different from the make-believe world of the crime dramas churned out by Banjax TV.

'Will you be wanting to interview us?' It was the voice of the ham actor again.

'Perhaps you could provide all your contact details for Sergeant Flint. If we need to speak to any of you, we can make contact in due course.'

Kirsten Baldwin had a desk in an anteroom near to Andrew Northam's office. She looked younger and even thinner sitting down.

'How long have you been Mr Northam's assistant?' Lydia began with a softening up question.

'A couple of years. I was headhunted.' She didn't offer any more of an explanation, content to bathe in the adulation she expected.

'And did you enjoy working for him?' Lydia continued.

'He was one of the best bosses I've ever worked for. He was hard-working and demanding but very considerate too.'

'Did he mention anything that was causing him worry, or concern? Did he ever mention that he thought someone wanted to cause him harm?'

'That's preposterous. He was a TV executive. Who would possibly want to kill him?'

I butted in. 'Someone certainly did. And it's our job to find out who that was.'

'Yes, Inspector. I didn't mean to sound uncooperative.'

'When did you see him last?'

Baldwin blinked away the emotion in her eyes that teared up briefly. 'Thursday afternoon. He had a meeting with some chaps from one of those American networks that wanted to commission the company to run a UK historical drama series. He was delighted and thrilled. It shows you, Inspector, how valuable the television industry is to Cardiff.' She added as an afterthought, 'and to Wales, of course.'

'I need you to be more exact about the timings.'

'That meeting took all morning. Then he went out for some lunch as he always did to a café around the corner and then he came back and spent most of the afternoon with some of the production team or on the telephone.'

'Do you know who he was meeting that evening?'

She shook her head briskly. 'I'm terribly sorry, I cannot help you. I don't look after his social calendar.'

Lydia pressed her. 'Did he not mention what he was doing? Did he give you any indication of whether he was busy or sitting at home watching EastEnders?'

'Never EastEnders, Sergeant.' She paused. 'I have no details of what he was doing.'

Now Lydia sounded borderline exasperated. 'But did he ever discuss things with you? Small talk? Did he go the gym or a specific restaurant?'

Baldwin gave Lydia a helpless look. 'Sorry.'

I cut in. 'How did he get on with other members of staff?' I decided to cast my fishing line a little further and possibly a little deeper. 'For example, were there difficulties with female employees?'

Baldwin picked up a ballpoint from her desk and turned it through her fingers. 'There were complaints from two of the actresses on one of the soaps we were producing. Typical bloody actors, thinking they were more important than anybody else. They made some unfounded allegations of improper conduct against Andrew.'

'What sort of complaints?'

She gave an embarrassed sigh. 'Touching and making lewd suggestions. All nonsense of course. Andrew could be a flirt but ...'

'Who dealt with those complaints?'

'It was somebody from HR.' Baldwin replied dismissively.

I glanced over at Lydia and she nodded her understanding that we'd need to collect any papers relating to both complaint.

'We'll need details of everybody that he met that Thursday. And a log of all his telephone calls.'

Baldwin clicked on a mouse and her monitor screen purred into life. As she searched for the information I slipped through into Northam's office with Lydia. I sat by his desk imagining the to and fro of conversations about some super-popular crime drama. I spun around on the chair and looked up at the triptych of modern art hanging on the wall behind his desk. I recognised the Cubist technique, so I tilted my head back and forth. It was no good, I couldn't see any form or structure.

A few moments passed before Baldwin appeared at the door of Northam's office. She gave Lydia a suspicious look as she finished examining the contents of a filing cabinet. She waved some sheets of paper in the air. 'Here are the details you need.'

In reception half a dozen of the staff we had spoken to previously were talking in hushed tones, but they fell into absolute silence and neutral stares as we made our way to the car and headed back to the middle of Cardiff.

I parked some distance away from Northam's flat. Old Victorian and Edwardian buildings built to service the industrial needs of coal exporters from Cardiff in the nineteenth century and the new blocks of flats sat cheek by jowl with the remnants of a council estate.

A different uniformed police officer stood inside the hallway, checking everybody who entered and left. The CSIs were probably still up there, I concluded. I walked past the entrance and on up to the end of the street with Lydia trotting behind me. 'Getting my bearings,' I said, when she gave me a quizzical look.

I scanned the buildings, searching for a CCTV camera conveniently trained on the door of Northam's apartment block. A pair of uniformed officers emerged from a nearby building and nodded over towards us. Their clipboards identified them as conducting house-to-house inquiries.

From their reports Wyn or Lydia or I would dig out some fragment that would help us track down the killer.

Most of the adjacent properties were occupied by offices although I knew that nearby a boutique hotel had recently opened. The owners had announced its opening in a splurge of advertising in the local newspaper.

'He must have let the killer in,' Lydia said as we stood on the pavement on the corner looking down towards Northam's apartment.

'He knew the person.'

I didn't wait for Lydia to reply before marching down the street for the entrance. The uniformed officer recognised us and we took the lift to the top floor. The crime scene investigators were still finishing in the bedrooms upstairs, dusting for prints mostly. I stood with Lydia looking into the bathroom.

'Was there blood anywhere else?' Lydia asked.

'No.'

'The altercation took place in the bathroom?'

'It looks that way.'

Lydia took a step nearer, almost standing on the threshold. 'Northam must have been overpowered very quickly. He wasn't a small man.'

I pointed towards the toilet and wash basin and then at where Northam's body was discovered. 'He was propped up against the wall.'

Lydia stepped inside, scanning the surroundings as she did so. 'There must have been two of them. One person on his own couldn't have overpowered him.'

Chatter from the two CSIs filled the hallway as they descended from the first floor. They greeted us, both telling us that they had finished their work. The investigators dragged the door closed behind them and Lydia opened the door to the sitting room exclaiming as she did so. 'Wow, this is an amazing room and what a view.'

My mobile rang as Lydia made for the sliding doors

onto the decking outside. I recognised Alvine Dix's number. 'I've been working on Carey's laptop. Something you should see.'

Chapter 24

Alvine Dix protected the forensic department based in the bowels of Queen Street like a scientist in an old B-movie shielding his Frankenstein-like creation. So there must have been a genuine reason for her request. Alvine's office had a small window covered with a battered vertical blind. Modern LEDs flooded the place with light.

'Why the urgency?' I asked, as Alvine waved Lydia and me to two visitor chairs by her desk.

'We were finalising the examination of Raymond Carey's laptop. One of my team did some work on identifying the folders and files. Most were the usual – Word documents, Excel spreadsheets for some projections and household expenditure. He had quite a lot of money invested in bitcoin, by the way.'

'Come on, Alvine, get on with it. We all want to get home. It's been a long day.' She narrowed her eyes at me as though it was the most reprehensible thing anybody had ever said to her.

'There are files hidden on his hard drive you need to look at.' She got up and beckoned for us to follow her. One of the junior investigators sat by a desk waiting patiently, a laptop open in front of him.

He straightened when he saw Alvine approach.

We found chairs and sat alongside him. She nodded at him and he reached for the mouse. Then the screen came to life.

'Carey had a particular taste for gay pornography and there are videos stored on his computer – legal, but barely. I had a recent case where videos had been stored where the owner had hoped he could hide them from prying eyes.'

'Not a lot of point in doing that if the laptop was ever part of police investigation,' Lydia said.

The blurry images of a bedroom emerged and he paused the footage, turning to look at me and Lydia. 'These are quite violent. Standard protocols mean we should forward them immediately to the task force dealing with violent sexual offences.'

Alvine cut in, 'Inspector Marco knows that. Just run the footage.'

He pressed play and we sat and watched in silence as the images filled the screen.

A double bed dominated a small room. A pack of cigarettes and a lighter sat on a bedside table, alongside a lamp that cast a faint glow. The wallpaper had peeled and you could almost smell the decay in the room. A man, completely naked, lay on his front on the bed, each wrist bound to the corner of the bedstead. His ankles were firmly secured to the legs of the bed, making his whole body spread-eagled on the sheet.

The footage, recorded on a handheld camera, caught the laughter and joking of the men standing around the bed. A sick feeling developed in my stomach as the camera moved to one side, the focus adjusting to take a close-up of the man's backside.

'How much more of this is there?' I said.

Neither Alvine nor the investigator replied. The footage ran on.

Two of the voices were clearly identifiable but there were no faces, not even in profile.

When the camera turned to look at one of the men standing by the bed, undressing, the sick feeling turned to bile as he climbed naked onto the bed. It was just about possible to see the face of this man: Raymond Carey. Nothing was left to the imagination as he squatted over the prostrate body and raped him. The only sound was the moaning from the figure lying on the bed and the movement on the mattress.

I had been standing, frozen to the spot for what felt like minutes.

'I've seen enough.'

'We can't identify the other two.'

The investigator added. 'There's a tattoo or birth mark on the victim's shoulder but the quality of the recording is poor, so I haven't been able to get a clear image. There's something else, Inspector.' He restarted the video.

The man who filmed Carey handed him the camera and more banter was exchanged between the abusers but the other two faces weren't recorded. I guessed this was Carey's private footage for his exclusive entertainment. The footage moved on and Carey neared the door and he was alone in the bedroom.

He paused at the bottom of the bed and he turned to the victim. Then he used a cheerful tone and said, 'See you later.'

'Christ almighty!' I snapped. 'Play that again.'

Lydia gasped as the words could be heard quite clearly.

Alvine responded, 'I thought that might be of interest.'

It changed everything. I stared at the frozen images on the screen. Was the victim on the bed our killer? We had to find him. Fast.

Lydia interrupted my train of thoughts. 'Can we be certain that only Carey and the victim heard those comments?'

The investigator frowned.

'Simple bloody question.' I sounded angry. I was angry. 'Carey was one of three men involved – if the other men didn't hear the words, they may not connect his death to this victim …. The man on the bed. So …'

Lydia finished the sentence for me. 'There could be more victims.'

Years ago, I would have gone straight for one of my favourite watering holes to down a couple of beers hoping it would erase the images of human depravity I had seen. Alvine sounded matter-of-fact. 'We'll do what we can to recover a voice file for each of the other two men. It might be possible for you to identify them that way.'

Shock was evident in Lydia's voice. 'It's truly evil.

Those men should rot in hell.'

I looked over at Alvine. 'Is there any way we can identify the man on the bed.'

'Doubtful. He obviously suffered a lot of injuries which would probably have taken quite a while to heal. We'll do what we can with the footage, but the lighting wasn't good and they made sure they didn't show his face.'

Lydia again. 'What sort of sad sick bastards would have done that?'

Then I turned to Lydia. 'Let's go.'

Standing on the pavement outside Queen Street, Lydia announced. 'God, I need a drink.'

The autumn air had chilled my skin but the change in temperature from the stuffy forensic lab wouldn't chase away the images we had both seen. She marched away and I followed her. A few minutes later she was standing at the bar at Lefties ordering a large gin and tonic. I settled for my usual sparkling water and we found a spare table.

'Carey was sick,' Lydia looked up at me. 'He and his two friends must've filmed that gang rape. And then he could watch it over and over in his spare time like the sick saddo he must have been.'

'We need to find the victim and identify the other men in that recording.'

'I'll get started first thing, boss.'

'And contact Plowman – he might know something.'

Lydia took a second large gin and tonic at a much slower pace than the first. We mulled over everything we knew about Carey and prioritised the work needed to be done in the morning: trace a voice file, unlikely; interrogate the intelligence database for any complaints of a multiple gang raped perpetrated by three men, possible, but unlikely; identify the men from the video footage, a long shot.

It was late when I bundled Lydia into a taxi. I was hungry and knew I had to eat or I wouldn't sleep. Although after seeing the footage earlier I doubted sleep would come easily.

Chapter 25

I sat in my car the following morning looking over at the apartment building where Judy Campbell lived. She would be preparing for work, another day in the recruitment agency where she worked placing chefs and waiters with hotels and restaurants. Lydia sipped the dregs of her coffee; she looked remarkably fresh and healthy, a world away from the way I felt. I had slept badly, images of being cross-examined in court about the way I had contaminated the crime scene at the Northam apartment woke me regularly: every police officer's nightmare. After giving evidence I spotted Alvine Dix sitting at the back shaking her head morosely as though I should have known better.

But it was the footage from Carey's laptop that dragged me fully awake, assaulting my thoughts. I stood under the hot shower for longer than normal until I had banished them into a dark corner.

When the low loader drew up behind me followed by a scientific support vehicle it was time to ruin Judy Campbell's morning, definitely her day and possibly even the whole week. I wondered how she'd explain her absence to her boss.

'The CSI lads are here,' I said to Lydia.

She nodded and slotted the plastic takeaway mug into a cupholder behind the gearstick of the centre console. We walked over to the property; a man in his seventies walking his dog and a youngster on a bike were the only people nearby. The entrance lobby didn't have a fancy video entry system, just a panel of doorbells with a number under each. A crackly voice emerged from the speakerphone, 'Who is it?'

'Judy Campbell?'

'Yes.'

'Detective Inspector John Marco Wales Police Service.'

'What do you want? I mean...'

'This is official business.'

The door buzzed and then clicked, and Lydia pushed it open and we took the stairs to the first floor. Judy Campbell stood in the door to apartment three, arms crossed, a defiant look on her face.

'What the hell is this about? I've got to leave for work in a minute.'

'We need to interview you under caution,' I replied. 'Now you can cooperate with us or I can formally arrest you and take you back to Queen Street.'

'This is preposterous.'

'It's not something I'm going to discuss here,' I replied with a determined edge to my voice.

For a few seconds we stood glaring at each other. Then she realised there was no alternative. 'I'll have to call the office.' She turned on her heel and went inside. I heard the muffled sound of a conversation and the words, 'I should be in later.'

We'll see about that, I thought to myself.

She returned to the landing clutching her coat.

'We'll need your car keys too. We have a warrant to seize the vehicle and have it impounded.'

Another dull lifeless stare. 'I don't believe this.' She scrambled through her bag and then jerked a hand at me with the fob.

We retraced our steps down the stairwell. Outside a team of investigators were waiting. I tossed one of them the key and Lydia and I led Judy Campbell to my car.

Campbell said nothing on the journey back to Queen Street. We booked in with the desk sergeant at the custody suite and deposited her in an interview room while a duty solicitor was organised to attend. We sat and waited. It gave me time to review the questions Lydia had prepared yesterday, and look again at the CCTV footage of Judy Campbell from the night Armsby died.

It was mid-morning when the solicitor arrived, and I rang the CSI team in the hope they had discovered some crucial piece of evidence I could put to Judy Campbell in interview. But the investigator chortled down the telephone, warning me not to expect any results until later that afternoon.

I checked back with Wyn about progress in identifying the woman Northam had met the evening he was killed. 'No luck so far, boss.'

We didn't have time to wait. 'Get a warrant.'

When Judy Campbell was ready to be interviewed, we traipsed back down to the interview room. The duty solicitor was a tired-looking man in his fifties with bulging eyes and spectacles that belonged in a 1950s movie.

Lydia placed the laptop on the table and once introductions had been made, I slotted the tapes into the machine sitting at the end and screwed to the wall. Cork lined the room, but it didn't dull the sound of the ineffective air conditioning – within an hour the place would be stifling, sweaty and smelly.

Once I was ready, I turned to Judy Campbell.

'We are investigating the murder of Frank Armsby.'

She pulled folded arms tightly to her chest and dipped her head slightly, defying me.

'Can you tell me about your relationship with Mr Armsby?'

'I didn't have one.'

'But you dated him. I'm sure most people would consider that to be a relationship.'

She gave me a quick disgusted snort.

'The man was a pig.'

'Tell me about the dates you had.'

Her solicitor whispered something in her ear. Then she straightened in her chair. 'We went out a couple of times. At the beginning he was nice enough. We went out to different restaurants.'

'We need the names and dates.'

She gave me another tired look. 'I can't be certain of

the dates and I certainly don't remember the names of the restaurants.'

Lydia cut in. 'Do your best.'

As Campbell dictated Lydia scribbled down the details. Campbell sounded mechanical, going through the motions, ticking the boxes.

'You made a complaint that Frank Armsby had assaulted you.'

Campbell used a scathing tone. 'He raped me, Inspector.'

The solicitor piped up. 'I hope you're not going to re-examine that complaint, Inspector. Because if you do this interview is at an end. Now.' I hadn't expected quite the vehemence from this timid man.

I paused for a moment tapping a hand on the file of papers Alison had given me relating to Campbell's initial complaint. 'The Crown Prosecution Service decided not to proceed. How did that make you feel?'

'I felt betrayed, as though nobody listened to me, as though the system protected the guilty.'

'Why did you go and see Frank Armsby?'

'I've told you before.'

I nodded my head at the machine, its whirring a gentle sound in the background. 'I need you to reply for the purposes of the tape.'

'Perhaps it wasn't the wisest thing to do but I needed to confront him, tell him how I felt.' The solicitor butted in again. 'Are you suggesting Miss Campbell's genuine anger at the failure of the Crown Prosecution Service to press charges turned to murderous intent?'

I gave the solicitor a kindly smile, but I wanted to say this was my interview and I would conduct it the way I considered best. 'Although we've spoken to Miss Campbell at the offices of DependAssist we need to record her responses so that we can eliminate her from our inquiry.'

I turned back towards Judy Campbell. 'Where were you

on the night that Frank Armsby was killed?'

Lydia took the question as the prompt for her to open the laptop on the table. Campbell and her solicitor gazed over as she clicked the monitor into life.

I looked over at Campbell, she still hadn't answered. 'Miss Campbell, I asked you where you were on the night Frank Armsby was killed?'

Was she going to continue her lie? Did she realise we could prove she hadn't told us the truth?

She thrust her chin out and smirked, 'I was at home as I told you.'

I stared into her eyes. Defiance wasn't going to work. Was she daring us? It was difficult to tell from the body language. I glanced over at Lydia, giving her a brief nod for her to take charge. It would give me time to watch Campbell.

Lydia turned the laptop so that Campbell and her solicitor could view the screen. Then she asked Campbell to confirm the registration details of her vehicle. Campbell spat out the information. Then Lydia clicked play and announced. 'This is CCTV footage from the middle of Cardiff on the evening Frank Armsby was killed.' She pressed pause and fiddled with the computer until she was able to highlight the number plate. All the while Campbell gazed on intently. 'Can you confirm that this is your vehicle?'

Campbell uncomfortably coughed her confirmation.

'This is footage of you visiting a petrol station and convenience store. So you lied to us about being in the flat all evening.'

She gaped over wide-eyed at Lydia and then at the monitor as though she hadn't contemplated we would have traced her movements.

Her voice cracked. 'But I was in the flat all evening apart from that I mean. I went to get some groceries. I don't believe this is happening.'

Lydia pursued the line of questioning. 'So you confirm it was you driving.'

'Yes, but I only popped out.'

'You were actually out for almost an hour. Where did you go?'

Campbell frowned at Lydia's question. 'I don't remember.'

The solicitor interrupted again. 'Is this your only evidence? Frank Armsby was killed in the industrial estate of Penarth Road. And you're suggesting Miss Campbell was responsible?'

I replied, 'We want to know why Miss Campbell lied to us about her movements that evening.'

'I didn't lie. I mean, I didn't kill Frank Armsby. I was in the flat, all evening, but I needed some shopping.... Surely you don't think?'

I continued with a serious tone. 'As you know Frank Armsby was knocked over by a vehicle and then we believe the same vehicle ran over him. We have a team of investigators examining your vehicle now and they'll be undertaking a detailed examination. If there is any evidence your vehicle was involved then they will find it. Now would be a good chance for you to consider very carefully the reply to my next question.' I paused and scanned Campbell's face hoping for cooperation, but I spotted tension in her jaw and an intense unblinking stare. 'Did you use your vehicle to kill Frank Armsby?'

'Don't be absurd.'

Lydia snapped the laptop closed and I announced that the interview was at an end. We left Judy Campbell and her solicitor. I reported progress to the custody sergeant, telling him we needed to speak to the investigators crawling over her vehicle before we could decide finally to release her.

I traipsed back to the Incident Room, Lydia following in my slipstream. She went to organise coffee as I called the CSIs – there was nothing to report, they hadn't made the breakthrough I had hoped for and an irritated voice told me they would contact me if there was any news.

Lydia returned and deposited mugs on coasters on my desk and sat down. 'What did you make of her, boss?'

'Did you see that vengeful look in her eyes at the end?'

Lydia nodded. 'She hated Armsby right enough.'

'But why did she lie to us about where she'd been?' I took the first sip of my drink.

'Maybe she didn't think it was that important?'

'I hate it when people lie.'

The telephone rang and I snatched at the handset. 'Amy Gould is here to see you,' the voice from reception announced. I turned to Lydia. 'Finish up your drink. Andrew Northam's victim is waiting to be interviewed.'

Chapter 26

The most striking thing about Amy Gould were her black rimmed spectacles that sat perfectly at the bridge of her nose. Her blonde hair parted slightly off centre curtained her face and her low cheekbones gave her an elongated appearance. She followed me through into the conference room near reception where Lydia was waiting.

'This is Detective Sergeant Lydia Flint.'

Gould's lips appeared not to move, but she squeezed out a brief 'good afternoon'.

'Thank you for coming in,' I said.

'Not at all.' The voice sounded confident, the accent a neutral English variety.

'We are investigating the murder of Andrew Northam.'

She nodded her understanding.

'You made a complaint that he had raped you.'

'And the case was dismissed.'

The lack of emotion unnerved me. I decided on a slightly different approach. 'Can you tell me about your relationship with Andrew Northam.'

'I first got to know Andrew Northam a couple of years ago. I work as a lawyer in a firm that specialises in media and entertainment law. His company were clients of the practice.'

She played the lawyerly detachment far too effectively. I wondered how she really felt?

'How often did you meet?'

'I suppose it depends on how you define "often". There were a few business meetings where we worked on some deal he was in the process of completing. He was a very driven individual and very ambitious.' Now she paused. Was this a crack in her armour?

'Did you meet socially?'

'Twice, Inspector.' She hesitated and I could see the pain behind the tough exterior. 'On the second occasion he invited me back to his flat in the Bay.'

She adjusted her spectacles, giving her time to compose her thoughts.

I didn't have the original file of papers from her case and I wanted to fast forward to the question I needed answered but first I asked, 'And that was the occasion when he raped you?'

She blinked rapidly. 'The apartment was luxurious and he was very flattering. He came on to me in the hallway.' Another pause. 'I'm sure you can get all the information you need from the CPS file.'

Lydia cut in. 'It must have been terrible. Have you had any support afterwards?'

Gould nodded confirmation before adding, 'There's a charity I was referred to – DependAssist. They've been supportive. Actually, I don't know what I would have done without them. I've been able to get my life back on track.'

Then she turned towards me. 'And, Inspector, I'm sure you'll want to know where I was when Andrew Northam was killed. I was on holiday in Stockholm.' She fiddled in her handbag and produced various documents, including a copy of her booking with the details of the flight from Heathrow and the hotel.

I stammered a reply, 'Thank you, that's very helpful.'

'I can imagine you might have thought I would want him dead.'

I didn't reply, neither did Lydia. Gould continued, 'He scarred me for life, Inspector. I'm not pleased he is dead, but I didn't shed a tear. The world will be a better place without him.' Then she got up. 'I do hope you won't need to contact me again.'

I scrambled to my feet. 'Thank you for your time, Miss Gould.'

'I'm not surprised she's so cold after what happened to her,' Lydia said as she followed me back to the Incident Room.

'I guess it's her way of coping.'

'He was a right bastard. There's nothing to differentiate Northam from the other two. They're all predators. It's disgusting.'

Amy Gould's name wouldn't be added to the list of persons of interest and her image didn't need to be pinned onto the board. The documents she left would be scanned into the system and marked as alibi.

I reached my office door before reminding Lydia to chase the CSIs about Judy Campbell's vehicle. I sat down at my desk as my mobile rang; I recognised Superintendent Cornock's number.

'I've organised a press conference this afternoon, John. Get over here soon as you can.'

Imagining the emails flying around between Cornock and ACC Neary and the public relations department made for the sort of policing I never wanted to be part of. I much preferred the sharp end – finding the evidence, putting together the motives and chasing down the bad guys.

Vanity made me look at my clothes. My jacket had definitely seen better days and I wasn't wearing a tie. And it meant that if I was to be sitting in a press conference my mother would see the television reports and within a day I'd have a critical comment that I needed to smarten up.

Returning to the Incident Room, I shared with Lydia and Wyn the announcement about the impending press conference before heading over to see Superintendent Cornock. This time there were two civilians from the PR department sitting in the visitor chairs in front of Cornock's desk. The civilian I'd met before looked equally terrified this time, although Cornock hadn't adopted the same angry expression as before.

David Wilkinson, the older civilian, used a loud, confident voice obviously hoping to be in charge. 'We've organised to get all the major news outlets to attend. How would you want to deal with the inevitable question that there might be a serial killer on the loose in Cardiff?'

'It's three deaths for Christ sake. None of them are linked,' Cornock said.

'Are there no similar features?'

Now there was a belligerence to Cornock's voice. 'By that do you mean – is the modus operandi of each the same?'

'Spare me the technical lecture, Superintendent.'

'There's nothing to suggest we've got the same killer at work.'

'Really?' Incredulity now in Wilkinson's voice. 'Do you expect the press to believe that?'

'It's the truth for Christ's sake. We've got a tentative link between Armsby and Carey to a man known for his organised crime activities. And Armsby and Northam had faced unsuccessful prosecutions for rape allegations. The circumstances of all three murders are different. I don't want any inflammatory headlines. Do I make myself clear, David?'

Wilkinson held up a hand in mock surprise. 'Okay, but don't let the press see how angry you are. Keep it factual. Don't give them any reason to build a conspiracy theory. I suggest we stick to the narrative: appealing for witnesses in relation to all three.'

Once Wilkinson had reminded Cornock of the time for the conference he and the PR assistant left. Cornock waved me to one of the empty chairs. 'I hate this fucking 24-hour news cycle. We have to feed the monster with morsels of information all the time.' He looked up at me. 'I hope you've got good news, something positive about the Northam inquiry.'

I struck an obliging upbeat tone. 'We can eliminate Northam's victim from the investigation. She was in Stockholm at the time.'

The superintendent gave me a pained expression, as though he was expecting something far more substantial.

'And we've interviewed Judy Campbell this morning and impounded her vehicle. As yet the CSIs haven't been able to link her car to Armsby's murder. But she lied to me about leaving the flat on the evening he was killed, and we still can't account for all her movements.'

'So, she's in the clear?'

I wasn't certain how to reply. I hadn't come to a conclusion about Judy Campbell yet.

Cornock continued. 'I spoke with Dr Margaret Fabrien. She'll be back tomorrow. God knows we need as much help as we can on these cases. But don't let the people in PR know we've got a profiler involved. The last thing we need is the press spinning this out of control. We've got an hour until the press conference, so you'd better bring me up to date.'

Cornock accompanied me back to the Incident Room, notepad in hand. Wyn and Lydia sat silently as they listened to my summary of the case, Cornock occasionally interrupting.

'Do you think we are dealing with one killer?' Cornock asked although it felt like a rhetorical question from his earlier conversation with the public relations officers.

'The only thing that links Armsby and Northam are the abortive prosecutions. Although they both used the same dating site as Carey. Wyn is working on establishing any links to all three men.'

'But one was in Bristol and the other was in Bridgend. It would be stretching coincidence to believe the same person had it in for both men. And there was no publicity surrounding the Northam case.'

Cornock got to his feet. 'Let's go, John.'

The room was too small and too stuffy for a press conference, especially when full of journalists. After the artificiality of video news conferences via video during the pandemic the level of banter suggested the reporters were pleased to be back in one room, even though their numbers were limited.

Cornock took charge, introducing himself and then me, sitting by his side. Before entering the room I had surreptitiously dragged my fingers through my hair, hoping I could make it look senior-officer like. But I probably made things worse. Wilkinson sat at the end of the table next to Cornock and after the superintendent had read the prepared statement, he invited questions from journalists that presumably he had pre-vetted. The opening questions were straightforward, giving us the opportunity of calling for the public's assistance and inviting anyone with information to come forward.

A journalist near the front who announced he was from one of the tabloids piped up, 'Three murders so close together suggests you might have a serial killer to catch. Would you agree?'

A pained expression creased Wilkinson's face and Cornock's in turn. Cornock scowled at the journalist. 'There is nothing to suggest the three men knew each other or that the murders are similar in any way. We are not treating it as the work of a serial killer. I'm sure you wouldn't want to unnecessarily worry your readers by suggesting that were the case.'

There were shocked faces amongst the hacks in front of us.

I could see Wilkinson pointing at another journalist whose face was well known from TV news broadcasts. He'd obviously been well-primed because the question was friendly, giving Cornock the opportunity to thank all the officers on the team investigating the deaths and the members of public who had already offered assistance. At that stage Cornock even stared into the camera, once again inviting anyone with any information to come forward.

A voice from the back filled the pause after he'd finished. 'Are these crimes linked to the appalling record of the Wales Police Service on investigating and prosecuting sexual and domestic offences? During the lockdown there was an epidemic of domestic violence which will have a profound effect on women and families for generations to come. When is the Wales Police Service going to face up to its responsibilities?'

Cornock glanced at Wilkinson, who gave him a I-don't-know-who-this-is look. I had to move in my chair to see the face of the reporter. I hadn't recognised the voice, but Jack Hughes' serious and intense face was unmistakable.

Cornock stood up, signalling the press conference was at an end but added, 'The Wales Police Service always welcomes any member of the public who has any information to come forward in complete anonymity.'

The Superintendent followed Wilkinson out of the room through the throng of reporters. He turned to Wilkinson. 'Who the fuck was that? Why can't you weed out these people?'

He hissed back, 'This is a free country, superintendent. We have a free press.'

I tackled Wilkinson once Cornock had left. 'That was a Jack Hughes and he's not a journalist. He works for a charity supporting victims of violent crime.'

Wilkinson looked surprised.

'Find out how he got a press pass.'

I didn't wait for a reply. I stormed off back towards the Incident Room.

It didn't surprise me that the press conference hadn't gone well. In my experience they rarely achieved anything. I opened the door into the Incident Room and Lydia looked over at me. Wyn jumped to his feet breathlessly exclaiming. 'You need to see this, boss.'

Chapter 27

'What have you got, Wyn?'

'I've been doing some trawling on the internet. I came across a website and there's a podcast linked to it. The website discusses in detail prosecutions of men for domestic abuse. Sometimes the names of the people are redacted but mostly there's lots of discussions about the failure of the CPS and how incompetent the police are.'

'How is this helping us?' Lydia sounded vaguely impatient.

'One of the main participants in the podcasts is Penny Larkham. She is one of the counsellors at the charity DependAssist.'

'I remember,' I said.

'Apparently there's a public meeting in Pontypridd tonight. This group calls themselves Justice for All. They want to raise the profile of the inadequacies of the WPS and the Crown Prosecution Service. They seem to be well organised although the website is a bit amateurish.'

Wyn clicked into the computer and opened the page for Justice for All. The logo looked unprofessional, as though someone with no graphic design experience had cobbled it together. The menu down the left-hand side had tabs titled Case Histories, Our Mission, and The Future. Wyn opened the pages he had found with details of Frank Armsby's failed prosecutions.

'Somebody had access to the information about the cases involving Armsby,' I said.

Lydia continued. 'That could only have come from the victims or from the CPS—'

'Or someone inside the WPS.' My comment met with two grim faces and silence. 'But that's hardly likely.'

Wyn picked up the thread. 'From everything I've read on the website it all looks second hand, anecdotal stuff probably from interviews with the victims and maybe someone attending at one of the court hearings.'

'Any mention of Andrew Northam?' Lydia said.

Wyn nodded.

I cut in. 'But that case was heard in Bristol and it was dismissed by a judge at a very early stage.'

Wyn again. 'There are numerous podcasts and video clips I haven't listened to yet. And there's a lot of material on the website we need to go through.'

'Send me the link. And what time is the meeting again?'

'Seven pm in a working men's hall in a suburb of Pontypridd.'

I turned to Lydia. 'I hope you haven't got anything planned for tonight.'

She gave me a world-weary shrug.

Back in my room the presence of Jack Hughes at the press conference was still annoying me. Tracking down David Wilkinson from the PR department proved taxing and I sensed my irritation building. I went from one extension to another until I eventually tracked him down.

'You're a hard man to get hold of.'

'Been a bit busy, Inspector.'

'Did you find out how Jack Hughes got a press pass?'

'Sorry, it's slipped my mind.'

I started counting, intending to reach ten but got to two before my annoyance kicked in. 'And why the bloody hell not?'

'Calm down—'

'Don't tell me to calm down.'

'Look, is he a suspect or a person of interest or is he somebody who wheedled his way into a press conference and asked a question you didn't like? I've got other things to do. I'll get one of our assistants to check him out.'

The line went dead as I gripped the handset tightly.

Wilkinson was right. I needed to get things into perspective.

Finding the person or persons who had scrawled 'see you later' on the mirror in Carey's dining room dominated my thoughts once the frustration at Wilkinson passed. We had an unidentified victim and the possibility that Carey's two accomplices were in danger.

And now there was Penny Larkham and her website naming the victims. There were probably others, equally well-intentioned and misguided people, behind the website and the podcasts she was running.

I spent time trawling through the various pages of the website reading the one-sided heavily opinionated pieces criticising the Wales Police Service and the Crown Prosecution Service. This was citizen journalism at its very worst: dangerous and populist. There were even images of Assistant Chief Constable Neary and one of the senior lawyers from the CPS responsible for the decisions not to prosecute.

When I read about the long-term damage to the mental health of victims I sympathised. The system was broken, of course, but fixing it would be difficult and criticising it is easy. Justice can be a fickle animal, rough and uncompromising and often unfair, but until someone could come up with a better system for prosecuting the perpetrators of domestic and sexual violence we had to make do with the protocols and procedures we had.

I became inured to the language of the website and its harsh prejudices and lopsided judgements. But did I really think that Penny Larkham might be responsible for the deaths of Frank Armsby and Andrew Northam? The circumstances of Raymond Carey's death suggested a depth of hatred and ritualistic violence the other murder scenes lacked. I requisitioned a police national computer check on Penny Larkham before I left Queen Street with Lydia.

'The women on those podcasts have certainly got it in for men,' Lydia said as she followed me across the car park towards my Mondeo.

I paused for a moment after we got into the car. 'I can sympathise in a way. If a woman has been abused by a husband or sexually assaulted by a complete stranger the system we've got for prosecuting is completely inadequate. Most women don't even come forward.'

I started the engine and drove out into the early evening traffic.

'Even so, boss, if the system needs to be changed then going through the right channels is the only way to do that. Exposing men by using a website and podcasts won't achieve anything. It's going to draw more attention to Larkham and whoever else is responsible.'

The Cwm Du working men's club was an old, ramshackle building. Weeds grew along the guttering, spilling down over the downpipes streaked green and brown. The front door was open and outside was a notice board advertising the Justice for All public meeting.

A set of double doors led off the hallway, their extravagantly glazed window panels gave me a glimpse into the room beyond. 'There's a decent enough audience.'

Lydia peered into the room. 'I'm surprised there are so many present.'

It reminded me of the frequency of comments added to the posts on the website blog and of the several hundred people that had liked the YouTube channel. Behind us the main door opened and the chatter from half a dozen women, and their presence, filled the hallway. Lydia and I slipped into the hall behind them and took our seats at the back.

As surreptitiously as possible I cast a glance through the assembled spectators and watched as Penny Larkham fussed about organising the paperwork on the table and then tapping the microphone checking it worked before announcing she wanted to get on with the meeting. As she did so Jack Hughes sauntered into the hall and took his place alongside her.

Lydia and I sank back in our chairs, hoping Larkham and Hughes wouldn't notice our presence. Being at the front of this sort of meeting it can be difficult to spot individuals' faces in the audience. Larkham was like a different person and that surprised me. She was filled with bile and loathing for all the institutions that created the legal system and the judiciary. I struggled to imagine how she could be an impartial counsellor. She would have known all about Frank Armsby from the sessions with Judy Campbell and the same would be true for Andrew Northam and his victim Amy Gould.

Had she decided to mete out justice where the system had failed?

Jack Hughes contributed in the quiet, measured tone and language I recalled from my first meeting with him in the offices of DependAssist. It made me wonder why on earth he was there. Was it to supply moral support to Penny Larkham? The level of her personal anger suggested no lack of self-confidence. I guessed he was there to add gender balance. There was at least one case referred to on the website of a male victim of domestic abuse.

The meeting continued with individual testimonies from victims, the voices often trembling as they recounted their interactions with the police and prosecuting authorities. Penny Larkham wound up with a reminder for everyone to keep up pressure on their local politicians about changing the law and that no one should avoid any chance of getting publicity for the cause.

Lydia and I slipped out once everyone got to their feet and we avoided the general invitation to have tea or coffee. I buttoned up my coat and pulled the lapels to my face as we left. I turned to Lydia. 'I think we pay Penny Larkham a visit in the morning.'

Chapter 28

Two emails reached my mobile the following morning as I pulled into the car park at the offices of DependAssist. The first told me that the PNC check on Penny Larkham had shown no criminal convictions and nothing of interest. The second from Superintendent Cornock confirmed that he had arranged for Dr Margaret Fabrien to consult again that afternoon. I should have expected the first – Larkham was too self-important to have a history of criminal convictions – and the second annoyed me. I didn't need any more input from Margaret and her presence was beginning to feel like an unwanted intrusion.

I shared with Lydia, sitting by my side, the details of both emails. She nodded her understanding. Then she jerked a hand towards the far end of the car park where Penny Larkham emerged from a silver Mazda sport car. She didn't notice us as she locked the car and hurried over to the office, important things to do no doubt. A couple of the admin staff arrived, and then Jack Hughes pulled up into a parking slot in an old red former Post Office van, the faded livery of its previous owner evident on the side panels. He didn't notice us either as he locked the vehicle and headed over to the main entrance.

I finished checking my emails and we walked over together to the office building.

'This won't take long,' I said, yanking the door open. I took the stairs up to the offices two at a time and breezed in pushing my warrant card into the face of the receptionist I'd seen before. 'I'm here to see Penny Larkham, now.'

She gave me a frightened look and as she tapped the extension number into the telephone on her desk I barged through into the offices, Lydia following behind. I found Penny Larkham and Jack Hughes deep in discussion in Larkham's office. She frowned when she saw me enter. I didn't bother looking for a chair to sit – I wasn't staying long. Lydia closed the door behind us.

'I want to know what the hell you're doing with this website – Justice for All.'

Hughes and Larkham exchanged glances. Then they turned to look at me, defiance blazing in their eyes.

'How dare you come in here unannounced. These are offices of a charity. You need to make an appointment if you want to discuss anything with us.'

'The campaign you're running could well be interfering with the lawful conduct of a police inquiry. You've posted confidential details on the website about the murders of Frank Armsby and Andrew Northam. And by coincidence the alleged victims of both men were clients here.'

'Are you suggesting we've broken any law or some ethical standard?'

'I want to know where you got your information.'

Larkham gave me a thin-lipped, snide smile. 'Sneaking into the back of our public meetings isn't going to help you, Inspector.'

I drew a long breath. I sensed Lydia stiffening by my side. I could almost hear her warning me to be sensible, calm.

'I've got three bodies in the morgue which means a multiple murder inquiry. And I need to catch the killer. Nothing you're doing is going to help.'

My comments must have flicked a switch in Jack Hughes' mind. He stood up abruptly and strutted towards me which caught me off-guard for a second. Penny Larkham reached out a hand to calm him. He stopped and spat out his comments. 'And what about Judy Campbell and Amy Gould? Did they get justice? And the same goes for all the other people who suffered from domestic and sexual abuse that the Wales Police Service have ignored and treated with utter contempt over the years.'

'Spare me the lecture, Mr Hughes. I want to know exactly how you got a press pass to the press conference yesterday.'

Now he crossed his arms, all smug and self-important. 'I applied, dead easy really. Didn't you like the question I asked? You weren't man enough to answer it and you're not man enough to admit the failings of the police.'

He shrank back as though he had used up all his energy to challenge me. He gave Larkham a tired-looking glance and sat back into his seat. Hughes' protestations gave Larkham the opportunity to gather her thoughts. 'I suggest you leave now, Inspector. Both of you. This is tantamount to police intimidation. I've got a good mind to make a formal complaint.'

I narrowed my eyes. Once we left she'd probably be celebrating with Jack Hughes and all the staff that she been able to get under my skin. I tried one last throw of the dice. 'If you publish anything else about any of my ongoing inquiries I'll put together a file for the Crown Prosecution Service to consider charges of perverting the course of justice against you. So if you want to make a complaint you go right ahead.'

And with that I stormed out taking Lydia with me.

We sat in the car for a few minutes allowing my temper to subside. Lydia ventured the comment, 'I think you might have goaded her a little bit too far, sir.' She only used 'sir' when she wanted to be formal. And she was right, of course.

I blew out a mouthful of air. 'Once I'm back in Queen Street I'll warn Superintendent Cornock he might get a complaint from Larkham.'

'How do you think he'll react?'

I turned to give Lydia an are-you-serious look. 'He will probably listen to her very politely and then tell her to go to hell.'

Lydia chortled. I started the engine and I drove into town. By the time I reached the car park at Queen Street my mind had been calmed by the journey. We threaded our way up to the Incident Room and Wyn looked up at us as we entered, a startled look on his face. 'You've got to see this, sir,' Wyn said. 'I've been working on the CCTV footage we recovered from the property across the street from Northam's apartment building.'

He clicked open the footage and the images of people walking in the street and the occasional car and taxi filled the screen.

'This footage was recorded the day before he died. It's early evening,' Wyn said.

I could see the time on the monitor – seven pm.

A few moments later a figure approached the entrance door and pressed the intercom. Even from the blurry images on the screen I recognised Jim White. His head pitched upwards slightly and then he pushed the door open and entered the building.

'I've been doing some preliminary work to identify if there is any link between Jim White and Andrew Northam, and apparently there was some joint venture company they had which is involved with a boutique hotel in Newport.'

'Another link to Jim White. We need to tackle him again. But before we do that I need to talk to the Super.'

I left the Incident Room and made my way to Cornock's office. He looked up at me as I entered his room, a gnarled, angry look on his face. 'I've spoken to Alvine Dix. She's sent me the footage. What sort of weird despicable people are we dealing with?' He waved me to a chair. 'I've told Alvine I need to know if she can identify the other two men. The poor bastard on the bed has gone to the top of the list of possible suspects. And can you blame him for what they did to him?'

I paused, gathering my thoughts. 'It's not an excuse for murder, sir.'

Cornock waved away my reservations. 'Of course not, of course not, I know that.'

'And we've also recovered some footage from the property across the street from Northam's apartment block that has a record of Jim White entering the building the day before he died. And White and Northam have a joint venture company running a boutique hotel in Newport.'

Cornock guffawed. 'Boutique hotel in Newport?'

I got to my feet. 'I'm going over to see Jim White.'

'And don't forget about Margaret Fabrien arriving after lunch. And John, this video may well justify a different team handling Carey's death.'

'I should tell you, sir, that we visited the offices of DependAssist, a charity that supports victims of abuse and sexual violence.' Cornock narrowed his eyes. 'Two of the employees have been running a website called Justice for All that has details of two of the murder scenes. I was hoping for their cooperation...'

'But?'

'There was a frank exchange of views.'

'Frank exchange of views you say.'

'Yes, it was... I may...'

'I'll deal with any complaint, John.'

Then he picked up a ballpoint from the desk and got back to his paperwork. I detoured around to the Incident Room, collecting Lydia, before heading down to the car park.

Luckily the traffic to Newport was light and we made the journey in good time. There was no need to rely on the satnav for directions as I recalled the route easily enough. The Audi Q5 was parked in the same place but there was no sign of the convertible sports car. Perhaps Laura was in the gym, pounding the treadmill, pushing weights.

The workshop on the ground floor was now fully occupied by a team of mechanics working on a convertible BMW 4 Series. Jim White was looking around shouting instructions and gesticulating when we entered from the entrance lobby.

'And what the fuck do you want?' He raised his voice.

'We need a word.'

'How about 'leave'?'
'Very funny.'

We stood exactly where we were, defying Jim White, who eventually barged past us for the stairs to the first floor. We followed in his slipstream and, in his office, he stood legs wide apart by his desk. There wasn't an invitation to sit down nor an offer of coffee.

'We're investigating the killing of Andrew Northam.'

'Oh, for fuck's sake. You don't think I'm involved with that too?'

'How well did you know Mr Northam?'

'Am I a suspect in his murder?'

'Please answer the question.'

'He was an "associate". I've done business with him occasionally and we have this current joint venture developing a boutique hotel in Newport.'

'Is it going well?'

He gave an angry sigh. 'If I told you it was none of your business what would you do? You'd better leave me alone, remove me from your list of suspects and any of your fucking lists come to that matter.'

'When did you last see Andrew Northam?'

Now he rolled his eyes.

'What could possibly be my motive to kill Northam?'

I stepped nearer to Jim White. 'If the joint venture isn't going as well as you'd expected you'd have the perfect motive. Perhaps Northam wasn't prepared to invest any more? Had he given you an ultimatum you didn't like? Maybe he didn't want to be involved with anything dodgy.'

'You really are scraping the bottom of the barrel now.'

'So when did you see Andrew Northam last?'

The answer wasn't hurried or forced. 'It was weeks ago. I can show you his emails.'

'Weeks ago,' I repeated. 'And where was that?'

'At the hotel of course.'

My mind kicked in – should I arrest him now on the

spot? I knew he was lying, but I couldn't justify his arrest for murder. Why would he be visiting Northam's apartment building? It was a question that wouldn't wait until I had Jim White in an interview room.

I took a moment to glare at Jim White. 'We have CCTV footage of you visiting his apartment building on the day before his body was found.' I stated this as slowly as I could.

It wrong-footed White. He gave me a dazed look which he morphed into a pleading, man-to-man response. 'You know how it is. I visit this friend of mine...'

I dragged out the discomfort for White with silence.

'She lives in one of the apartments.'

'Her name?' Lydia snapped. White dictated the full details which Lydia jotted in her notebook.

He turned to me. 'Can we keep this between us? I mean Laura doesn't need to know does she?' There was even a scrap of humanity in his question.

'And we discovered your fingerprints in Armsby's car. Do you care to tell me how they got there?'

He sounded deflated now, realising there was nothing he could do to avoid unpicking his life. 'I was with him a few days before he died. We had lunch, talked shite and he gave me a lift. Satisfied?'

I avoided answering. We left Jim White, and back in the car I turned to Lydia as I fired up the engine. 'You'll need to check out the 'friend' later.'

She nodded. 'I don't like him. But I'm not certain he's capable of bludgeoning Andrew Northam to death.'

'Maybe not, but he'll be certain to know somebody who could. We need to work on the background to this hotel development and establish the names of some of White's known associates.'

Back at Queen Street I dictated detailed instructions for Wyn to build a comprehensive picture of Jim White's financial dealings with Andrew Northam. He'd need help from Boyd Pearce in the economic crime department. It meant a call to the inspector in charge. As firmly as I could I made clear to Boyd Pearce's boss that a multiple murder inquiry took precedence over any investigation by the economic crime department.

Chapter 29

Margaret Fabrien arrived very soon after lunch. She made herself comfortable on one of the chairs at a desk in the Incident Room. She focused intently as I outlined the circumstances of Andrew Northam's death, Lydia and Wyn occasionally piping up with comments. A thick black A4 notebook was open in front of her and she took notes using an elegant, thin fountain pen.

Wyn had arranged for all the CCTV footage and details of the allegations against Northam to be added to the computer in the room Margaret would use but she didn't go there directly after our briefing but followed me into my room.

'Tell me what you think.' She pushed the door closed and sat in one of the visitor chairs.

'We've got a killer to catch.'

She raised an eyebrow. 'So you do not think that there are multiple killers?'

I could listen to this sort of French accent all day, and all night.

'All three men were involved in sexual assaults. It's the only thing that links them apart from a connection to a man called Jim White, a notorious white-collar criminal.'

Margaret was nodding. 'I do not think that Superintendent Cornock agrees with you. The implications of having a serial killer are perhaps uncomfortable for him. I believe he would prefer if a different person was responsible for the death of Mr Carey.'

'We shall need to discuss matters once you've watched the video and considered everything.'

'Of course.'

'Will you be staying this evening?'

She shook her head. 'I have another meeting tomorrow with the Metropolitan Police.'

For the rest of that afternoon I chased our operational support department for details of any allegations of a male gang rape in the past few years. I spoke to three senior intelligence officers who promised to get back to me with any relevant information. Telephone calls trickled in over the next couple of hours – there had been several individual male rape allegations, none of which had resulted in a successful prosecution. I made a mental note to ask Alison what the success rate of prosecutions was for male against male sexual assaults. And Southern Division's intelligence officers couldn't help either.

Wyn hot-footed it into my room announcing he had information about the boutique hotel in Newport and Lydia followed him, standing at the threshold listening to him as he shared the details. 'Although the project ground to a halt during the lockdown when building work couldn't take place, since the easing of restrictions work has recommenced. I've spoken to Detective Sergeant Boyd Pearce who tells me the hotel doesn't feature in their inquiry. And I've done some digging around with journalists I know and none of them have heard about financial problems at the hotel.'

'Okay, but we still check out the possible alibi witness.'

Lydia announced, 'I've already called the number, boss. Nothing so far.' She continued, explaining that her efforts to identify the victim in the footage from Carey's video, as well as the other two men involved, was proving equally unsuccessful.

Disappointment laced with frustration filled my mind. But was I wrong to believe White was involved because of what I knew about him? Was I guilty of being too keen to implicate White? I still had no link to the gun that had killed Carey so I tapped out another message to Terry – *Any news? Contact me.*

The final disappointment of the afternoon was a detailed report from the forensic department who had spent a full day on Judy Campbell's car. There wasn't a single shred of evidence to prove her vehicle ran over Frank Armsby and nothing in the samples removed could prove a link to Raymond Carey and the PPE-suited visitors to his home.

I wandered out to the Incident Room and over to the board, surveying the faces of the three dead men. Then I read the names of Armsby and Northam's victims. Did they know each other? Had Judy Campbell and Amy Gould somehow decided to dispose of their attackers and at the same time rid the world of Raymond Carey for good measure. It didn't make sense. But I knew that the answer probably was in the images and information in front of me.

I returned to my office, and moments later Margaret knocked on my door, entered unbidden and sat down.

'I have watched the footage... It is very bad. Have you been able to identify the victim?'

'Not yet. We are examining our records for complaints of male on male assaults, but they are rare. And few result in prosecutions and even fewer in successful convictions.'

She nodded.

'I would suggest you concentrate on identifying offenders with a violent disposition. The anger demonstrated by the attack on Carey points to somebody with a ferocious temper. And the words that were scrawled on the mirror are a link to the circumstances portrayed in the footage. Have you identified the other two men?'

I give another shake of my head.

Margaret read my mind. 'It must be frustrating. The three unidentified men have to be your immediate priority. But these sorts of sexual predators will take pleasure in sharing videos like this.'

Facing the prospect that we may never bring the culprit or culprits to justice invaded my thoughts. It was too vile to contemplate.

'I think you are mistaken to believe this is the work of a single killer. The deaths of Frank Armsby and Andrew Northam are different and in my opinion you should be looking for a different culprit. The depth of the depravity evidenced by the injuries to the body of Raymond Carey suggests a deep-seated anger. And the individual would most certainly have been involved in something like this in the past – possibly even previous convictions and also a history of mental instability.'

I wanted to add – and that rules out everybody who has surfaced in the inquiry so far.

Margaret continued. 'The murders of Armsby and Northam are vigilante-style killings. You will probably find the culprit amongst either their victims or individuals assaulted and scarred by sexual or domestic violence.

'We've interviewed Judy Campbell, Frank Armsby's recent victim, who can't explain part of her movements for the evening involved but there's nothing to suggest her vehicle was responsible for the hit and run which killed him.'

'And can you link her to the death of Andrew Northam?'

'No, and his victim was in Stockholm on holiday at the time of his death.'

Margaret took a moment to ponder. 'I still think the different murder scenes all suggest a different killer. I'm sorry if this disappoints you, John.'

She gave me a kindly smile. 'I shall need to leave soon. I have a train to catch.'

'I'll walk you over to Central Station.' I volunteered.

She smiled. We left Queen Street and threaded our way behind the St David's Centre and then down towards the old brewery quarter. When we arrived at Queen Street the notice board announced her train had been cancelled. 'Damn. Now I have over an hour to wait.'

'Time for a coffee?'

She smiled at me again. Her face lit up as her mouth creased open and her lips puckered.

We walked to an Italian place I'd been to a couple of times. 'My mother likes this place,' I said. 'The owner imports coffee direct from Milan.'

We settled into a small table by the window and Margaret ordered a sandwich and a coffee. I did the same.

'You have a wonderful accent,' I said. 'How long have you lived in the UK?'

The smile turned to a blush. 'My father is from England and he met my mother when he was in Paris. They run a hotel in Caen.'

'How did you get into this profiling business?'

'It was part of my PhD studies and I decided to develop it as an academic interest afterwards.'

'Do you enjoy your work?'

She rolled her head as though the answer was going to be ambiguous. 'It is always pleasing when bad people are locked up. It is not so good when innocent people suffer. I am glad I can help.'

The sandwiches arrived in good time and between mouthfuls we got to know each other. She was fascinated by my family history and even more impressed I knew Lucca, my mother's hometown, where she had spent holidays as a child camping with her parents.

I settled the bill, waving away her offer to pay for the sandwich and coffee. 'The least the WPS can do.'

We walked back to Cardiff Central Railway Station and I watched her make her way through the barrier, her smooth gait giving her whole body a graceful swaying movement.

I wondered if I'd ever see Margaret Fabrien again. I didn't have to wait too long for the possible answer because as I stood milling around on the concourse my mobile rang and I recognised the number for operational support. I pressed the handset to my ear. 'Detective Inspector Marco?' Margaret had disappeared up the staircase towards the platform for the eastbound, London train.

'You're needed at a crime scene.'

Chapter 30

I jogged back to Queen Street, pinning my mobile to my ear at the same time. Lydia answered after a couple of rings. 'I've just heard, boss.'

'Get as much detail as you can. I'm en route back to Queen Street.'

I finished the call and by the time I'd reached the car I was sweaty and out of breath. I checked my phone again. Operational support had messaged me with the address and postcode. I heaved off my coat and threw it into the back. I pressed my mobile into the hands-free cradle and quickly punched the postcode into the satnav.

I fired the engine into life and drove east for Rumney. Once I got nearer the suburb I paid more attention to the detailed directions from the disembodied voice filling the cabin. It directed me through various avenues and crescents until I saw the flashing lights of two marked police cars. I drew up on the pavement a little distance away and left the car. The terraced properties were set back and below the road. When I reached number fourteen I flashed my card at an uniformed officer. I stopped and looked at a Mercedes taxi parked on a square of concrete at street level, built over the original garden. Another officer stood nearby preventing anyone from accessing the pavement immediately in front of the house. In due course the whole place would be cordoned off by the crime scene investigators and their fluttering yellow tape would mark the perimeter. It was too cold for neighbours to mingle and gossip in groups outside, but I guessed that WhatsApp messages or texts would be bouncing around the properties.

I noticed Lydia's car approaching from the other direction. She hurried over to join me after locking her vehicle. 'I got here as soon as I could, boss. I went to see David Plowman but he wasn't home.'

'I've only just arrived.' I tipped my head towards the front door. 'Let's see what we've got.'

I took the few steps to the entrance, snapping on latex gloves. I asked the uniformed officer on the threshold. 'Do you have any idea when the CSIs are due to arrive?'

'They should be here any minute.'

'What's the victim's name?'

'Mark Wyatt. He's in the back bedroom.'

'And who found the body?'

'A neighbour who lives round the corner. We told her to expect you.'

In the hallway I glanced up the stairs, wondering what to expect. The staircase carpet was thin with age and at the top I spotted a box room immediately to my right. It looked empty. The other two doors in the landing were for the other bedrooms.

I pushed the rear door open with my toe and Lydia followed me inside. Examining the crime scene meant every one of my senses peaked as I took two steps into the room dominated by a bed. I could hear the chatter from outside, I could smell the dust and decay from the ancient carpet. Death always created a tacky sensation in my mouth.

Wyatt lay stark naked on the bed, his head staring upwards at the ceiling. His hands had been tied to the corner of the bedstead behind him and thick ropes attached his ankles to the bottom splaying out his body like a starfish.

'Jesus,' Lydia said quietly. 'It's just like Carey.'

I moved cautiously nearer the bed. There wasn't much room to manoeuvre and I didn't want there to be any chance I'd contaminate the crime scene. I looked down at the body, realising the cuts scarring his lower body and genitals replicated the frenzied attack perpetrated on Raymond Carey. A thick cotton cloth had been stuffed into his mouth. No one would have heard him scream although I hoped that someone might have heard the gunshot. The single bullet wound to the chest mimicked the horror at Carey's property.

'It's the same MO as Carey's killing,' I announced. 'We need to find this bastard.'

I turned to look at Lydia but my attention was taken by the words scrawled on a mirror above a cabinet – 'see you later'. I jerked my head at it and Lydia gasped when she saw it.

'No question,' I said. 'It's the same killer.'

She didn't reply but turned her head to look out of the door at the sound of conversations at the front of the property. I could hear Alvine Dix and Paddy McVeigh talking. We left the bedroom and joined them in the hallway downstairs.

'Good evening, John,' Paddy said formally.

'Hi, Paddy,' I nodded a greeting at Alvine.

'What have you got for me, Marco?'

'The victim is Mark Wyatt. It's the same MO as the killing of Raymond Carey.'

'So the press is right then. We do have a serial killer in Cardiff.'

'It's not...' I didn't bother finishing my sentence. I wasn't going to debate with Alvine the technicalities and definition of a serial killer. I dropped the tone of my voice slightly and fixed her with determined eyes. 'We need to stop whoever was responsible. Fast. So I need the full forensic report by the morning.'

Alvine was momentarily taken aback. 'We'll do what we can. But I am one investigator down as it is.'

'Well get someone off their rest day, for Christ's sake. I want the investigation finished by tomorrow morning and I need the report on my desk before lunch.'

Paddy piped up. 'Can I go and see the body now?'

'He's in the back bedroom.'

Paddy stomped up the stairs, Alvine following behind.

The ground floor of the property was like a thousand other former council houses in Cardiff and all over Wales. The sitting room was functional with a space for a dining table and chairs at the rear. We paused for a moment inside. A stale, tacky smell hung in the air.

'Place hasn't been cleaned for months,' Lydia wafted a hand in front of her nose.

A large screen television had pride of place with a sound system that looked expensive. I ran a hand over the material of the sofa: it felt cheap, the sort that could be changed every couple of years for the latest special cut-price deal. Looking out of the rear window I noticed a garden that fell away to a thicket of trees.

Through in the kitchen several doors of the wall units hung off their hinges and their cracks and scratches suggested they were new twenty years ago. The back door was ajar, and I guessed the killer had accessed the house from the woodland at the bottom of the garden. Calling at the front door would have been far too risky.

Lydia yanked open the door to the fridge. 'Typical bloke.' I glanced over and noticed the dozen or so bottles of German lager stacked inside.

I needed fresh air so I motioned for Lydia to join me outside. I took the steps up to the pavement, fumbling for the packet of cigarettes in my jacket pocket. I couldn't remember whether it was the fourth or fifth or maybe even the sixth of the day. Seeing Wyatt's body made restricting my cigarette count seem irrelevant. I enjoyed the sensation of the smoke filling my lungs and nicotine invading my body.

I stood outside with Lydia. 'We need to ask Plowman if he knows anything about the video.'

'I called his place of work when I couldn't reach him – apparently he's visiting friends in London.'

'Message him and tell him to contact us urgently.'

Lydia stood up wind from me, but it still didn't stop her from turning up her nose. 'I don't see the point.'

'Sorry?'

'Of you smoking five a day. Why don't you give up? You'd feel so much healthier, boss.'

I cast a mournful sort of glance at the property. 'It's a

The Cardiff Lockdown Murders

coping mechanism, I suppose.'

Paddy wasn't long, and joined us on the pavement. 'No question in my mind that it's the same killer who dispatched Mr Carey. I'd say you've got one sick individual to arrest. I'll be doing the post-mortem first thing in the morning John, so get to the mortuary by eight.' And with that he was gone.

It was late, too late to start any meaningful house-to-house inquiries. Tomorrow all the standard protocols would kick into place. The estate would be flooded with uniformed and community support officers but for now we had Wyatt's neighbour to see.

The sequence of house numbering was all out of order. Frustration built as I tried to find Wyatt's neighbour's home. Eventually we found the right property. I knocked on the door and heard a shout from inside and seconds later a man opened the door and glared at us.

'Detective Inspector John Marco and Detective Sergeant Lydia Flint, Wales Police Service. We'd like to speak to Mrs Kane. I understand she found the body of Mr Wyatt.'

He gave our warrant cards a cursory examination then jerked his head for us to enter.

'The missus is in the kitchen.' He led us to the room at the back.

Mrs Kane was sitting by a table at one end of the extended room. A slice of lemon sat delicately on top of a pile of ice cubes in a tall glass, the clear liquid inside providing comfort, by the way Mrs Kane nursed her drink.

'It's the cops, love,' the man said.

She barely acknowledged our presence, returning her gaze to the glass in front of her. Lydia and I sat down. 'When did you discover Mr Wyatt?' I announced.

'I do the laundry for him.' The accent was like her husband's: Cardiff born and bred.

'Did you see anybody leaving the property?'

She shook her head.

'Do you know if he has any family?'

Another shake of the head.

The man piped up. 'He's a bit of a loner. Nobody knows much about him and he hasn't lived here long.'

'How well do you know him?'

She shrugged now. 'I do the laundry for him: ironed his shirts, that sort of thing. I'm not in any trouble, am I?'

'No, of course not Mrs Kane. Do you know anything about his personal life? Does he have girlfriend?'

Mr Kane snorted. 'No girlfriends, pal. But I've seen blokes going in and out of the house.'

Lydia made her first contribution. 'Do you think he was gay?'

'Who am I to say, love. Each to their own, I say.'

I turned to look back at Mrs Kane. 'Do you know if he had any other friends in the neighbourhood?'

'I dunno. He was a taxi driver and a lot of people knew him.'

I stood up and made to leave but when I warned Mrs Kane that officers would be calling to take her fingerprints to eliminate her from our inquiry she looked terrified. I reassured her it was routine. As I reached the door of the kitchen into the hallway Mrs Kane raised her voice. 'Did he suffer? I mean all them...'

Even though Pat Kane wasn't related to Wyatt, I needed to spare her feelings. 'He was shot so it would have been quick.'

I saw the barest flicker of relief on her face before we left.

Chapter 31

I left the mortuary the following morning after watching Paddy McVeigh carve up another cadaver. Paddy's comments about the nature of the injuries sustained by the body had sickened me and although I had been tempted to leave before the examination was complete, I had stuck it out.

The second cigarette of the day found its way to my lips. Then I sparked the Zippo to life and drew deep lungfuls of smoke into my lungs. I'd already texted Terry once that morning telling him we had to meet and as I reached my car I pulled the handset from my jacket and tapped out a second message – this time more urgent, more belligerent.

I thumbed out a message to Alison, too, suggesting we meet on Thursday after work. I had to hope that I could get the evening off. Our abortive date seemed far more than five nights ago. And I was beginning to lose track of the days – bad sign, so one night off would be well deserved.

I finished my smoke and ground the cigarette butt into the tarmac by the front tyre of my Mondeo. Getting into the car I reached for the ignition as Alison replied: *Thursday is fine with me. Looking forward to it. X.* I drove back to Queen Street. It was still early, and the roads were quiet. Since the pandemic I'd noticed the buses were less crowded and the traffic lighter – more people were working from home. During the journey I glanced at a message on my mobile on the hands-free cradle. It was from Superintendent Cornock telling me he expected an update.

In the Incident Room, both Wyn and Lydia were on the telephone and from their conversations I guessed they were coordinating the preliminary house-to-house inquiries. Wyn mentioned my name a couple of times and when I looked over at the board I could see that someone had found an image of Mark Wyatt. It looked ominously like a picture from police national computer records.

I trooped off to the kitchen, made a coffee and returned

as Wyn was finishing his conversation. Lydia stood by the board.

I sat down in one of the chairs near an empty desk. 'Did you get the photograph of Mark Wyatt from where I think you did?'

Lydia nodded. 'I did a PNC check this morning, sir. He was sentenced to five years for assaulting a man six years ago. After his release halfway through the sentence he moved to Cardiff.'

'Where is he from originally?'

'Nottingham. I've already put in a request to speak to the senior investigating officer.'

'Excellent.' I looked over at Wyn. 'Have you got all the house-to-house inquiries organised?'

'I'm expecting a preliminary report by lunchtime.'

'And has anybody seen a forensic report from Alvine?'

Neither officer nodded so I assumed it might be languishing in my inbox. I got up and took my mug through into my office. Once my computer was booted up I checked through my emails. No sign of anything from Alvine Dix – perhaps she would take me literally at my word and send the report at the end of the morning.

I sipped on the coffee as I deleted redundant emails and spam. Lydia appeared on the threshold of my office. 'I've spoken to White's alibi witness for his visit to the apartment building and she confirms his version of events.'

I sat back in my chair. 'So he's in the clear for Northam's murder.'

'Looks that way. Do you want me to tell Boyd Pearce not to waste any more time on White's finances?'

Lydia was right – focusing on White was a distraction now and a sliver of doubt developed in my mind that I had allowed White to be too prominent in the inquiry.

'Yes, do that.'

Lydia left and I reassured myself that the time spent on White had not been wasted and hoped that Boyd Pearce would discover enough to prosecute him.

Finishing my drink, I heard activity from the Incident Room and Wyn's conversation with two other voices. Then Wyn shouted through the open door of my office. 'Something you should see boss. The CSIs have been through Mark Wyatt's laptop.'

I joined him by his desk where he was clicking through with his mouse. His face suggested he knew exactly what he was looking for but his sombre expression gave me an uneasy feeling. 'I have the name of the file we need.'

Moments later he let out a dull exclamation. 'Here it is, found it.'

Then he clicked into the folder and then into a video file. A sense of foreboding crept into my mind as I watched, for a second time, on a different laptop, the assault perpetrated by three men on an innocent man tied to a bed. 'Christ, Wyatt must have been one of the other men.' The footage was identical to that recovered from Careys's laptop. Voices but no faces other than Carey's.

'We can't be certain Wyatt was one of them unless we can check his voice against this recording,' Lydia said.

And I knew exactly where we could get that. 'Call the SIO in Nottingham and ask them to send us a copy of one of his recorded interviews. And don't let them give you any excuses about being too busy or any of that crap.' I turned to Lydia. 'This afternoon we're going to go over to Wyatt's house. In the meantime, I'll see if we can get a recording of Carey's voice.'

I go back to my room and dug out the fancy business card Carey's superior gave me when we met him in the bank. I dialled his direct number. Ford sounded mildly surprised when I introduced myself.

'How can I help, Inspector?'

'I know this sounds a little unusual, but we need a sample of Raymond Carey's voice. Perhaps there might be colleagues at work who could identify his voice from a recording we have.'

'We can do better than that, Inspector. I'm sure he featured in a video for a continuing professional development course for some of our junior staff.'

I fist pumped the air. 'When can you get that to me. I need it as urgently as possible.'

'I'll do what I can.'

'Excellent, thank you.'

Mid-morning I listened to Wyn's summary about the preliminary results of house-to-house inquiries around Mark Wyatt's home. It meant wading through a mass of statements to unearth a gem of information we could use.

A map had been opened on the desk. I noticed the woodland behind Wyatt's property – perfect cover to access the house.

'I've still got to go through all the CCTV footage from outside Northam's flat,' Wyn said.

'Somebody must have got in,' Lydia said.

I got to my feet. 'All we have to do is find how and who.' I grabbed my coat from the coat stand and rejoined Lydia. Wyn's reference to the CCTV footage triggered a train of thought. 'We need a comprehensive list of everyone who accessed the apartment block on the day he died.'

'Okay, boss.'

Minutes later Lydia and I were stationary at a set of traffic lights, the pulsing of the indicator the only sound in the cabin. A message bleeped on Lydia's mobile and she read the details before announcing. 'Detective Inspector Ian Smith from Nottingham Police will speak to you tomorrow. I had to really hassle the admin staff to organise that for us. And they've promised to courier us the tapes of Wyatt's interviews.'

The traffic light turned green and I followed the road round and sped off in the direction of Rumney. The residents of the estate where Wyatt lived obviously didn't merit a proper mobile incident room as the neighbourhood next to

Raymond Carey's home had. But there were police cars and several uniformed officers milling around, clipboards in hand.

Two officers stood on the pavement outside Wyatt's home. Lydia and I greeted them formally before taking the steps down to the front door and entering the property. An earlier email from Alvine confirmed they had finished, but the final sentence had notified me that my request for her to call additional resources would impact on her budget. Sometimes Alvine Dix could be a real pain in the backside but I decided that if Cornock raised the issue I'd tell him that Alvine could go to hell. I was the SIO, this was the fourth recent murder and budgets could go to hell too.

There'd be photographs of the house from every conceivable angle and we'd probably need more space on the board in the Incident Room to accommodate them. But there was nothing like standing in the actual crime scene.

'He must have known the killer or killers,' Lydia said. I nodded; she was getting accustomed to reading my mind.

'Using the front door would have been too risky.' I entered the kitchen. 'Maybe Wyatt let them in...' I paused my train of thought. 'If there'd been a struggle, we'd have found some sign of it: scratches on the walls – but I didn't spot anything.'

'The place isn't exactly out of a good housekeeping magazine.'

'Why does Wyatt go upstairs with his killer?'

'Wyatt wouldn't have argued with a man pointing a pistol.'

Lydia was right. A gun always changes things.

'He must have been scared shitless.'

Lydia nodded.

I continued. 'The post-mortem report for Raymond Carey indicated that he had been struck over the head but there was no suggestion of an assault on Mark Wyatt. There's no way a single person could have tied him up.'

'People can be resourceful, boss.'

I opened the back door and we left the house, striding down the garden. A section of the post and wire fence at the bottom looked rotten, so I pushed one of the posts and it almost buckled. It was easy enough to hold down the top wire for Lydia to clamber over it. I followed her and we scrambled down into the thicket of trees and shrubs. From Wyatt's garden it looked impenetrable but soon a narrow path led to a steep section. It reached a clearing and after a few yards the tree cover thickened again before a gravelled path branched into two directions. I pulled out my phone and got the compass to work. Walking northwards would take us away from the housing estate where Wyatt lived so I opted for a southerly direction.

Soon enough it led onto a larger flat section where the incline decreased and the woodland thinned into surroundings perfect for an afternoon stroll. I spotted a man being hauled by a Labrador. I stopped and asked where he had come from. He gave me a puzzled look and told me the car park was only a few yards away. I pressed on, Lydia trotting behind me.

We emerged into a car park with room for three cars only. We paced down the tarmac road leading up to it and eventually found ourselves in a housing estate. Instinctively I looked around for CCTV cameras. I couldn't see any immediately.

I reached for my mobile and barked instructions for the house-to-house team to get down here.

Chapter 32

It was late in the afternoon when I pulled up behind two marked police cars in the street near the woodland. A young officer stood by one of the vehicles, clipboard in hand, ticking a list attached to it. He stiffened as I approached and launched into a summary of the house-to-house inquiries. I held up a hand. 'Highlights only, please.'

'Not much to report I'm afraid, sir.'

A sergeant I vaguely recognised came up to us. 'Glad to see you, Inspector.'

'Are you making much progress?'

He chortled. 'We've encountered a lot of time wasters. Sam here has the names of people we need to follow up. A couple of dog walkers use the paths in the woodland regularly but haven't seen anything. We've done all the houses in the immediate vicinity to the car park and we're going to spread back now along the rest of the estate.'

'Give me the details of the individuals to contact.' This was the sort of policing I enjoyed. Talking to people, gathering evidence and building the case piece by piece. There'd be setbacks, of course, but somebody had seen something important.

I found Mr Bolton power washing the paving slabs that lined a small area at the side of his property. When he spotted me, he stopped and stared at my card. 'How can I help?'

'It would be most helpful if you could spare a minute.' Activating my be-really-nice-and-polite button would have impressed the trainers of Southern Division who always stressed the importance of good public relations.

Bolton leaned down and switched off the machine and nodded towards a small rear gate. 'We can talk in the kitchen.'

He dragged off his boots and pointed at the brush matting by the door, encouraging me to clean my shoes before entering. I duly obliged and entered the neat, well-ordered environment. 'I'm investigating the murder of Mark Wyatt.'

'There's been a lot of gossip going around about him – I don't believe half of it.'

He waved at one of the chairs by a table.

'I understand that you regularly walk through the footpaths in the woodland.'

Bolton nodded. 'I do a circular route around there a few times a week. Getting out of the house after my wife died does me good.' He tapped his head indicating that exercise helped him deal with the grief and loneliness.

'We believe the killer might have accessed Mark Wyatt's property by climbing over the fence at the bottom of his garden. I was wondering if you've seen anything unusual in the past week or so. Somebody you haven't seen there before perhaps. An unusual car in the small car park.'

Bolton pondered then frowned. 'I can't say I've noticed anybody.'

'Do many people use the area?'

'There are some regulars. And some of the kids ride their bikes which is a bloody nuisance. Have you talked to Katie from the nature conservancy group that looks after the woodland?'

'No, do you have her details? How often does she visit?'

'I'm not certain. Quite often though.'

Bolton got up and from a cupboard retrieved an address book. He flicked through it until he found the entry he needed and dictated the contact telephone number for Katie and her email address.

I stood up. 'Thank you very much for your help.'

Bolton followed me outside, dragging on his Wellingtons, obviously intent on finishing the task in hand when he added. 'I hope you catch whoever did this. Is it true that he was...?'

'The information you've provided has been very

helpful.' It was another anodyne comment. Bolton gave me a brief nod of acknowledgement and got back to his power-washing.

Of the other two addresses the sergeant had given me one of the properties was still empty and at the other the neighbour saw me approaching the front door and shouted over, 'There's nobody there, mate. They're on holiday in Tenerife.'

I spent a few minutes tracking down the sergeant, and spotted him leaving another property, a fierce-looking woman in a housecoat standing on the threshold as he did so. I listened to his complaints about people's disinterest and lack of community spirit.

Afterwards, I drove through the estate towards Wyatt's home, keeping an eye out for any kids cycling around, but I was disappointed. I drew up by Lydia's car and I noticed her in the distance talking to a couple of officers. An important looking man in an ill-fitting suit was standing alongside them gesticulating emphatically. I walked over.

Lydia introduced me. 'Detective Inspector Marco this is Councillor Luke Holroyd.'

Holroyd's voice was a decibel too loud. 'This is my patch. Everybody in the area is very concerned about what has happened. What can you tell me?'

'We have several different lines of enquiry. As you can appreciate—'

'Don't give me any of that flannel, Inspector.'

'It's only been a few hours since Wyatt's body was found and we've completed the post-mortem and the forensic report. We are now investigating—'

'Is there going to be an arrest soon?'

'It's too early—'

'Give me straight answers for Christ's sake.'

If only you'd let me answer a single question, I thought of replying. Instead I counted to five. Petty demagogues like this were common in the world of local politics but I couldn't offend him despite the obvious pleasure it would have given me.

'If you let me have your contact details, I can make certain the public relations department of Southern Division of the Wales Police Service will provide you with full details of every development.'

He gave me a disgruntled look.

'And you can contact Superintendent Cornock for an update.'

The name of a superior officer appeased him and he gave me his card with all his contact details. Once Holroyd had left, I turned to Lydia. 'Have you made any progress?'

'Nobody saw anybody approaching or leaving or entering the house. And both his neighbours weren't home on the afternoon he was killed. They were at work.'

Then I gave Lydia the details for Katie. 'I spoke to a witness who told me there is nature conservancy organisation that monitors wildlife in the woodland. I want you to contact her and find out if she's seen any unusual activity'

Lydia nodded and we made our way back to the car.

'Let's get back to Queen Street.'

Chapter 33

I reached Queen Street promptly the following morning in good time for my prearranged telephone call with Detective Inspector Smith.

I spent time reading the bare details of the previous convictions from the PNC search against Mark Wyatt's name. Then I read again Alvine's report and I studied the photographs of the bedroom. The letters daubed on the mirror were a chilling reminder of Carey's murder and it reminded me that we still had to contact Carey's partner.

Lydia arrived and poked her ahead around my door. 'Good morning, boss.'

'Has Plowman been in touch?'

'Nope – sorry, boss.'

'Make it a priority. If he's the third man in the video, then his life may well be in danger.'

At the agreed time I dialled Smith's direct line.

'Detective Inspector Ian Smith.'

I couldn't immediately make out his accent: middle England, not a strong as Birmingham but more pronounced than Yorkshire.

'It's DI Marco, Wales Police Service.'

Smith sounded almost pleased. 'I hear that Mark Wyatt is no longer with us.'

'I understand you were the SIO on the case where he was convicted several years ago.'

'At the time I was attached to the task force dealing with sexual offences. The force rotates officers into that department. Mark Wyatt was a nasty piece of goods. He attacked this eighteen-year-old lad in a lane in one of the quieter neighbourhoods of the city. We recovered evidence from the scene that implicated Wyatt.'

'Did you interview him?'

I sensed Smith recoiling at the memory. 'At first he denied any involvement until the weight of the evidence became abundantly clear to him. He was depraved and it surprised me the sentence was only five years. I always thought he would reoffend in a big way and that, next time, he would be locked up for a lot longer.'

'Do you know if he had any connections to Cardiff?'

'None that I was aware of.'

I interrogated Smith about every detail relating to Wyatt's life. His work, his friends, acquaintances, family background: everything unearthed by the police investigation. Smith's personal recollection would add colour to the paperwork. Otherwise it could take days to consider every piece of information. Time we didn't have.

'Why did you need the original tapes of the interview?'

'We recovered footage from Wyatt's laptop which recorded a brutal multiple gang rape of a man strapped to a bed.'

'Jesus.'

I continued. 'Voices can be heard, and we need to identify who they were.'

'And you think the victim of that assault may be your killer?'

'The same footage was on the laptop recovered from the home of another murder victim – a man called Raymond Carey. We haven't found a link to Wyatt, yet, but one must exist.'

'Best of luck with that.'

'If we can categorically identify one of the voices as belonging to Wyatt it'll mean progress.'

Smith added, 'It's always sad to hear about a murder but... nobody will grieve for Mark Wyatt. He was an evil bastard.'

'Will you inform the victim from his original crime that he's been killed?'

Smith let out a long sad breath. 'No need, Inspector. Very soon after Wyatt was convicted and sent to prison, he killed himself. I even went to the funeral. His mother was in bits.'

The Cardiff Lockdown Murders

We let a troubled silence fill the void in the conversation. A successful prosecution could never erase the events from the victim's mind. Protecting the innocent wasn't part of our job but it still appalled me whenever something like this happened.

'That's tragic,' I said eventually.

After thanking Smith I rang off, my thoughts focusing on the task in hand. And I had yet to hear from Terry, despite my texts. So I called him. 'I can't talk now Marco,' Terry managed in a breathless whisper, 'I should have some news tomorrow.' The call finished abruptly and I stared at my mobile, wondering what exactly Terry was doing.

After my call with Smith I needed a coffee but Wyn stopped me en route to the kitchen.

'There's an expert calling this afternoon to listen to the recordings.'

'Good work.'

'And I've done some more work on the footage from the CCTV camera outside Northam's apartment block.'

'And?'

'I've been trying to track down everybody who accessed the property in the hours before he died. We know he returned to the flat on Thursday evening after he finished work. There's no sightings of him leaving afterwards so I worked back. There are over two dozen people who've been in and out of the building. I've identified some of them. They're all linked to either ownership of the flats or they were guests or staying at the apartments.'

'But?'

'On Thursday morning a cleaning company arrives, a van draws up outside and a cleaner hauls out a trolley that he moves towards the main door. He's in uniform but we don't get sight of his face. It's as though he's hiding from the camera. The van stays outside and after a few minutes the cleaner leaves.'

'What's so mysterious about that?' Lydia said.

'I double checked with the managing agents and I rang the company that has the contract. They weren't due to clean and tidy the common parts for another week.'

'So why the hell were fake cleaners there?' I trotted back to my room shouting to Wyn and Lydia as I did so. 'Let's get back there now.'

I grabbed my coat and made for the car park. After the short drive down to the Bay I pulled the car onto the pavement outside the apartment building. On the journey I'd made contact with the cleaning company demanding they send a representative with a key in case none of the occupants were home.

I pressed the intercom for each flat and was rewarded with a dull electronic signal. I cursed; I should have known that the owners wouldn't be at home at this time of the day. I turned to Wyn. 'Call that bloody cleaning company again.'

I listened to a one-sided conversation, my annoyance increasing by the lack of understanding. 'Should be here any minute, boss,' Wyn said.

We didn't have to wait long for a van to pull into the street. An operative jumped out and ran down the pavement towards us. He fumbled with the key and let us in. As we entered, I turned to him. 'Don't go anywhere until I tell you.'

I stood for a moment in the silent hallway. Now that we were inside, I had the opportunity of thinking, considering exactly why fake cleaners wanted access. 'Let's assume the killer wanted to surprise Northam. There might be a storeroom somewhere where he could hide until he went up to Northam's apartment later that evening.'

'But he didn't stay in the block long.' Wyn reminded me.

My mind accelerated through the options. It struck me that somebody had pointed out the obvious before. 'What if there were two killers?'

Lydia and Wyn looked at me as though I was losing the

power of rational thought. I continued regardless. 'The cleaning trolley we saw earlier must have room for someone to hide. After all they weren't bloody cleaners. So if there is a store room somewhere one of them could have stayed hidden inside.'

'And when I saw the trolley being removed it was probably empty.'

Lydia picked up the thread. 'But that doesn't explain how the second person helped the first attack Andrew Northam.'

I looked around and the alternative struck me then. 'There must be a rear entrance.'

Marching down the corridor took us past various numbered apartment doors. But there was nothing to suggest there was another entrance, so we doubled back to the main hallway. Another long passage heading right and we passed the doors to four flats before the passageway doglegged left. Doubt niggled that my solution had any merit until we reached the end where a frosted glass window allowed in meagre grey light.

Alongside it was a half landing reached by three steps and at the end was a doorway with a simple Yale lock. All the apartment doors we passed had fancy five lever locks. Wyn and Lydia were behind me and all three of us stopped and looked at the door. I turned to Wyn. 'Get the cleaner back here with their keys.'

His footsteps reverberated as he raced down the corridor. Seconds later he reappeared with the same cleaning operative. 'Get that bloody door open. And don't touch anything.' He did as instructed and then got out of our way. Lydia and Wyn followed the same precaution as me by snapping on latex gloves. It was a narrow space converted to store cleaning equipment and a meter box for the electrical supply for the common parts. And more than enough room for a person to sit and wait.

In the far corner I spotted a door to the rear. It had a bar that opened only from the inside.

I looked over at the cleaner. 'Give me the keys. You can leave now.'

He opened his mouth to complain but thought the better of it.

Despite Alvine Dix's complaints that the storeroom wasn't a crime scene I insisted she allocate two CSI investigators. Within half an hour they were dusting the place. Once they were finished, I returned to Queen Street with Lydia and Wyn. We sat mulling over my theory of how the killer accessed Northam's apartment. Wyn had printed out an image of the man he had seen on the footage. He looked professional enough to go unchallenged.

'Does this mean we are looking for a man in relation to all these killings?' Wyn said.

Lydia, insightful as always, added. 'It could be a man and a woman working together. If the boss is right and one of them stayed in the cupboard all day the other could have been let in through the rear entrance the night Northam was killed. Then they go up to his flat and...'

Chapter 34

The telephone rang on Wyn's desk and I listened to the one-sided conversation before he announced, 'Charles Griggs, the voice analytics expert, is waiting downstairs.'

'Have you been able to isolate the voices from the video footage?'

Wyn nodded. 'And I transferred the recording from the Nottingham City Police interview into a digital file so we can play them on a laptop for Dr Griggs.'

'He's a doctor?' Lydia said.

Wyn sounded knowledgeable. 'Not the medical kind. The PhD kind.'

Before seeing Dr Griggs, I checked my emails, pleased that Alvine had sent me her report. A smile creased my lips when I read the results of the fingerprint analysis, but I wasn't exactly certain how Cornock would react.

Wyn stood at the threshold of my office, laptop in hand, prompting me that we didn't want to keep Dr Griggs waiting. We trooped down to a conference room near reception where Dr Griggs was waiting. He was an earnest-looking man in his fifties with thinning hair, a suit fashionable thirty years previously and battered shoes.

'Dr Griggs, I hope you'll be able to help us. We have sample voice recordings from two men, both of whom are of interest to us in a live inquiry. We then have a recording from a crime scene and we need to identify if any of the voices match the two men.'

'I can only do my best,' Griggs replied, like an academic who has been passed over for promotion. I turned to Wyn and nodded. He opened the laptop and Lydia and I sat opposite Griggs and Wyn. The voices from the footage was played first. It sounded vile and grotesque even without images to accompany it. Griggs made a pained expression. Then he darted me a glance. 'What is this, inspector?'

'I can't explain the details.'

'It sounds perfectly despicable.'

I nodded at Wyn, adding for Griggs, 'Constable Nuttall will play the two recordings we can confidently say belong to two different men. The first we'll call man A and the second man B. Please confirm if you can match the voices to the first recording.'

Griggs managed another troubled expression. 'It's not that easy you know. I mean it might take me some time to do this properly.' He reached into a bag by his side and removed a pair of headphones. 'It's much easier and more effective if I use these noise reduction cans.'

Wyn slotted a memory stick into the USB socket of the laptop and clicked play.

Griggs's face was a picture of focused intensity. He listened to a sample of each recording. Then he asked Wyn to replay them all again as he jotted notes onto a pad. It was after the fourth replay before he turned to Wyn. 'Please play the original of each identified voice.'

Wyn did as he was told and Griggs continued with his simultaneous note taking and listening.

I knew Superintendent Cornock wanted an update and I wanted some positive developments from this expert to share with him. Griggs took his headphones off and looked over at me. 'I shall need more time to be certain. And I would like to have these digital recordings sent to me so that I can listen to them properly. But my preliminary analysis is that two of the voices in the first recording match the voices of man A and man B.'

A large piece of a difficult jigsaw slotted into place.

'Thank you, Dr Griggs.'

A smile crossed his face for the first time.

Superintendent Cornock gave me a pained look after I'd finished explaining the position regarding Mark Wyatt and Raymond Carey.

'What are you suggesting?' He measured his words carefully. 'There's no chance we're going to make a public appeal for the third man involved in a brutal sexual assault to come forward. How the hell do you think that would play out?'

'I've got Wyn and Lydia cross-referencing all the contacts in Wyatt and Carey's mobile and laptop to see if there's any person in common who might be the third man in the video and a possible victim.'

'But it could be chasing a needle in a haystack, John. You have no idea where this video was taken, how old it is, or anything.' He threw the ballpoint he was turning through his fingers onto the pile of papers on his desk. 'It's our job to find the person who killed these men.'

'If we identify the third man, he might lead us to the individual they assaulted—'

'And how exactly is that going to help you solve the murders of Armsby and Northam? Please don't tell me they are linked to another gang rape Carey and Wyatt perpetrated.'

The superintendent was right, of course, so I added. 'We've also established how we believe the killers accessed Northam's apartment. A cleaning storeroom on the ground floor has a small rear entrance. We believe there were two of them, at least one was a man and the circumstances of his death suggest that two people were involved.'

'Jesus, so we have a pair of nutcases stalking the streets of Cardiff.'

'And fingerprint analysis there confirms that whoever was in the storeroom was also in Carey's house.'

Cornock slumped back in his chair. He sounded tired when he blew out a mouthful of air. 'So we can link Northam and Carey. We can link Carey and Wyatt. I've asked Dr Fabrien to return tomorrow and unless you can make some meaningful progress, I shall have to allocate a separate team to one of these inquiries. All I know, John, is that *if* we've got two different killers it justifies two teams. Fresh minds and all that.'

I opened my mouth to say something but decided against it.

Superintendent Cornock's rebuke reverberating in my mind helped me focus on reviewing everything. I had a couple of hours to spare until my date with Alison and after texting her to arrange a time and place to meet I settled down at my desk. I set out a sheet of paper and wrote the name Armsby on the top and Judy Campbell alongside it adding a question mark. She had motive and she had lied to us about her movements on the evening Armsby was killed.

Raymond Carey and Mark Wyatt's death had been brutal and ritualistic. I scrawled their names in the middle of the sheet circling them twice. I added – 'Third man' and 'Victim' to either side. Dr Margaret Fabrien and Superintendent Cornock were convinced they were the work of different individuals to those who had killed Armsby and Northam.

Northam's name and the circumstances suggested a killer out for revenge. What would the profiler make of the discovery of fingerprints linking Northam's crime scene to Carey's?

Would she still be convinced that two different killers were at work?

I walked out to the Incident Room and sat looking at the images on the board. All of the victims had been perpetrators of sexual violence and that made them connected for me, despite the differences and despite Dr Fabrien's professional opinion.

I read the time. I had to get home, shower, change and hope I'd be good company for Alison.

Chapter 35

The lighting at Bruno's Bistro was subdued and the customers discreetly tucked into tables unobserved by other diners. I had eaten here a few times, often spotting colleagues with guests who weren't their partners. These were occasions salted away in the favour bank and so far I hadn't had occasion to use up my credits. But being a detective meant knowing when I could sensibly cash in my chips.

The maître d led us to a table and I held Alison's elbow as I shepherded her to her seat. She beamed back. Alison gave the waiter an order for a Pinot Grigio and I had my usual sparkling water. No ice, no lemon.

She scanned the menu. 'Do you recommend anything, John?'

'The steaks are always good.'

I found myself staring over at her and noticing the perfect proportions of her mouth and the warmth of her smile. Her make-up was perfect, the pale red lipstick made her lips look sumptuous. She looked over and fixed my eye contact for a fraction longer than she needed. 'I shall have the langoustines, they are one of my favourites. And a steak.'

The waiter arrived with the drinks and left with our orders.

'I'm going to switch my mobile off tonight.' I placed the handset on the table.

'How is the investigation going? There's been a lot of gossip about the circumstances of two of the deaths in particular – the ones in their own homes.'

'They were very brutal.'

'Is it true they were tortured before being shot?'

There was something vaguely reassuring in a discussion with Alison about work. Relaxing was easier knowing she was familiar with the stresses and strains of the life of a police officer. Even so I lowered my voice slightly. 'I've never seen anything like it. And it sickened Lydia.'

'I hope I'm not speaking out of turn, but Chief Superintendent Harper has got wind of your recent meeting with Penny Larkham at the offices of DependAssist. She's been making threats to officially complain about your conduct.'

I almost hissed my reply. 'Did you know that the victims of Frank Armsby and Andrew Northam were Larkham's clients? She was one of the few people to have known the details of their crimes – sorry, alleged.'

Alison chuckled at my self-correction.

'I know what it's like when somebody complains too vociferously – it makes you suspect they are involved. I'm sorry, we shouldn't talk about work.' Alison sipped her wine and give me another warm smile. 'Tell me about yourself, Inspector.'

My Italian ancestry intrigued her over dinner. At least we shared a continental connection – her mother was from the Netherlands and her father worked as an architect in Chepstow. Alison rolled her eyes as she listened to a summary of my family's business background. 'I can't believe your father really makes ice cream.'

'Papà even has a contract to supply the prisons.'

She demolished the langoustines with accomplished elegance. Whenever I ate them the shells shattered, sending shards all over my shirt and trousers and if I tried to squirt lemon juice over them I got covered in the stuff.

She didn't notice me turning up my nose at her blue steak. It reminded me of the comedy line that a good vet would bring it back to life. Mine was medium to well-done and the fries were thin and crisp. I listened as she talked about the various teams where she had worked in both Cardiff and Newport.

I kept being drawn back to her eyes and her broad, warm smile. The same waiter cleared away our dishes and took an order for two crème brûlées that arrived with delicately sliced fresh strawberries. 'Strawberries are never the same out of season.' It was Alison's only criticism of the meal.

I didn't want the evening to finish. It made me realise I needed more time off and especially time to spend with Alison.

'Let me show you some of Cardiff Bay. Then perhaps I can make you coffee?'

She gave me another of her intense smiles. I paid the bill and we left. She put her hand through my arm and drew herself closer to me than was justified even by the chill autumn evening. I pointed out the Barrage that kept the fresh water inside Cardiff Bay and I promised to walk with her to Penarth once the case was over. In the distance lights dotted the top of the cliffs on which the outskirts of Penarth perched. Alison spotted the Millennium Centre and asked me to read the words carved into the outside. I made a stumbling effort with the Welsh words, excusing my poor pronunciation, before we sauntered over to the Parliament building and then around to the Norwegian Church.

It was a short walk from the waterside area of the Bay up to my apartment block. And the nearer I got to my home the more I found a tingling flooding my body and my heartbeat pounding. As I fumbled for the door key to the main entrance, I grazed her hand and sensed the warmth of her skin like a stab of electricity. We took the lift up to my flat and only then did I think about whether the place was tidy and was the bathroom clean enough?

I opened the door and I shrugged off my coat and helped Alison with hers.

Then we stood for a second gazing at each other, exploring and suggesting at the same time. I reached a hand to her face and drew her towards me. I leaned in and kissed her on the lips finding her hand curling around my neck. She deepened her kiss, gently stroking me with her tongue.

I tugged her blouse as she unfastened my belt. Then we didn't hesitate and we yanked and pulled furiously at each other's clothes. We left them on the landing as we headed for the bedroom where I closed the door.

Chapter 36

Alison pulled on a white shirt from my wardrobe, its tails brushing the top of her thighs. She kissed me lightly on the lips before announcing she was going to make the coffee I'd promised her the previous evening. I chuckled and gazed over at the alarm clock. It was still early, and I headed off to the shower as I heard Alison organising herself in the kitchen. It had been a while since the place had experienced a woman's touch.

Chatter from the television in the sitting room drifted through the open door as I left the bathroom. I was buttoning up my shirt when the flat doorbell rang and it puzzled me as to who might be calling at this time. I left the bedroom and watched as Alison's slim perfectly proportioned legs glided over the carpet.

I was halfway down the landing when she opened the front door.

'Good morning,' Alison said.

There was silence for a moment. The possibility that Lydia was there came to mind and I juggled the explanations and justifications for Alison's state of semi-undress before deciding it would be none of Lydia's business. When I reached the door, I stared into Jackie's face as she was blinking rapidly her mouth slack, a little lost for words.

'John, I'm sorry to call so early but...'

Alison sensed the mutual discomfort and stood to one side before walking back into the flat, where I heard the bathroom door close behind her.

'Jackie, I can explain.' I was beginning to sound like someone from a second-rate soap opera.

Now her voice hardened 'We're both adults. You don't owe me any explanation.'

'It's not what—'

She raised her hand and I stopped mid-sentence.

'I wanted to talk about Dean. But it can wait. I'll call your mother to explain about the holiday.' Abruptly she left, striding for the staircase. I closed the door and padded back into the kitchen where Alison joined me as my coffee dribbled into an espresso cup.

'I'm sorry if I created any embarrassment.'

'Jackie is my ex.' I said simply as though it was explanation enough. I rolled my eyes. 'Coffee?'

She gave me one of those confident smiles, reaching over to give me a brief kiss on the lips. 'That'll be lovely.'

I left Alison making herself at home, telling me that she had a late start that morning. I took a moment sitting in my car to look up at the apartment building. I smiled. Waking up with Alison by my side made me feel human again. As though the activity of the past two weeks was detached from real life of loving and being loved. I wanted things to be different with Alison and very soon I'd need to tell her all about Jackie and my drinking. No secrets, I resolved, tapping the steering wheel – I would be a better person.

Driving into Queen Street gave me time to think. Jackie would probably call my mother. My mother would then call me. But whether Jackie would mention Alison wasn't a certainty and I certainly wasn't going to call my mother and tell her about my private life. Perhaps it would make my mother realise that trying to engineer a reconciliation between Jackie and me wouldn't work. I took the stairs to the Incident Room and found Lydia and Wyn discussing the priorities for the morning. Pleasantries exchanged I reached my office depositing my coat on the stand.

Margaret Fabrien was arriving later so I needed to prepare. I sat waiting for my computer to boot up when a message reached my mobile and fishing it out of my pocket I read Terry's request to meet.

I grabbed my coat and rushed out of my office into the Incident Room calling to Lydia and Wyn. 'I need to go.'

Terry was halfway through a massive mug of thick brown tea when I slipped into the bench seat opposite him at one of his favourite haunts on City Road. His gaze darted around.

'This is the last time I do you any favours, Marco.'

In the world Terry and I inhabited things were never that simple and I didn't bother to reply.

'I've got someone for you to meet.'

'This had better be a valuable use of my time.'

'But there can't be any comeback.'

'Comeback?'

'You don't investigate her.'

'Her?'

'She calls herself a service provider.'

I hissed a response. 'What the fuck do you mean?'

'Somebody wants a service and she provides it.'

'Are you talking about guns?'

Terry jerked a glance around the café and spat out his reply. 'Not so loud.'

Meeting an individual who would admit selling a gun and doing nothing about it might raise some tricky questions. I needed to balance the urgency of tracking down the killer against the expediency of identifying someone dealing in guns.

'Do you want to meet her or not?' Terry whispered. 'Because she is doing this as one big favour to me. Afterwards the favour bank is all used up, Marco.'

I looked over at him raising an eyebrow as if to say you-know-it's-never-over-don't-you?

'So why is she your new best friend?'

'Like I said, she owes me.' He finished his drink. 'Let's go.'

We stood on the pavement outside. Terry turned to me. 'Your phone needs to be switched off.' He pushed a shoulder bag in my direction it's top flap open. 'Drop it inside. Don't worry, you'll get it back when we're done.'

Reluctantly I turned the phone off and dropped it into his bag.

His pace quickened as he took one junction after

another. Occasionally he looked around and back behind us as though he half expected to see a marked police car following us. At the end of a road he darted into a convenience store and jerked his head for me to follow him. He dawdled around the display counters near the door, casting the occasional glance outside. Once he was satisfied I hadn't arranged some surreptitious surveillance he nodded his head towards the rear of the building. He shouldered open the door and we entered a storeroom in the bowels of the premises. And then out to a small yard that led onto a narrow lane. It led down behind a row of terraces and at the bottom he pointed the remote at a Ford Fiesta and wordlessly jumped into the driver's side. I joined him and he sped off. He repeated the convoluted journey in the car as he had done on foot from the café taking various junctions and casting anxious glances into the rear-view mirror.

'This is all bit James Bond isn't,' I said.

Terry kept looking straight ahead. 'Like I said, no comebacks.'

Eventually Terry got to the main roundabout where North Road meets the A48. He drove north up Northern Avenue past Whitchurch and on to the Coryton interchange on the M4. 'We are we going Terry?'

He didn't reply but pressed on up the A470.

He indicated left into the Treforest Industrial Estate and repeated the exercise of dawdling and driving into dead ends, making three-point turns and returning along the same journey to flush out any possible surveillance. 'Nobody is following us, Terry.'

He chose a road running parallel to the main A470 through Hawthorn and skirted around Rhyd y Felin before taking a left for Pontypridd. Now he could either take a left to the Rhondda valleys or double back into the A470 and on for Quakers Yard and Merthyr. He did neither. He took a route around the back streets of Pontypridd.

He pulled the car to the edge of the road near the

pavement.

'I'll wait for you here.' Terry used a businesslike tone. He nodded at the black van parked fifty metres away on the opposite side of the street. 'Get into the passenger side.'

'I hope this is going be worth it.' I reached for the door handle and jumped out.

The transit was ten years old, dabs of rust decorated the wheel arches and the door groaned a complaint as it squeaked open. I got in. It smelled, really badly, as though it had never been cleaned. I hauled down the window a couple of inches.

I waited. I looked over at Terry. He hadn't moved.

It must have been ten minutes before the rear door of the van creaked open and someone got inside. Wire mesh covered the small hole in the plywood panel between the seating cabin and the back making it pointless trying to identify the individual behind me.

'Inspector Marco.' It was a woman's voice, Cardiff accent.

'Terry says you might have some information for me.'

'There's something you need to know. This meeting didn't take place.'

A man in a shell suit, his stomach straining at the material, passed the van, drawing heavily on a cigarette. Terry was still sitting, sphinx-like, in his car.

The woman continued. 'I did some business a while ago for a product that can be difficult to source. I like to keep this sort of thing confidential. There's a telephone number that might help you.'

I spotted scraps of paper and pencils on the dashboard and scrambled to jot down the details.

Then I heard the rear door squeak open. Seconds later a car roared into life and sped away.

I sat looking at the digits, wondering if all this secret agent stuff was really justified.

Chapter 37

Margaret Fabrien arrived half an hour after I'd returned from my meeting with Terry and his mysterious contact. I heard the unfamiliar lilt and accent so I left my room and joined her and Lydia standing before the board. Margaret turned and smiled. I noticed for the first time that one eyebrow was slightly higher than the other and her nostrils were flared too. Her light brown hair had been pulled tightly behind her head and a long ponytail hung down over her shoulders across a white blouse and navy jacket.

'I'm sure you didn't expect to be back quite so soon,' I said.

She rolled her eyes. 'Superintendent Cornock's message was very urgent. I had to make excuses to the Metropolitan Police. The inspector in charge wasn't happy.'

'There has been another death.'

Margaret nodded seriously.

I stepped over to the board and pointed at the image of Mark Wyatt. 'Wyatt was killed in circumstances similar to Raymond Carey. He was tied to a bed and then mutilated before being shot. And the words "see you later" were written in lipstick on a bedroom mirror.'

'Ah, I see.' Margaret used a serious tone that matched her frown.

'Wyatt lives on an estate of houses so using the front door would have been risky. We believe the killer gained access through woodland at the rear of the property. It leads down to another residential area where the killer could have parked his car.'

'You're assuming it is a man.'

I looked over at Margaret, as did Lydia. Wyn looked a bit nonplussed.

Margaret added. 'It is always sensible to keep an open mind.'

'We've put everything together from what we know about Wyatt's murder. And we've also established that

Northam's killer got access to his flat by using a storeroom with a door to the rear yard of the apartment block. We have CCTV footage showing a person pretending to be a cleaner entering the building.'

'Interesting.' Margaret sounded intrigued. She turned her attention back to the board. It was a mixture of mugshots, photographs of the crime scene and threads and connecting information. In the middle of all this information there was a thread we hadn't identified. 'It had been my view that more than one killer was at work, but the death of Wyatt should encourage a fresh evaluation. I can only give advice of course. But let me summarise.'

She pointed at the photograph of Frank Armsby. 'At first I considered his murder was a straightforward case unconnected with the violent sadistic nature of the injuries perpetrated on Raymond Carey.' She moved a hand and jerked a perfectly manicured finger with the nail painted a delicate pink at the image of Carey. 'There was a depth of emotion and hatred and violence associated with the circumstances of Raymond Carey's death. It must have been horrific.'

'And the video footage links directly to Mark Wyatt.'

'Can we definitely say that Mark Wyatt and Raymond Carey were killed by the same person?' She answered her own question. 'I think that must be correct. And establishing that Raymond Carey and Mark Wyatt are the voices on that footage does point to their victim as a likely suspect. But, as you know, John, men like Wyatt and Carey are probably serial offenders. They may have assaulted other men.'

'And how does Andrew Northam fit into this then?'

She frowned and turned her gaze to Northam's picture. 'A violent attack.'

I could sense Margaret was moving towards confirming her previous conclusion that there were two unconnected killers. Inevitably it meant a different detective inspector and a new team would take over one of the inquiries. I had even reconciled myself to that possibility. It might even be for the best.

'Do you have the details of the alleged assaults perpetrated by Armsby and Northam? There is something else I wish to explore.'

Lydia and Wyn took a few minutes to find the paperwork relating to the prosecution of Frank Armsby. Lydia set them out onto the table in the Incident Room. Unpacking the documentation took time but I eventually identified the circumstances surrounding Judy Campbell's complaint. She had been working late at an office building on an audit where Armsby was the accountant for the company. The staff had left for the evening leaving the two of them alone. There was a deadline to meet and Campbell hadn't wanted to face criticism from her immediate superior about delays with the work being completed so she had stayed on. Armsby had offered to buy her a drink after they had finished but as she got to his car he bundled her into the rear seat where he attacked her.

Margaret was sitting by my side as I shuffled the statements and documentation. Occasionally I read out a summary and Margaret nodded knowingly. When I realised that the scene of Armsby's crime was a business address three units away from the builders' merchants where his body had been found I paused. 'You won't believe this.' I shared the details with Margaret.

Again, another informed look crossed her face.

'We need to look at the file of Amy Gould, please.'

Lydia replied. 'We don't have all the information for Gould's complaint, boss.'

But I knew someone who did.

I found my mobile and called Alison, inviting her to join us.

She arrived a few minutes later, her hair glistening and she gave me another of her warm smiles. I hoped none of the team noticed.

'Alison, thanks for coming on short notice,' I tried to sound formal without pulling rank. 'Can you outline the circumstances of Northam's assault on Amy Gould?'

'He invited her back to his apartment.' Alison said flatly, although I guessed she was thinking about last night. I certainly was. 'And he came on to her and he pushed her into the bathroom where he raped her. I thought her evidence was compelling and she would have made a great witness but—'

'Bathroom?' Lydia said. 'That's where he was killed.'

'It's coincidence, surely,' Wyn added.

Margaret moved nearer the board, her silence speaking volumes. 'I do not think it is coincidence. I would suggest the deaths of Northam and Armsby are replicating in some way the scenes of the crimes they committed against their victims.'

I blew out a lungful of breath. 'And the murders of Carey and Wyatt are replicating the scene from that dreadful footage.'

Margaret nodded. I joined her by the board.

Wyn piped up. 'Judy Campbell has an alibi – sort of – for the night of Armsby's death.'

I picked up the thread. 'And we know Amy Gould was in Stockholm at the time Andrew Northam was beaten to death in his bathroom.'

'I have revised my opinion,' Margaret announced. 'I believe you are looking for the same killer.'

I stared over at the board. 'We need to identify a common thread.' I turned back to face the team. 'Judy Campbell seeks counselling from DependAssist, and she insists we speak to her at their offices. But then she lies to us about leaving the apartment for the early part of the evening Armsby was killed.'

'Why did she do that?' Lydia said.

I continued. 'Amy Gould is assaulted by Andrew Northam in the bathroom of his apartment. And we know he was killed there. There's a definite pattern.'

Lydia again. 'And we know Amy Gould was also counselled by DependAssist.'

'Penny Larkham.' I announced slowly. 'She's the only link to both Armsby and Northam.'

Alison joined me and gazed at the maze of information and data and photographs on the board. Then she pointed at Caitlin Prior. 'I've seen this woman before.'

I gave her a troubled look.

'She was at the trial of Frank Armsby and Andrew Northam. She was sitting quietly at the back. Why the hell would she do that?'

I turned to look at the faces of Raymond Carey and Mark Wyatt. 'Still doesn't give us an explanation for the deaths of Carey and Wyatt. Penny Larkham didn't know anything about them, surely?'

I paused for a moment, a dozen different priorities bouncing around in my mind. 'We need Penny Larkham and Caitlin Prior's phone records. Today. As soon as. There must be something we've missed. Let's get details of all the vehicles registered in Larkham's name as well as those registered to Caitlin Prior. And get one of the tech guys down here. I want the video footage of that cleaner going into Northam's apartment block checked over again.'

Chapter 38

Alison left soon afterwards, and Lydia followed me back to my office and sat in one of the visitor chairs.

'I still haven't traced Plowman,' Lydia said.

'Does he respond to messages?'

'No.'

'Does his employer have any other contact details?'

Lydia shook her head, her face creased with worry. 'He told them he was staying with friends in London.'

'Family?'

'None we know of.'

'Get a search done for Plowmans in London and get uniform to call at his home. They can ask the neighbours too.'

Lydia nodded. 'How did you get on this morning?'

I pulled the scrap of paper with the eleven digits of the mobile phone and placed it on my desk.

'I want this number checked. It belongs to someone who bought a gun.'

Lydia whistled under her breath. 'Shouldn't you make a formal report. I mean...'

'Nothing to report – it could be a wild goose chase.'

Lydia gave me a world-weary turn of the head acknowledging that I really should know better.

I demolished a sandwich at my desk for lunch in the middle of reviewing everything we knew about Penny Larkham. She might well have a client who had been assaulted by Carey and Wyatt and I couldn't ignore the possibility that Carey and Wyatt's victim had killed both men. It meant that Larkham had information we needed.

I found the result of the PNC search against her name and something made me stop and double check the date of birth. Larkham didn't look fifty-nine – the age on the paperwork. So I resubmitted the search requesting details of known aliases.

It was mid-afternoon when Wyn shouted his

enthusiasm. I stood up and left my office.

'We've had the results of the triangulation of Penny Larkham and Caitlin Prior's mobile numbers. We can track both women to Penarth Road on the evening Armsby was killed and to the Bay area at the time that Andrew Northam was killed.'

'Good work. Anything to link them to Carey and Wyatt?'

'Not yet, boss. I'm working on it.'

'I think it's time we spoke to both women.'

I got back to my room and read the enhanced PNC search waiting in my inbox. Now it was my turn to sound eager. 'You won't believe this.'

Wyn and Lydia appeared at my door and even Margaret joined them, drawn by the sounds of progress.

'Larkham changed her name a few years ago – she was previously Penny Hinton and guess what? She was convicted of grievous bodily harm when she assaulted a former lover.'

Margaret nodded wisely. 'A history of violence is always indicative of a predisposition to reoffend.'

My mind began to prioritise. I turned to Wyn. 'Invite Caitlin Prior in for another chat. Lydia and I will get Penny Larkham in.'

Lydia and I descended the stairs to the car park as I tapped out a message to Alison. *Thanks for your help. Developments this afternoon. Loved last night. Speak soon X*

As we pulled into the car park outside the offices of DependAssist Lydia looked through the windscreen. 'It beggars belief Larkham might be involved.'

'She's the only direct link we have to the deaths of Armsby and Northam.'

'But that suggests a different killer was responsible for Carey and Wyatt. Dr Fabrien thinks it's the same murderer at work.'

'I don't like loose ends. Why would Caitlin Prior be

present at the trial of both Northam and Armsby?'

'Even so, boss, Larkham's a counsellor who expects people to trust her with confidential information.'

We left the car and walked over to the offices of DependAssist. Jack Hughes was on the reception desk, working through a pile of paperwork and he gave us a sullen look as I asked him to tell Penny Larkham we needed to speak to her.

He scooped up the phone and announced our presence to Larkham.

Moments later she appeared in reception and ushered us through into her office.

She sat down and motioned for us to do likewise. I stood and got straight to the point. 'We'd like you to come to Queen Street to assist with our inquiries.'

She frowned and her forehead creased deeply. 'What's this about?'

'We can explain once we reach the police station.'

'Am I under arrest?'

'Cooperating with our inquiries.' I sounded upbeat.

She stood up reluctantly and followed us outside. We made the short journey back into the centre of Cardiff.

Once she had been safely deposited in an interview room, I made my way back to the Incident Room where Wyn was waiting. 'I've put Caitlin Prior into interview room three.'

'Penny Larkham is in seven. Any luck with the ANPR results?'

'It could take some time, boss. But I did a full PNC check against Caitlin Prior. There is no history of any convictions or violence.'

I spent an hour with Lydia preparing for the interview with Penny Larkham, honing and polishing the questions and tactics. Until we were ready, she could languish in the interview room, waiting and worrying. It is always a good strategy to let a potential suspect sweat a bit and as Larkham had been through the mangle of a police interview and all its technicalities I needed every advantage possible.

Lydia slid a fresh bottle of water over the table at Larkham when we arrived for the interview. She gave her a brief smile of thanks.

I sat in one of the uncomfortable rigid plastic chairs and set out the papers in front of me. Although it wasn't an interview under caution, I had decided to take the precaution of having it tape-recorded so after removing the packaging from the tapes I dropped them into the cassette in the machine. Once the beeping noise had finished, I turned to Penny Larkham.

'We're investigating the murder of Frank Armsby and Andrew Northam. Could you explain to us exactly what your work is with DependAssist?'

She frowned, calculating, I guessed, how much aggression she could get away with. 'I am a trained counsellor and my work involves providing professional assistance to the victims of sexual and domestic abuse.'

'Did Judy Campbell and Amy Gould seek your help?'

'I think you can dispense with the absurdity of asking questions you know the answer to.' First sign of aggression, now all I had to do was get under her skin.

'Please answer the question.' I was reasonableness personified now. I'd be smiling at her in a minute.

'Counselling victims is what I do, Inspector. It's my job.'

I opened the file of papers in front of me. 'Did Judy Campbell discuss with you the detailed circumstances of the alleged assault against her by Frank Armsby?'

'There was nothing alleged about it,' Larkham retorted. 'And you should know I cannot discuss the details of what was discussed with me confidentially.'

I tried a different tack. 'I don't want you to breach any confidentiality. But surely you can confirm that Judy Campbell discussed with you where the assault took place?'

'Where are you going with this?'

Lydia stopped scribbling notes at this stage and replied. 'We could always apply to a magistrate for a warrant to requisition the records of your discussions with Judy Campbell. I do hope that wouldn't be necessary.'

A worried look crossed her face. 'You could never get a warrant in those circumstances. It would be unethical.'

'Murder is the most heinous crime, Miss Larkham,' Lydia continued, rather formally. 'We were hoping you might cooperate with us.'

Larkham pouted, but I watched her mind working. Was she calculating how much she could tell us? What assumptions had she made so far about what we had deduced? And was I staring at Armsby's and Northam's killer?

'Judy Campbell and Amy Gould shared with me the circumstances of their assaults. But as I'm sure you're aware, both Frank Armsby and Andrew Northam faced prosecutions and those details would have been public knowledge.'

Her first mistake. The facts of both cases hadn't been mentioned in court before they'd been dismissed by the judge in each case. Was it more than simply justifying to herself its disclosure to us?

'Are you familiar with the industrial estate near Penarth Road where Frank Armsby was killed?'

'No, I'm not, Inspector.'

'Have you ever been there?'

'No, I don't think I have.'

'And are you familiar with the apartment block where Andrew Northam lives?'

'Again, Inspector, the answer is no and if you ask me if I've ever been there the reply would be the same.'

Now I looked directly into Larkham's eyes. I wanted to see exactly how she was going to react when I asked my next question. 'We've been able to do some preliminary work triangulating your mobile telephone.' She looked worried, but was it the sort of worry a murderer might tolerate? 'And we've discovered you were in the vicinity of Penarth Road and Cardiff Bay, near Andrew Northam's apartment, on the evenings both men were killed.'

Now she looked over at me perplexed. 'This is absurd. Are you suggesting I was responsible for killing both men?'

'The location of the original assaults committed by Armsby and Northam were known to you and we can place you near the scenes.'

Larkham shook her head.

'Armsby and Northam were killed in violent circumstances. And is it true that several years ago you were convicted of grievous bodily harm when you assaulted a former lover?'

Now Larkham took time to reply measuring her words. 'That was a long time ago and I have changed as a person since then. I've retrained.'

'Why did you change your name?'

'I moved away from London, too many bad memories.'

'Were you trying to hide your past?'

'Don't be absurd.'

'Tell me about your relationship with Caitlin Prior.'

She even tensed her fist on the table in front of me but quickly hid it when she realised I'd noticed. Changing your identity and moving didn't change the nature of the person sitting opposite me.

I continued. 'The website Justice for All you run is responsible for spreading information about current police inquiries which is most irresponsible and could well be impeding our work. Were you aware that Caitlin Prior met Frank Armsby on the night he was killed?'

There was no flicker of surprise on her face. The meeting must have been pre-planned.

'Why did she meet him?'

No response.

I stood up deciding it was time for me to speak to Caitlin Prior. But before leaving I turned to Penny Larkham. 'Assisting us with our enquiries may stick in your craw but we want the same as you – to catch abusive individuals. And making our task harder doesn't help.'

Larkham gave me an icy glower as I left.

Caitlin Prior gave me mostly simple, monosyllabic replies. She wasn't riled or troubled by the implication she might be involved in a double murder. Hardly anybody in my experience can keep completely emotionless when faced with a police interrogation. The stress in her body must have been off the scale and her heart would be ramming against her ribs but she was cool and unperturbed.

'Is there any crime in attending at court?' She asked when I challenged her presence at the hearings when the cases against Armsby and Northam were dismissed. She was right, of course, but her presence there was unusual.

When I asked about her relationship with Penny Larkham she looked at me and then through me. I even tried asking her about the vehicles she owned and she didn't raise an eyebrow or make any objection when I insisted they be examined forensically. 'I doubt that I could object in any event,' she had said.

Finally, I asked about her date with Armsby. I took time to outline all the evidence we had including the footage of her arriving at the restaurant.

'We were hoping to trap him.'

I took a moment to let the significance sink in. 'Trap him? What the hell do you mean?'

'The WPS are useless in prosecuting abusive men so the only way is to get eyewitness evidence that no prosecutor or judge could ever challenge.'

'You must be mad. And who do mean by 'we'?'

Prior smirked. 'Penny and I were going to make certain that next time Armsby would be going to down.'

'Do you realise the danger you were facing?'

'It's better than doing nothing, which is what the WPS is good at.'

We left Prior and Larkham festering in their respective interview rooms.

Chapter 39

I didn't want to watch the video we had recovered from Raymond Carey's laptop more than was absolutely necessary. It appalled me that human beings could inflict such pain and terror on each other and record everything for some macabre pleasure. The unidentified third man in the video needed to be locked up for a long time and if the victim was the killer then the same fate awaited him.

It amazed me how Peter Kelly, a civilian from the forensic department, could abide watching the footage. He said little, but clearly enjoyed the geeky intensity of his work.

Lydia joined me as we stood behind him, watching him fiddling with the controls enhancing the quality, adjusting it until an image of the man on the bed appeared on the screen. 'Can you see the blotches on his arms and shoulders?' Peter said.

I squinted at the monitor. 'It's a bit blurred.'

'I've seen that sort of image before. It looks like psoriasis.'

'And have you been able to make any progress with the footage of the man spotted outside Northam's apartment building?'

'Sorry sir. He was deliberately keeping his face hidden.'

'Can you be certain it was a man?'

'From everything I can see about the way the person walks and holds himself there is no doubt it was a man.'

I trooped back to my office and Lydia and Wyn followed me.

I sank into the chair by my desk. 'Is there anything from the ANPR cameras?'

'I'm waiting for the results, sir,' Wyn replied.

'What do you want to do about Larkham and Prior?' Lydia said, sitting down on one of the chairs; Wyn remained standing by the door.

I looked over at Wyn. 'How did you get on in

Larkham's office?'

'That Jack Hughes bloke is strange. He got really difficult with me about accessing a list of Larkham's clients.'

'Did you get the details in the end?'

'Yes, she's been counselling twenty-six recent clients in relation to either sexual or domestic abuse offences. And quite a few of them were as a result of a prolonged series of assaults during the lockdown. Once the restrictions were eased the courts were dead busy with applications for injunctions for men to keep away from their partners.'

Lydia sounded reflective. 'It's depressing isn't it? Why do men act like that?'

Wyn continued. 'It wasn't just women that she counselled, there were two men who had been assaulted by their wives.'

I interjected. 'No record of male on male assaults or men being counselled?'

'None, boss.'

Lydia turned to face me. 'Are we going to warn all these twenty-six individuals that they should be careful?'

'We don't need to tell them how we got their identities or disclose the link to the DependAssist charity.'

Wyn and Lydia nodded.

'Get that done and in the meantime we wait for the CSIs to complete their forensic examination of Larkham and Prior's vehicles. For now we release them on bail.'

As Lydia made to leave, I asked, 'Any more news on Plowman?'

'I sent him messages and uniform have been to his home, but he wasn't there and the neighbours haven't seen him.'

'Damn – we need to find him.'

Lydia nodded and left to organise the necessary paperwork for Larkham and Prior's release. I settled into the last few hours of the day, pondering the identity of the third

The Cardiff Lockdown Murders

man from the video on Carey's laptop.

It must have been someone common to Carey and Wyatt I reasoned. And being unable to contact Plowman I had to assume it might be someone else. I started with Wyatt's laptop, hoping there might be a 'Pictures' folder in the hard drive. Everyone kept digital photographs these days and it didn't take me long to find it. I unearthed some borderline illegal images and shots of groups of men in a bar somewhere drinking heavily and all the images had been stored into organised folders – 'Düsseldorf' was the name of one, 'Majorca' another and the photographs contained inside covered several different years.

Then I turned my attention to Raymond Carey's laptop. This time there was more order and neatness to the arrangement of the picture files. He had everything stored by year and within each folder were subdivisions for the month and then for the locations of photographs. I didn't find anything questionable and the gallery could have passed for the contents of anybody's holiday snaps. There were pictures of Carey and Plowman somewhere in the Brecon Beacons I guessed by the look of the windswept hilltops. Others of them on a beach relaxing in the sun.

I searched for faces common to Wyatt's photos but didn't find any. Establishing all the possible links in common would take hours

By eight pm I got up, stretched my back and then walked out into the Incident Room. Wyn turned to face me. 'I've spoken with all of the men linked to Larkham's clients. A couple of them became really aggressive, demanding to know how we got their names. I told them it was confidential police business. They've all been warned to take their personal safety carefully and if they notice anything suspicious they are to contact us immediately.'

'Good.' I paced over to the board and stared at the slip of paper that I had pinned under Carey's name. 'Do we know if this phone has been switched on yet?'

Wyn double checked his computer and shook his head. 'And it's a pay-as-you-go phone, sir. It's not registered to anybody and it was bought for cash at a local supermarket.'

'There should be a law against that.'

Wyn chuckled, although I meant it deadly seriously. Lydia joined me by the board. 'I've heard from the CSIs as well and they've confirmed that neither Prior's nor Larkham's vehicles has any evidence of a collision with Armsby.'

'They might have cleaned the car thoroughly after killing him.' I knew I sounded as though I were clutching at straws. I probably was, but there was something wrong about Larkham and Prior. I looked at the still image of the man posing as a cleaner outside Northam's apartment. 'What if he is connected to Prior and Larkham in some way. Let's look at their telephone records again. Are there any common numbers – somebody that we can connect to both women.' But it was late – too late to achieve much else. I had a briefing with Superintendent Cornock first thing the following morning, which meant an early start.

A text from Alison bleeped on my mobile as I reached my office door. *Glad to help. I'll look forward to the next time. A x.* The prospect of seeing Alison again made me smile far more than the prospect of my meeting with Superintendent Cornock in the morning.

Chapter 40
When I woke my legs were splayed over the bed, the duvet an unruly mass. I glanced over at the alarm clock – it was still early. Immediately I started prioritising tasks for the day – I had a meeting with Superintendent Cornock and I needed to prepare. I showered, dressed and organised an Americano. I was eating toast as the sound of activity somewhere in an apartment above me percolated through the building, reminding me that most families would be relaxing on a Saturday. Cardiff City were playing away from home so I'd catch the result later – I hadn't even checked if the game was on television.

I reached my Mondeo and thought about Larkham and Prior. Annoyance stabbed at my mind – at them for believing that on their own they could make a difference, and with the system for failing victims of domestic and sexual abuse. Plowman's lack of contact worried me, and I decided on a detour to his home.

The weekend traffic was light, and I made good time. I pulled up outside the house, which had a deserted feel. I left the car and I peered in through the front window after fisting the door and not getting a reply. I undid the latch on the rear gate but the back door was locked and, staring through the kitchen window, I couldn't see any sign of life, so I drove to Queen Street.

I reached the Incident Room and dawdled by the board. The silence gave me time to think. The grotesque images from the scenes at Carey and Wyatt's home dominated the board. The telephone number from Terry's mystery contact had to be followed up – another task for Wyn that morning. I cast a glance over at the details of Mark Wyatt and realised that I hadn't read the results of the house-to-house inquiries.

Settling down at my desk I opened my computer and found the report. I read the usual language about following the standard protocols before turning to the conclusions: there were still residents that hadn't been contacted. It reminded me that Mr Bolton, the man I had interviewed, had given me the name of a woman who visited the woodland as part of a nature conservancy charity.

I scrambled to find any record of contact with her. Nothing.

I rang her mobile number. She answered after two rings. 'Hello?'

Introductions out of the way, I said, 'I need to ask you about the woodland in Rumney which is at the rear of the house where Mr Wyatt was killed.'

'Look, I'm on my way to the woodland as it happens. Can I meet you there?'

'Of course.' I stood up and grabbed my keys and jacket.

After a fifteen-minute journey I reached the car park by the woodland entrance but it was empty. I didn't have to wait long and Katie arrived in an old Fiesta, its exhaust clattering. I got out and walked over towards her. She gave me an intense gaze without bothering to look at my warrant card.

'I'm tying up loose ends. We suspect that Mark Wyatt's killer accessed his property through the woodland.' I jerked my head at the trees alongside us. 'Have you seen anybody unusual here in the past week or so. Some out of the ordinary activity?'

'It's mostly locals who walk here.' She pondered for a moment. 'But come to think of it I did notice a van here a couple of times and I've never seen it before.'

'Can you describe it?'

'Red and old and more battered than my car.'

Her description made me pause as my adrenaline spiked, remembering where I had seen a similar vehicle. I asked slowly, 'It may be very important, but can you remember anything else about the van?'

She stared at my Mondeo as though it helped her focus.

'I'm sure it was an old Post Office van. You could still see a trace of the livery.'

The Cardiff Lockdown Murders

I fumbled for my keys. 'You've been very helpful, thank you.' I left Katie and rushed back to Queen Street.

'There could be hundreds of old Post Office vans,' Lydia sounded a note of caution.

I was standing by the board in the Incident Room.

Wyn was clicking his mouse as he nodded agreement. 'A friend of mine has one, boss. It's done massive mileage, but it was dead cheap.'

'Even so I want a full search against Jack Hughes as well as a PNC check and find out if he owns a red van. And I called at Plowman's home first thing but there's no sign of him.'

'I'll try and contact him again.'

'Do some more digging into Plowman. We need to find a voice file for him. If he is the third man in the video, we need to find him.'

I was halfway back to my office when Wyn announced in an excited voice, 'The mystery mobile has just switched on.'

'Excellent, where the hell is it?'

'It's reaching The Hays near the St David Centre.'

I didn't waste another second. 'Lydia, let's go. Wyn, keep an eye on that signal. And keep me posted with its movements. And notify the Super I'll be late for his briefing.'

Once we were outside Queen Street, I jogged down Charles Street and then round the side of the Metropolitan Cathedral before skirting the St David's Shopping Centre. I paused when we reached The Hays and spoke to Wyn.

'The signal is going down Royal Arcade.'

I nodded at Lydia in the direction of Cardiff Central Library and then we ran. I got to the entrance of the Royal Arcade and rushed in, my mobile pinned to my ear, shouting for updates from Wyn.

I cast the occasional glance into the various outlets in

the arcade but Wyn had been silent and by the time we reached the bottom I stopped and yelled into the phone. 'Where the hell is the signal now?'

'It's been switched off, boss,'

'Check it again.'

I surveyed the surroundings shops and city centre buildings hoping I could recognise somebody – perhaps it was Caitlin Prior or Penny Larkham or even Jim White. I took a few more steps into the middle of St Mary Street, Lydia gave me an odd look. I turned to face her. 'Signal's gone dead.'

'Why the hell would that happen?'

I decided against returning to Queen Street and paced up St Mary Street. At the junction of Wharton Street, I glanced left and I saw the imposing structure of the Principality Stadium and to my right the route back to The Hays and then Queen Street. I didn't have to make a decision, as my mobile rang and I recognised Wyn's number.

'It's in the market.'

I turned to Lydia. 'Come on!'

The market building was in the middle of the city and was home to hundreds of stallholders. The user could be inside on purpose – trying to confuse us, lay a false trail, like something from a thriller movie.

I darted into the entrance and passed the meat and fish and fresh vegetable counters. I still had my mobile Superglued to my ear. Wyn regularly confirmed that the signal was still in the central market. Calling it would be pointless; my number would be unfamiliar. I couldn't risk the mobile being switched off. I tried to look incognito sauntering around the hall pretending to talk into my mobile. Lydia did likewise and when we neared each other we avoided contact and kept scanning the faces of the stallholders and their customers. We needed the mobile to be in a less crowded location.

We had prowled around every single stall by the time I heard Wyn's voice again. 'It's moved, boss. Now the system tells me it's in the Queen's Arcade.'

'How the hell did that happen?'

The Queen's Arcade was on the opposite side of The Hays and meant the user had at least a five-minute advantage on us.

'The triangulation can be unreliable, sir,' Wyn replied.

'Well get the bloody thing to work properly.'

I found Lydia and we sprinted over towards the entrance of the Queen's Arcade. Once inside I thrust the mobile to my ear as Wyn exclaimed, 'It's on the move again. It's going out into Queen Street.'

I motioned for Lydia to follow me in the direction of Queen Street. We bolted through the arcade and at the end I pushed open the doors and dashed out on to Queen Street almost colliding with a group of elderly women. I made stumbling apologies as they gave me bewildered looks. I heard Lydia mentioning we were busy and on police business. I stood in the middle of the pedestrian area and spoke to Wyn.

'There was a break in the signal, but it's restarted now. It's going towards the Kingsway.'

Buses used the area and my heart sank at the prospect the mobile and its user might conveniently find a bus leaving the city centre. 'Call operational support and find out what marked police vehicles are available in this immediate area. Keep this line open, Wyn.'

I was breathless and sweaty. A painful blister had developed in my right foot. I couldn't remember when I done this much exercise before. I reached the corner of Kingsway and Greyfriars Road where buses collect passengers in an area dominated by hotels and car parks.

I put my mobile to my ear again. 'Where's the signal now?'

Wyn hesitated.

'What the hell is wrong, Wyn? Do have a signal or not?'

'I thought it was on the Kingsway, but I've lost it... No... hang on... It's just reappeared.'

I gave Lydia a despairing look.

'Is it moving? I mean has it boarded one of the buses. There are dozens of them here.'

'I don't think so.'

'Check it again. We can't lose the signal.'

Wyn sounded excited when he replied. 'Got it. It's gone under the underpass. It shows the person walking up to City Hall.'

'City Hall. Now.' I yelled at Lydia and sprinted for the pedestrian underpass that led under Boulevard de Nantes.

When we emerged on the other side, I spoke to Wyn again.

He was calmer. 'It's passed City Hall and it's outside the National Museum.'

Lydia and I raced towards the museum.

'Where is it now?' I interrogated Wyn as we stood on the steps.

He sounded mystified. 'Inside, boss.'

Inside the grand Edwardian entrance hall I stood ignoring the inquisitive gaze of staff. To my right was a small shop and a counter selling coffee and tea and muffins and beyond it a staircase to the first floor and the exhibition areas. To my left was another staircase and ahead of me was the entrance to the cafeteria on the lower ground floor.

I called Wyn again. 'Do you have any data now on where the signal could be?'

'Sorry boss. It shows it as being in the building.'

The system had been unreliable before – could I depend on it giving us an accurate reading now? I didn't recognise anyone sitting by the tables near the counter, but I didn't know who I was looking for. I marched over to the shop and stared in – pointless, I know, but I was going through the motions.

I couldn't wait until the signal moved again. I couldn't close the National Museum of Wales in the hope of tracking the user. Why does anybody visit the National Museum of Wales? To see the exhibits and the fantastic paintings, but I wasn't going to jog through each exhibition room searching for a person with the mystery mobile. That would be a one-way ticket for a complaint to Superintendent Cornock and a severe dressing down.

I also came to the museum if I wanted to sit in solitude and think. In the café. So I ran over to the enormous glazed doors and pushed my way through and took the steps down to the basement level. Lydia was behind me. I took two steps and saw a familiar face. But not a face I was expecting to see that afternoon.

I turned to Lydia and whispered, 'I'm going to call the number.'

I fidgeted with my mobile and seconds later we heard another mobile rang.

I walked over to the table dropping my mobile on the surface. Judy Campbell looked up at me.

'Are you expecting a call?' I said.

Chapter 41

I told the sergeant at the custody suite to extend Judy Campbell the warmest of Wales Police Service's hospitality. I had reasonable grounds to suspect she had been in possession of an unlicensed firearm. And because she lied to me before and had given me the runaround when I wanted to interview her about Frank Armsby I wasn't going to give her any quarter.

I was back in my office sipping a cup of coffee, looking at the two mobiles we had recovered from Judy Campbell sitting on a tray on my desk.

'While you were booking Judy Campbell into custody,' Lydia said nodding her head at the mobile that had rung at the café of the National Museum, 'I had the tech guys check the phone for fingerprints.'

'Anything?'

'There were only two other numbers on that mobile. Both pay-as-you-go and unregistered.'

'And the other phone?' I asked.

'That's her regular mobile,' Wyn said. 'I was going to start work on that when you arrived.'

'I'm getting a warrant authorised so we can search her property. Once I'm back I want the results from her mobile. And then she can explain herself.'

'What are you expecting, boss?' Lydia said.

'Hopefully, the gun kept neatly in a bedside cabinet.' I stood up, my attempt at humour falling completely flat.

Less than half an hour later I was parking opposite Judy Campbell's apartment. I gathered my thoughts, pulling together all the loose threads. If Judy Campbell was working with somebody else, I needed to be careful and drawing attention to her by executing a search warrant might alert that other person. 'I'll go in first. Follow me in a couple of minutes.'

Lydia frowned but nodded.

I left the car and, as inconspicuously as possible, I

strolled over to the apartment. I let myself in and left the door on the latch. I donned a pair of latex gloves and found the kitchen. The cupboards had breakfast cereal packs, bags of teabags, jars of instant coffee and the usual selection of tinned food. After a few minutes I heard Lydia entering the flat and she stood in the doorway surveying the scene. 'Success?'

I shook my head. We finished a methodical search before moving through into the lounge. The TV and sound system looked reasonably new, as did the sofas. Framed photographs adorned the wall and I gave the shelving units a cursory examination by flicking through some of the books and rearranging the ornaments. But there was no gun.

Half a dozen men's shirts hung in the wardrobe of the bedroom. I stared at them and wondered who they belonged to. 'We'll need the CSIs to see if we can get any DNA evidence from these clothes.'

'Could be a boyfriend, or perhaps she likes to wear men's shirts,' Lydia said.

I made certain she didn't see me smiling to myself. I closed the wardrobe door. Lydia was rummaging through a bedside cabinet, having already opened and examined the drawers of cupboard. 'It looks... well, ordinary.'

I pulled the door closed and we hurried back to Queen Street.

'You were right, sir,' Wyn said. 'Jack Hughes owns an old Post Office van.'

The constable eased himself into one of the visitor chairs in my room. Lydia hovered around the threshold, an unfinished mug of coffee in her hand.

'I've been through the second mobile we recovered from Judy Campbell's possessions. One of her regular contacts is Jack Hughes who works at the charity DependAssist. They meet up regularly. The texts are a bit cold and formal and there's nothing to suggest they are an item.'

'Campbell must have met Hughes when she went for counselling,' Lydia said.

A darker scenario developed in my mind. 'Did Jack Hughes and Judy Campbell meet on the night Armsby was killed?'

Wyn looked puzzled. 'Let me check the CCTV footage from outside her flat.'

'We'll check Campbell's mobiles,' I said beckoning for Lydia to sit down.

I picked up the mobile used to contact Terry's acquaintance. 'Let's try this one.' I found my way to the messages section. 'There are a couple of texts that evening to one of the two numbers on it. All rather cryptic – *Are you there? All OK? Wont b long.*'

Lydia asked, 'And there's no name for the other user?'

'It was to the second of those pay-as-you-go numbers.'

Uncomfortable and heavy pieces of the inquiry jigsaw slotted into place. 'Do we have a photograph of Jack Hughes?'

Lydia stared over at me. Her silence was answer enough.

'We'll need all his personal details from his HR file.'

'I don't think we'll get much cooperation from Penny Larkham.'

'Call her and tell her we require all their personal records as part of the investigation. And tell her we need them today but don't say anything to suggest he's a suspect.' I scrambled to my feet. 'But in the meantime, let's have a look at the images from that video on Carey's laptop and the footage from outside Northam's apartment.'

When we reached Wyn's desk he turned and gave us a positive nod. 'I've found the footage from outside Campbell's apartment. I've spotted the red van.'

'Show me,' I said.

I leaned over Wyn's shoulder and glared at the monitor.

He clicked play. 'It was nine forty-five when the van comes into view on the road near her flat.' Wyn pointed at the screen. 'Here the vehicle stops, and you can see someone get inside.'

'Can you tell who it might be?'

'We'll need to get the tech guys to enhance the image.'

'Good work, Wyn. It looks like Campbell and Hughes have some explaining to do. Let's look at the footage from Carey's laptop.'

I lost patience with Wyn as he fumbled with the mouse. 'Get on with it, Wyn.' He mumbled apologies and eventually the sickening images from Carey's laptop emerged onto the screen.

'Does the figure on the bed look like Jack Hughes?'

Lydia frowned. 'Do you think he could be working with Judy Campbell?'

I continued to stare at the screen, willing myself to find some recognition between the prone, moaning body and the administrative assistant I had seen at the offices of DependAssist. 'Move on to the images from outside Northam's apartment.'

Wyn clicked open the footage and we watched in silence as the cleaner arrived and then departed.

'It could be Hughes,' Lydia said. 'But it could be a hundred other men. We can hardly identify him from that footage.'

'Dammit. See if you can get this footage enhanced.'

'The tech guys have done what they can.'

'Well tell them to do it again.' I stalked back to my room deciding we needed to talk to Judy Campbell. I returned to the Incident Room, notepad at the ready, gesturing for Lydia to follow me.

The custody sergeant had organised for Judy Campbell to be placed in an interview room with her solicitor. I was going to make this as brisk and as businesslike as possible. She would either cooperate or not.

Max Harris was a regular from one of the specialist criminal legal defence firms in Cardiff. Solid and dependable, he rarely interrupted unless I was seriously out of line and he always got good results for his clients.

'Good to see you, Max,' I said sitting down, placing the papers on the table. Lydia carefully positioned the laptop in front of her. Harris and Campbell gave it a wary look.

'Detective Inspector Marco.' It was said without any emotion – just a simple statement. He wouldn't want to give Judy Campbell the idea we knew each other well.

Once the opening formalities had been concluded and the machine was recording, I turned to look at Judy Campbell. 'Why do you have two mobile telephones?'

She didn't reply.

'One of the mobile telephones we recovered is connected to the sale of an illegal firearm. Do you know anything about that?'

She kept her eye contact direct. There was something unnerving in that.

'Can you tell me about the nature of your relationship with Jack Hughes?'

Now I watched the mist of uncertainty creep across her eyes, drifting over her face. She shifted uncomfortably in her chair. 'You do know who I mean? Jack Hughes who works at DependAssist.'

Most people's instinct is to reply to questions. All she had to do was tell the truth and she duly obliged. 'Yes, of course, I know Jack from the charity. They supported me at the time of my complaint against Frank Armsby and when the decision was made not to prosecute.'

'Now tell me – are you lovers?'

The hardness in her eyes returned. I circled around their relationship with a few more questions all of which she dodged or occasionally confirmed with a simple yes. What I really wanted to see from her reaction was what else she knew about Jack Hughes. 'We recovered a graphic and violent video from a laptop owned by Raymond Carey who was killed in his own home by a single gunshot.'

On cue Lydia opened the lid of the laptop.

I stared at Judy Campbell's face and her eyes and the curl of her lips. If she hadn't seen the video before she'd be disgusted and appalled, everyone would. But if she knew about the video, perhaps Jack Hughes had shared the details of his ordeal then she'd be detached, able to deal with the images. Lydia continued as I sat back. 'The video shows three men assaulting another man who is tied to a bed. I'll show you some of the footage where one of the men assaults the man on the bed. If Jack Hughes is the victim then the three men involved have committed serious criminal offences.'

Judy listened to Lydia's outline and rolled her eyes as though what Lydia was saying to her was completely pointless.

'We need your help to identify these three men.'

Lydia moved the laptop so that Campbell and Harris could view the footage. I studied her face and it told the story I thought it would. She knew about it, I was convinced. There wasn't the instant, undisguised abhorrence at the images, although we were watching the worst of human depravity. Harris's face registered the depth of his revulsion.

Once it was finished Lydia turned to Judy Campbell. 'Do you know the names of these men who assaulted Jack Hughes?'

Campbell gave a snide mean-lipped grin but said nothing.

I nodded at Lydia for her to open the laptop and once she had the footage on the screen I turned to Campbell. 'This is footage from outside your apartment block. Jack Hughes' vehicle stops and someone gets in. It's about an hour or so before Frank Armsby is killed. Is that you getting into his car?'

She stared at the images.
Really hard.
Then I saw fear in her eyes.

Chapter 42

'What did you make of that, boss?' Lydia said.

'She knew about that video.'

Lydia nodded. 'I agree.'

I pushed open the door to the Incident Room. 'We've got to arrest Jack Hughes before the custody time limits for holding Judy Campbell expire.'

'If you're right, boss, and he is involved with Campbell then he'll be spooked if he can't get hold of her.'

Wyn was on his feet as we reached his desk. He held up a sheet of paper. 'I've recovered the personnel file from DependAssist. It took a bit of wrangling. Larkham insisted on calling her lawyers before she'd release the information. I spoke to this solicitor with a plummy accent who told me I'd have to sign a receipt for all the documentation I removed.'

'Great work.'

I read the time on the clock screwed to the wall near the board. It reminded me again that if Judy Campbell were released, Hughes would be forewarned.

'I'm going to read these papers. In the meantime, I want you to check again the connection between Carey and Wyatt. There's something we've missed. That third man is a target. And call Plowman again.'

I left Wyn and Lydia focusing on the tasks I'd allocated.

Jack Hughes' curriculum vitae portrayed a peripatetic career moving from various admin roles, never staying with one employer more than a couple of years. He was in his late thirties, single, with no dependents and his next of kin was a Mrs Backhouse with an address in Barry. The regular appraisals concluded by the chief executive of the charity were a bland recording Hughes' lack of interest in professional development or advancing his career.

I noted a section that referred to his attendance record and any 'special health requirements'. After closing the file I turned my attention to identifying the third man from the video but something made me realise I had missed something of significance. Quickly I found the section with details of Hughes' regular medication for psoriasis.

I bellowed at Wyn and Lydia. Seconds later they appeared in my office. 'Hughes has psoriasis.' I tapped the papers on my desk. 'It's in his personal records.' They both gave me a baffled look.

'The man on the bed in the videos, for Christ sake, he's got blotches all over his arms – the tech guy pointed it out to us. Get the police surgeon to come in here and have a look at the video. Now.'

Wyn scrambled back to the Incident Room. Lydia announced. 'I've gone through everything we know about Carey and Wyatt and we can't link them at all. And Plowman still doesn't respond.'

'I suppose those sorts of men take precautions – they delete messages and hide their tracks.'

I got to my feet. 'What do we know about Plowman?'

'He was pretty cut up about Carey's death.'

'Very cut up – he sounded terrified, didn't he?'

'What are you thinking, boss?'

'He was upset, of course... but it was one hell of a reaction.'

Lydia frowned at me – I knew she could see where my mind was going. 'You don't think…?'

I marched out to the board as Wyn entered with one of the regular police surgeons. It diverted my attention from David Plowman, and it took Wyn only a few seconds to load the video. The surgeon curled up his lips in disgust as he watched the footage.

'I need to know if the blotches on that man's arms could be psoriasis.'

The surgeon nodded. 'Could be. There's no telling where psoriasis can break out on the skin. You can't identify that person?'

'You've been very helpful, doc.'

'Only too happy to assist. I happened to be at the

station. One of your guests knocked himself out on the cell toilet.'

I rolled my eyes as though it were an everyday occurrence. Once he'd left I stared at the picture of David Plowman at the bottom of the board under Raymond Carey's details. And then I looked at Jack Hughes' driving licence photograph. Are you the victim of this appalling abuse?

'We've got to arrest Hughes on suspicion of murder,' I said turning to face my team. 'And we need to find Plowman. I'm going to talk to the Super.'

Superintendent Cornock listened patiently as I outlined how I could justify issuing a warrant for the arrest of Jack Hughes. 'You better be right about this, John.'

'And I'll need an armed response team.'

'I agree. I'll get that organised immediately. You'd better prepare.'

I left Cornock pleased we'd made progress and hoping that if Plowman was going to be Hughes' final victim we'd be in good time to prevent a further death. Back in the Incident Room Wyn and Lydia were eating a sandwich each, both had a can of soft drink open on the desk in front of them. I wasn't hungry but I cracked open a can and took a mouthful of the sugary drink. 'Good work today. We've got a long night ahead of us.'

Chapter 43

Two uniformed officers in a marked police car followed us from Queen Street. Two more accompanied Wyn to Plowman's home. We met up with the armed response vehicle, a BMW 5 Series, at a prearranged point a little distance from Hughes' home. The radio crackled with confirmation they were ready. The marked police car led the way, lights flashing, siren blaring.

The ARV drew up outside a parade of shops, all closed apart from a takeaway pizza restaurant doing a thriving trade from the gaggle of youngsters dawdling outside. After leaving the BMW, one of the officers shouted at the group to disperse as his colleague reached for their weapons from the boot. Lydia and I left our vehicle and dragged on our protective clothing and hung back as the armed officers smashed the lock of a door next to the entrance of a newsagent. They galloped upstairs, Lydia and I following, listening to their shouted warnings.

Once the armed officers were satisfied the place was empty, they retreated down the stairs. We entered. The place stank of stale food and dirt and grime.

'This place is a shit hole,' Lydia announced as we moved from the kitchen into the lounge area. There were half-open takeaway pizza boxes, discarded bags of McDonald's and at least a dozen crushed tins of cheap lager.

'Let's get back to Queen Street.'

As we ran over to the car my mobile rang. I recognised Wyn's number.

'Better get over here, sir.'

The marked police car and the armed response vehicle pulled up ahead of us outside Plowman's property. Wyn stood outside with two uniformed officers. We joined him as the armed officers readied themselves, although I suspected they wouldn't be needed.

Wyn looked pale and drawn. 'He's inside – upstairs.'

Shock and disgust mixed in his voice.

Radios crackled around me and the lights from the police vehicles bounced off the windows of the surrounding houses. Groups of neighbours huddled on their driveways. I shared a heavy glance with Lydia. Fear gripped me.

Inside two armed officers stood in the landing clutching their automatic weapons – both nodded at the front bedroom simultaneously. I gathered my breath and entered.

I shouldn't have been shocked. It shouldn't have been a surprise. Even so, my stomach lurched at the sight of David Plowman naked and spreadeagled on the floor. The injuries were the same as I'd seen inflicted on Raymond Carey and Mark Wyatt. Long determined slashes by a sharp knife disfigured his lower abdomen and genitalia. A dirty rag been stuffed into his mouth and instead of a single bullet wound there were two, one in the centre of his forehead and another in the chest.

Lydia stood by my side, a look of horror on her face. 'This is... He is... We need to...'

I finished the last fragment for her. 'Let's get back to Queen Street and talk to Judy Campbell again.'

We passed Alvine Dix and two crimes investigators on the path leading out from the property.

'Get me a report as soon as you can, Alvine. He's in the front bedroom.'

'Same as before?' Alvine said.

I didn't bother replying.

A single thought dominated my mind – had I contacted Plowman he might be still alive. I should have protected him. If only I had made the connection sooner. I was feeling dizzy now – despair wrenching at my conscience. Down the street beyond the crime scene perimeter tape I saw the Caernarfon Castle pub. Light poured from the windows and I could sense the welcoming arms of that first pint of beer comforting me.

I started walking. I heard Lydia say something, but I

ignored her and continued.

I reached the door and without hesitating I went straight inside. A wall of warmth enveloped me like an old friend chiding me for an unwelcome absence. It drew me to the bar. My head was pounding – the images of David Plowman fresh and urgent. I ordered a pint of Brains and a whisky chaser and both appeared miraculously with little delay. My heart ached at the thought that Plowman had a family who would grieve. I reached over to the drinks but someone's hand intercepted mine. I turned and saw Lydia.

'This isn't a good idea.'

I couldn't see my face, but I knew I was grinning inanely. The voice of Dave Grohl singing the Foo Fighters' version of 'Times Like These' filled the bar. It made me think of Jim White.

'I wasted time on White. We should have...'

'You were perfectly justified in following that lead.'

I wanted to share Lydia's certainty.

I left my hand where it was, but she withdrew hers. I wanted so much to drink the beer. I didn't deserve to be a police officer – a man had died because of me.

'We did everything we could to contact Plowman,' said Lydia again, her voice soft and utter reasonableness. If only things were that simple.

I tightened my fingers around the glass: it chilled my fingertips.

'Don't, sir.' Now Lydia's voice was firm. 'Plowman could have contacted me. God knows I left enough messages.'

The whisky glistened in its glass.

Lydia leaned in towards me. 'Think about Jackie and Dean.'

I turned to face her.

'They need you.' She gave me a motherly look. 'We need to catch Hughes, boss.'

I glanced back at the pint on the bar and my throat

thickened. Lydia was right of course. But what harm could one mouthful do? I'd asked myself that before many times. A moment of realisation kicked in. One mouthful led to one drink that led to a second until I couldn't remember how many I had drunk. And then I'd be rolling out of the pub and arguing with the staff and anyone else daft enough to engage with me.

I backed away from the bar and I drew my hand over my mouth. It still felt gummy with saliva but alcohol wouldn't drive the guilt and remorse away. Catching Hughes might.

'Let's get back to Queen Street,' I said before turning and making for the door.

Wyn stood bolt upright when I entered the Incident Room. 'We need to stop this madman.' I made for the board gathering my thoughts. 'Contact the men you identified as possible targets again. Warn them to be really careful.'

Wyn's voice trembled slightly. 'Do you think Hughes could be after them?'

'Get it done and find another officer to help you if you have to. We don't have any time to waste. In the meantime, we're going to talk to Judy Campbell again. She may have information about other properties Jack Hughes may be using.'

I was angry enough to do some serious shouting at Judy Campbell. When we arrived at the custody sergeant's desk, I told them to get her into one of the interview rooms. I dismissed his suggestion that her solicitor be called. As he delegated for one of the officers to fetch Campbell he turned to face me. 'Do you think this is sensible?'

'Sensible?'

'Maybe we should be waiting until Judy Campbell's solicitor has arrived.'

'I need to know now where Jack Hughes might be. She's the only person who might know. Hughes could be carving up some other poor bastard right now. He's probably realised we've got Campbell and decided on some sort of fiendish killing spree.'

Lydia raised an eyebrow.

I barged into the interview room where Campbell had been taken as she stifled a yawn. 'What's this about?'

I didn't bother sitting down. 'Just tell me where the hell he is?'

She smirked and then sighed dismissively. Bad move – I leaned on the table staring down at her. 'We've been to David Plowman's place and I've seen your boyfriend's handiwork. He's going down for a long time and so are you.'

'You've got no idea.'

'I'm going to give you one opportunity to assist us with the inquiry. It's a take it or leave it situation, Judy. You help us now and I tell the Crown Prosecution Service you assisted. But if you don't then you're going to face so much shit you won't know where to turn.'

My urgent and frantic tone was giving her pleasure. I gripped the edge of the table. 'You're sick, fucking sick.'

'And you're part of a system that's flawed, evil. It doesn't deliver justice. It needs to be torn down from the top to the bottom. Completely changed. People like you, the prosecutors, the judges and everybody else involved in the system is corrupt and wicked.'

'Tell us where he is, Judy. And I promise you we'll make certain the prosecutor is aware of your cooperation.'

She sniggered as though my request was pathetic and my pleading contemptible. 'One last chance, Judy.'

Her mouth looked pinched; her jaw tight as she spat out the words. 'Fuck off.'

I stormed out of the interview room telling the custody sergeant to put her back into her cell.

I kicked the door of the Incident Room open in my temper. Superintendent Cornock was standing by the board staring at the photographs and the mass of information pinned to it.

'I've just been to see Judy Campbell, sir.'

'And?' The desperation in his voice mirrored my emotion precisely.

'I was hoping she'd cooperate and give us some idea where Hughes might be. But she laughed in my face.'

Wyn piped up. 'I've spoken with all of the twenty-six men on the list, sir. I've told all of them to be super careful.'

'Are any of them more likely to be targets than others?' Superintendent Cornock said. 'Is there a pattern?'

I moved round so that I could look at the image of Armsby and then Northam. 'Hughes has disposed of the three men who assaulted him.' It sounded shocking when it was said like this. 'Northam's case was dismissed by a judge in Bristol. Both of Armsby's cases were thrown out by a court here in South Wales.'

The noise around me lessened as I focused my attention on what we knew about Frank Armsby. Cornock said something, I'm certain, but I didn't hear it and Lydia raised her voice too. I heard my pulse beating in my neck.

Slowly I saw in sharp focus who might be the possible final victim. A judge had dismissed the charges against Armsby at his first trial and a jury acquitted him at his second. Judy Campbell's hatred of everything in the system must have been reflecting how Hughes felt. And he had access to the details of every victim Penny Larkham had counselled.

'What's the matter, John?' Cornock said.

I ignored the question reaching into my jacket pocket and finding my mobile. I thumbed through my contacts until I reached the number I needed. I pressed the mobile to my ear and listened to the call ringing, unanswered. It was exactly as I'd feared. I turned to Cornock and my team.

'Judge Patricks was the presiding judge at both of Armsby's trials. I've called his home – it doesn't answer. We need to get the armed response vehicle back there. Now.'

Chapter 44

Judge Patricks lived in Cyncoed, an affluent suburb of Cardiff, and I arrived in the street outside his detached home seconds before the armed response vehicle pulled up at the pavement. Two authorised firearms officers jumped out and repeated the procedure I had seen earlier, of opening the boot and reaching for their weapons.

I got out of my Mondeo with a nagging sense of foreboding dragging at my mind. The fact that the landline number to the house and the judge's mobile hadn't been answered set my nerves on edge. Perhaps the house phone had been left off the hook – perhaps Richard's mobile had run out of battery. Perhaps I was clutching at straws.

Lydia was standing beside me as the senior of the two officers checked in with Superintendent Cornock. If they had reason to suspect that life was threatened, they didn't need authority to use deadly force. Thankfully, the good people of Cyncoed were at home watching television or getting an early night. It was unnerving to see two armed police officers marching up the drive and approaching Judge Patricks' front door.

They hammered and shouted. No response.

I was tempted to jog round to the back door but protocols demanded both armed officers were in charge of entry to the property. When nobody appeared at the front door they rushed to the back. A patio of high quality slabs stretched the entire width of the rear and steps lead down onto a perfectly manicured lawn.

One of the officers shouted over to me. 'Door is open. We're going in.'

He pushed the door open with his left foot and shouted a warning, pointing the automatic rifle ahead of him. They swept through the darkness of the ground floor shouting as they checked each room.

Both officers stamped upstairs, their boots echoing around the stairwell. I followed them, Lydia behind me. I was beginning to think Judge Patricks and his wife were away on holiday. I could live with the embarrassment, just. Someone clicked on the lights and by the time we reached the landing a soft glow lit the space. The officers took a room each and shouted a warning as they entered with their weapons held high. At the far end of one of the corridors I heard a shout. 'In here, Inspector.'

My mind sagged. I'd seen enough blood and gore in this investigation. And facing the possibility that Richard Patricks or his wife were lying pinned to the bed or the floor was too sickening to contemplate.

I rushed down towards the door and inside saw both officers kneeling over a woman. Her hair was smeared in blood, but she let out a brief moan and my knees wanted to give way underneath me. I turned to Lydia. 'Call an ambulance.'

'Mrs Patricks. I'm Detective Inspector John Marco. Do you know where your husband is?'

She struggled with the help of the officers to get to her feet and sat on the edge of the bed. She gave me a helpless look. 'Somebody broke in.'

'Did you see who it was?'

She gave me a blank look.

'Was it a man or woman?'

She croaked a reply. 'A man... But I didn't see his face.'

'We'll get you some water before the ambulance arrives.'

'Where is Richard?'

'How is Mrs Patricks?' It was the first thing Superintendent Cornock asked when he entered the Incident Room.

Lydia replied 'The paramedics who attended didn't think she was badly injured. They've taken her to the hospital for a check-up. She'll probably be kept in overnight.'

'And the CSIs are going to the house now,' I added.

'Let's hope they find some fingerprints. And the judge had a CCTV camera tucked away out of sight covering the front and rear so we're hoping to recover the footage.'

'Where the hell has he taken Judge Patricks?'

I had thought of nothing else on the journey back to Queen Street.

'What do we know about Hughes?' Cornock said.

'He's worked in various admin jobs for the past dozen or so years. Single, lives in a rented flat in Thornhill. The name of a sister was mentioned as the next of kin on the human resources file from DependAssist. We'll need to talk to her.'

'I'll put the armed response unit on standby. Don't take any chances, John.'

As Superintendent Cornock breezed out of the Incident Room I recognised Alvine Dix calling my mobile. 'I've sent you some footage from the judge's house you need to look at.'

The line went dead.

I hurried to my office, clicking into my computer. It took an interminable time to come to life and even more for me to click through into my inbox until I found the footage she had sent me.

I moved the monitor so that Lydia and Wyn could view it at the same time. We watched in silence and in horror as the old Post Office van reversed up the drive towards the rear of Judge Patricks' home. Hughes hadn't bargained on the concealed CCTV cameras recording his every movement. He left the van and, after forcing the back door, went inside. Moments later he pulled and yanked at Richard Patricks, forcing him out of the property, his hands bound, a balaclava over his face. He pushed the judge against the panels of the vehicle before yanking open the rear doors. He bundled Richard inside, slammed the rear closed and drove away into the night.

'I want an alert for that van circulated force-wide and

The Cardiff Lockdown Murders

get officers to help you interrogate the ANPR system. It's less than an hour since he's taken Patricks. We need to find him.' I turned to Lydia. 'Let's go and talk to Hughes' sister.'

Once we'd parked outside the terraced property in Barry I glanced at the dashboard clock. It was almost ten-thirty pm. Judge Patricks had been missing for an hour and a half and the possibility Hughes had done his worst had spun a tight knot of bile in my stomach. Lydia reached for the door handle. 'Let's hope somebody's in.'

We trotted over the road and hammered on the door. We heard the television and then a light illuminated the hallway, flooding through the small glass panels in the door. Warrant cards at the ready, I didn't care what Hughes' sister would make of us. I wanted to know whether she had any idea where he might be keeping Richard Patricks. A broad chested man in his forties wearing a tight T-shirt opened the door, a woman lurked behind him at the threshold of one of the rooms.

'Detective Inspector John Marco and Detective Sergeant Lydia Flint.' I gave the man enough time to scan our warrant cards before I pushed my way in.

'What the fuck?'

Lydia closed the front door behind us. 'Now listen to me.' Despite his toned shoulders and bulging muscles, the man cowered. 'I need your help. And I don't want any crap.' I turned to look at the woman standing a few feet away. 'Are you Jane Backhouse – Jack Hughes' sister?'

She nodded confirmation. 'What's he done?'

'Your brother is suspected of being involved in several murders.'

Her eyes opened wide and she struggled for breath, leaning back against the door frame. Her husband or partner or boyfriend, I wasn't certain, and didn't care, helped her into the sitting room and she sat on the sofa.

'We know Jack has been responsible for abducting a

judge this evening from his home in Cyncoed.'

'Are you certain?' Jane snorted. The man sitting by her side opened his mouth to say something, but I cut in.

'We've got him on CCTV. No question at all. And we are pretty sure he has murdered five other people. So if you want to help your brother I need to know if you have any idea where he might be.'

Jane gave a helpless sort of look. 'I don't know... I mean, we're not that close.'

'Do you know if he has any property? Somewhere out of the way – maybe a workshop.'

Jane shook her head again. It was the man by her side who piped up. 'He talked to me a while ago about helping out in the arcade I run. He was after some Saturday work. Over the winter we do maintenance mostly.'

I got to my feet. 'Get your keys – you're coming with me.'

Chapter 45

Backhouse led us down onto Barry Island. The shops and cafés were all closed. A car full of youngsters, music blaring, drove passed us as we parked, and two late-night walkers made their way towards the promenade overlooking the wide beach. The last time I had been here was for coffee and cake and a stroll on the sand. Now I was here for something very different.

A salty wind blew up off the sea and cut through the warmth of my jacket. Backhouse stood outside a small, shuttered arcade. 'I rent these three units. I don't think he'd be able to get access.'

The shutters over the front were still securely fastened with padlocks and I took a step back and gazed up at the buildings. Then I crossed the road and stood opposite, calling Wyn. I had to know whether he had uncovered more details about Hughes.

'We've spoken to someone who knew him at his last employment, boss,' Wyn said. 'He said that something happened to Jack Hughes before he started working for DependAssist. He became very odd, withdrawn, cut himself off from friends.'

'Did he know where Hughes might be going?'

'Apparently he liked to walk the footpaths of the Gower peninsular. He rented a cottage there are couple of times.'

'Bloody hell, that's the last thing we need. Contact holiday letting agencies in the area.'

'At this time of night?'

My concept of time had evaporated completely. Wyn wouldn't be able to get any information until the morning – I had to hope that that wouldn't be too late.

I crossed the road and rejoined Lydia and Backhouse.

'There's a rear entrance, boss,' Lydia said.

'Show me.'

'Do you think we should get the firearms officers down here?'

I paused for a moment, wondering how long it would take them to reach Barry. I needed to follow protocols, but I needed to prevent another death even more.

'I'll call it in, but in the meantime we'll do what we can.'

My conversation with Superintendent Cornock was brief. His reply equally terse. 'I'll deploy the ARV immediately.'

Backhouse led us to the rear of the building and down a few steps until it opened out onto a gravelled area. In a corner were a collection of wheelie bins. In the distance I could hear train movements and I guessed the last service was arriving or leaving from Barry Island railway station. Backhouse had already reached one of the rear doors, keys in hand, but he looked shocked when he realised he wouldn't be needing them. He pulled at the unlocked door and we stared in.

I turned to Backhouse. 'You need to stay here.'

He nodded his understanding.

I switched on the torch that I'd brought with me from the Mondeo and illuminated the passageway ahead of us. I could see a staircase that doglegged to the left and up to the first floor. I gently pushed open a door to my right and the light danced around the contents. Massive floor-to-ceiling shelving units were crammed with boxes of toys and trinkets but there was no sign of human activity.

I retreated and nodded soundlessly for Lydia to open the door behind her. She did so silently, and her torch illuminated another stock cupboard that led into a small kitchen and toilet, the smell from both overpowering. I put a hand to my mouth hoping I wouldn't gag.

We took the stairs and entered a makeshift office. There was a computer and two screens as well as shelves screwed to the wall with lever arch files all neatly arranged in alphabetical order. We were at the same level as the pavement and beyond the shutters would be the Mondeo and the street. Several large glass display cabinets held dozens and dozens of different sized teddy bears and push penny machines. Rows of one-armed bandits stood to attention criss-crossing the room. I could imagine the place a wall of noise and activity in the height of summer but now it was deadly quiet.

We crossed over into the second part of the building and the sound of movement drew my attention. I turned to Lydia raising a finger to my lips as a gesture for her to be silent. She stuck her head out hoping it would help her to listen more effectively. But there was silence, and I wondered if my mind were playing tricks.

After a few seconds we moved again, threading our way through the slot machines and arcade games. I picked up my pace as I saw a door in the far corner. I guessed it led down to the basement area. I eased down the handle and opened the door slowly, pulling it towards me, but it creaked in protest so I stopped. I could sense Lydia stiffening as the door would have warned anybody downstairs. When I heard movement below, I knew we had been detected.

I yanked open the door and bounded down the stairs. But I was too late, the rear door flapped open uselessly and, stepping outside, I saw the lifeless body of Backhouse. I rushed over and searched for a pulse, and he groaned. Satisfied he was alive I darted back inside. Lydia was already on the telephone requesting an ambulance and trying to untie Richard Patricks at the same time. He looked up at me, relief and anger on his face. 'Thank Christ you've found me. Did you catch him?'

'Lydia will take care of you.'

I ran back to the front of the shops and then sprinted towards Harbour Road and, in the distance, I watched Hughes, arms flailing, heading for Barry. I wasn't going to let him evade capture for a second longer than I needed to, so I ran.

Instead of heading directly down Harbour Road he cut

left, skirting the Athletic Cricket Club ground and then on to a car park that edged onto Barry Harbour. I couldn't see the van, so I dismissed the idea he might be returning to it. Perhaps he had moved it after manhandling Richard Patricks into the building. If he was going to make an escape in his van, the armed response team would soon stop him.

Hughes didn't stop at any of the parked vehicles and accelerated diagonally across the car park towards the footpath that led along the side of a spit of land that created the harbour area. He dropped out of sight for a while until I saw his running figure again. Eventually his route would bring him back into the main section of Barry Island from where he'd started. So I couldn't work out what he was doing. I pressed on, my heart pounding against my ribs.

Ahead, a small breakwater fingered its way over the sand at the mouth of the harbour. I was gaining on him but when the path turned left he had disappeared. I couldn't see him anywhere. He wasn't on the breakwater, so I scanned my surroundings frantically. Then I spotted him scrambling down the rocks towards the sand.

I set off in pursuit.

By the time I landed on the sand he had reached the end of the breakwater.

I shouted a warning, but it had no effect and he picked up his pace. Clear of the breakwater, I noticed the tide was far out and luckily the sand was firm underfoot.

Hughes slowed and got caught up in a section of softer sand. I cursed when the same thing happened to me, but I changed direction and ran to my right. It worked, and I found myself accelerating and making ground on Hughes, who had reached the opposite side of the harbour. He glanced over at me and as he did so he stumbled, momentarily losing his balance. And, more importantly, I gained on him. He ran over towards a concrete slipway and then up for the Knap and the houses surrounding the old swimming pool area and the Marine Lake.

By now I was closing on Hughes.

Soon enough I'd catch this bastard.

I ignored the possibility he was carrying a gun and that I really should call the armed response vehicle.

He ran along the edge of the Marine Lake but he tripped and stumbled again. I was getting closer and closer. Hughes was tiring, casting glances over his shoulder.

He slowed again, blowing out painful lungfuls of breath. When I was near enough almost to reach out I hurled myself towards him and we both fell headlong into the Marine Lake. The water was shallow but he coughed and spluttered his surprise. I dragged him onto the path. I took a couple of seconds to catch my breath. Then I turned to the prone figure. 'Jack Hughes, I'm arresting you on suspicion of murder, you do not have to say anything but anything you do say...'

Chapter 46

I stood in the sitting room of the Backhouse family home with Lydia. It was late, very late. Only adrenaline kept us from falling over. Mr Backhouse nursed a large lump on the back of his head and dented pride. His wife looked stunned, her eyes unable to focus on anything and I promised to see if we could organise a family liaison officer to speak to them in the morning. En route back to Cardiff Lydia and I checked with the hospital, which confirmed Richard Patricks was sleeping soundly.

Superintendent Cornock insisted on speaking to me after Hughes was processed and it meant a debrief in the Incident Room until the early hours. I got back to my flat, and although my mind was still fully engaged my body ached. I lay down on the bed fully clothed, deciding I needed a moment before I could summon the energy to undress. Three hours later I woke with a start and, after discarding my clothes in a pile on the floor, crawled under the duvet.

I arrived at Hughes' flat early the following morning. Two marked police cars were parked near the parade of shops and two uniformed officers stood outside the entrance. I noticed Lydia parking near a scientific support vehicle and I waited until she joined me.

'Did you sleep much last night, boss?' Lydia said.

'Not much. What about you?'

'So-so, I suppose.'

I carded both uniformed officers and entered Hughes' apartment where we found Alvine Dix and her team taking the place apart.

'Detective Inspector Marco.' Alvine announced in an upbeat tone. 'You'll be pleased to hear we've discovered a hazmat suit secreted in the bottom drawer of one of his cupboards. I'm willing to bet the fragment we recovered from the home of Raymond Carey comes from this suit.'

'Excellent. Anything else?'

'Give us time.'

The Cardiff Lockdown Murders

Lydia and I took in the surroundings more carefully than we had the previous evening. There was detritus everywhere. In the kitchen, in the bedroom, in the bathroom. He lived a slovenly, pathetic lifestyle. Would Hughes actually admit he was the man tied to the bed in the footage we recovered? A half-decent lawyer would advise him to confess, using the repeated and violent assault he'd experienced as mitigation. He'd still face a life sentence in prison but if he cooperated the recommended minimum term might be reduced.

We left the flat and returned to Queen Street. We had an interview to conduct.

A dozen pieces of A4 paper with different headings, bullet points and notes scribbled on them were spread over my desk. Lydia and Wyn sat in the visitor chairs, each having contributed regularly to the interview plan with Jack Hughes. A full search hadn't turned up the gun. I had 'firearm' printed in large letters on a single sheet. I moved it around as I tried to determine how best to introduce it.

I read the report from the CSI team confirming Hughes' van had been recently cleaned, really deep cleaned.

I sounded exasperated. 'It's totally out of character for his van to be pristine. The flat where he lives is like a pigsty.'

'There's bound to be evidence Judge Patricks had been inside.'

'I know, I know, but it would have been good to have the final piece of evidence confirming he killed Frank Armsby.'

Lydia sounded reassuring as she tapped on the sheet of paper with 'fingerprints' written in capital letters. 'The material fragment recovered in Carey's home from the hazmat suit belonging to Hughes and his fingerprints in the store cupboard at Northam's apartment building are going to be conclusive evidence he was responsible for both deaths.

And I guess once the tech guys have been able to put together an analysis of Hughes' build and gait and then compare it to the man seen leaving Northam's apartment building he's not going to have a hope in hell of avoiding a charge of murder.'

I nodded. But I wanted an admission, something I could take to the Crown Prosecution Service' that meant Hughes would be facing a long prison sentence. I could wait, of course, until all the forensic analyses had been completed and in the meantime there'd be no question of releasing Hughes – there was enough evidence to charge him with an assault on Mrs Patricks, the abduction of Judge Patricks and possibly even attempted murder.

A strategy formed in my mind. I didn't need to try and trap Hughes, I concluded.

I needed to get him to confess.

I was ready by the end of the morning. I distilled the chaotic notes into a few simple bullet points. I visited the bathroom before leaving for the Incident Room and filled the wash basin with hot water and doused my face, drawing a damp hand through my hair. There were bags under my eyes, my skin grey and tired. I was going to sleep for a week after this was finished.

Lydia and I made our way down to the custody suite.

'His lawyer's arrived,' the custody sergeant announced when he saw us.

Once I had organised the tapes and all the paperwork had been completed, I turned to Lydia.

'Ready?'

She nodded and we headed down the passageway towards the interview room.

Michael Vance was another of the regular solicitors we saw at Queen Street: a flashy dresser with a liking for loud pinstripe suits and severely cutaway collars. That morning he had a tie with burgundy stripes. I introduced Lydia and he nodded an acknowledgement.

The Cardiff Lockdown Murders

We sat down. Hughes wore one of Queen Street's standard, all-white one-piece suits. The crime scene investigators would be doing a microscopic examination of all his clothes.

I noticed for the first time how young Hughes looked – his skin wrinkle-free and healthy. There was wariness in his eyes. I organised the tapes into the machine and once the bleeping sound finished, we were ready to start. It gave me a valuable few seconds to gather my thoughts and look into Hughes' face. I didn't want to forget he was a killer.

'It must have been terrible,' I said. 'I cannot imagine the ordeal you suffered.'

The frowns on the faces of both men opposite gave me the satisfied feeling that I had wrong-footed them from the outset. I didn't want to be kind to Hughes but it suited me fine if he thought I was. I continued in the same vein. 'We know Raymond Carey and Mark Wyatt and David Plowman were vicious and predatory. I'm sure the more we dig into their backgrounds the more we shall unearth about their unsavoury characters. They've probably assaulted other men.'

Ingratiating myself with Hughes appeared to be working, as he mellowed slowly like an ice cube melting on a cool work surface.

'Did you seek counselling after the assaults?'

I could tell Hughes wanted to shake his head and engage with me but something held him back.

'It can't have been easy knowing they had filmed you. It must have been enough to turn your stomach.'

I fidgeted with the papers in front of me, giving myself a little time and allowing Hughes to absorb the last few statements. Then I produced the photographs of Carey, Wyatt and Plowman, pushing them over at Hughes. I lowered my voice slightly and leaned over the table. 'We know that these men were responsible for assaulting you in the most despicable, evil way.'

I could see the revulsion on his face mixed with exhilaration. The three men wouldn't be assaulting him ever again, or anybody else for that matter.

'They...'

I didn't respond, Hughes had more to tell me. I had to wheedle it out of him very slowly.

'Which one of them did you meet first? Was it Raymond Carey, the bank manager?'

The brief look of surprise on his face told me I was wrong. I retreated slightly. 'But we know about Wyatt's stretch in prison. And I've spoken with the detective who investigated him several years ago. Wyatt was a foul individual.'

Relief filled Hughes' face, as though my statement came as welcome confirmation of everything he knew. I continued in the same vein. 'And Plowman was in it with Carey.'

Lydia took her hand off the laptop on the table in front of her waiting for some invisible cue to open it and show the footage. But I wasn't ready for that just yet.

'Jack, I understand that you suffer from psoriasis.'

He frowned.

'The official photographer from Southern Division took photographs of your back last night.' I produced half a dozen printed images that I pushed over the table, replacing the photographs of the three dead men.

'I'm sure you know why I had these taken. And I don't want to cause you any more distress but we recovered footage from Raymond Carey's laptop that shows a vicious assault by three men on another man. We believe that man was you. The man flat on the bed has patches of psoriasis over his arms and shoulders. They are identical to these images of you.'

I paused for a few seconds. I looked over at Vance giving him a subtle warning. 'I want to play the footage and then I'd like you to confirm whether it was you that the three men were assaulting.'

Lydia flipped open the laptop. I kept direct eye contact with Jack Hughes. His nostrils flared and he held a hand to his jaw that trembled slightly.

'No,' Hughes said.

Lydia paused as she was booting up the laptop.

We waited for Hughes to continue.

'I don't want to see it.'

'Is it you?'

He nodded briskly and he squeezed his eyes shut as though it would help him blank out the memory.

'I still need you to look at a still image from the footage. I want you to confirm it was you for the purpose of this interview.'

Lydia organised to show him a single frame. He stared at it for a few seconds before looking away. 'That's me.'

'Did you complain to the police about the assault on you?'

He laughed in my face. 'Complaining about a bank manager and a journalist! You must be joking.'

I turned to the second stage of my plan.

'Now tell me about Judy Campbell.' I tried my best to sound like Hughes' favourite uncle.

He must have expected me to bang the table and demand a confession from him. 'I've read the CPS file and I've reviewed all the evidence.' The tape recording wouldn't register my fleeting smile that suggested her case should not have been abandoned. 'She had regular counselling with Penny Larkham. Presumably she shared with you the details of the appalling assault by Frank Armsby.'

He opened his mouth to say something but thought the better of it.

'Do you have a close relationship with Judy?' I maintained my avuncular tone.

He blinked briskly. 'We had so much in common. The system let us both down. And everybody's conspiring against ordinary people like us. Frank Armsby and Judge Patricks and the police. Nobody looks out for us. We never get justice.'

'Did killing Raymond Carey give you justice?'

Hughes' lips twitched slightly, and he dragged a hand over his mouth, but I noticed the grin developing behind it.

'Carey was surprised when he saw me.' Now he sounded smug. 'It was easy once I was inside the house.' He leaned forward. 'I wanted him to suffer. I wanted him to experience the pain he caused me.'

'Did Judy help?'

'We both did it. We both made certain justice was delivered.'

Answering my questions meant the difficult part of the interview was over. Hughes explained how he and Campbell had overpowered and mutilated and then killed Wyatt and, finally, on his own, Plowman. Lydia made the occasional contribution. Everything about Hughes sickened me. I sensed Lydia's abhorrence too. Vance said little, but his skin had lost its florid colour. Hughes' relationship with Judy Campbell developed into a mutually-fuelled paranoia that led them to justify their killings.

After I outlined everything we knew about Northam, I asked, 'Why did you kill him?'

'I told her about Northam.' Pride filled Hughes' voice. 'He was a predator who lived a lie. He deserved to die for what he did to those women. And it sickened me when a judge released him – dismissed the charges against him.'

Finally, I asked about Armsby. 'We have footage of you collecting Judy from outside her home on the night before he was killed.'

Hughes answered simply. 'He was a monster.'

From what I had learned about Armsby I knew Hughes was right.

'We've recovered your van and it's been cleaned.'

It was a statement, but Hughes answered the implied

question. 'That was Judy's idea.'

'Did you run him over after Judy had agreed to meet him outside the builders' merchant?'

'Yes, she told me everything. All about what he had done to her and the other women she knew about.'

I paused when he finished the last sentence.

Despite everything that had happened to him and to Judy Campbell they were murderers. They deserved to be locked up for a long time. He even confessed to buying the gun and throwing it into Barry docks once he'd killed Plowman. By the end of the interview I had looked into the face of a man driven to the depths of evil. I was glad it was over, glad he wouldn't walk the streets for a long, long time.

Chapter 47

The October half term school break soon arrived. I had booked three days holiday to take Dean to stay with my parents in their caravan in Tenby. On Saturday I walked the Cardiff Bay Barrage with Alison, eating cake and drinking coffee lazily in the cafés of the Bay. We spent Sunday afternoon making love before enjoying a long shower where I could run my hands over her naked shoulders and around her perfect breasts.

The paperwork needed to complete the file for the Crown Prosecution Service had been finished in good time and after the holiday there'd been meetings with the senior Crown prosecutor responsible for the case. Judy Campbell and Jack Hughes would be pleading guilty and a judge would impose long prison sentences with minimum terms, ensuring they'd be middle-aged on release. I had promised myself I would switch off that weekend with Alison and that I would try and relax for the few days I was to spend with my parents.

I collected Dean from Jackie's house early Monday morning. She was brusque, avoided eye contact, and Dean's bag and clothes were already waiting in the hallway. Our conversation was perfunctory and after loading the car I left with Dean for the journey to Tenby. It was only after the M4 motorway ended and we'd passed the junction for Andrew Northam's country pile, that I felt the vestiges of the investigation loosening and floating away like an early morning mist.

That evening Mamma made one of her special chicken cacciatore stews Dean loved so much. The following morning, we all set out for a long walk before a generous lunch and a stroll through the town. Kicking a ball around the beach wasn't quite the same wearing an autumn jacket and feeling the chill of the wind against your face. But Dean loved it, as did Papà. Mamma had been unusually reticent, and it was teatime on Tuesday by the time she broached the subject of Jackie. Papà had diplomatically taken Dean to buy ice cream and she had orchestrated for me to help her with the evening meal. 'What happened with you and Jackie?'

It was one of Mamma's clever open questions. I often thought she would make a great detective – most mothers would. Did she know about Alison?

She didn't wait for me to answer and continued with, 'I thought you and Jackie were... getting on better.'

'There's too much history... I don't know if it would ever work again, properly, I mean.'

She gave me an intense look. 'I only want what is best for you and Dean. I always liked Jackie, John. And I don't think—'

'I know I didn't treat her as well as I should have done.' It surprised me I'd actually admitted that to my mother. 'I don't want to make the same mistake with Jackie again.'

'I don't want her to be hurt.'

'Of course.'

Papà and Dean arriving back brought the conversation to a natural conclusion. I had been scolded; I had made an admission of my own failings to my mother. Now we could both move on.

During our stay I slept a lot, watched too many animated films with Dean, and cheered Cardiff City as Papà and I enjoyed reruns of some of their old games.

On the last evening I sat with Papà on the wooden decking outside the caravan as Mamma organised pizzas with Dean. Papà was making good progress through a six pack of Peroni, and he had bought me some of the alcohol-free versions. I didn't particularly like them – they reminded me of the past, but I drank a couple to keep him company. We sat in our windproof jackets, their collars pulled up against the autumn chill blowing off the sea.

'That big case finished?' Papà said.

'Yes, thank God.'

'I don't know how you relax, how you switch off.'

I waved a hand in the air. 'All this helps.'

We talked about nothing in particular – family, the ice cream business, the old café in Pontypridd and it felt good to be chewing the fat with him. My mother's pizzas were terrific, I don't remember having anything like Dean's appetite as a boy. The following morning, I drove back to Cardiff, rested and pleased that Dean and my parents had enjoyed their time together.

Chapter 48

On the morning Jack Hughes and Judy Campbell were due to be sentenced several weeks later I chose my best suit – it had been dry-cleaned especially – and paired it with a white shirt and sombre striped tie. I had even visited the barber in anticipation of the hearing. I arrived at Queen Street promptly, taking the stairs to my office at a normal, sedate pace. The board in the Incident Room had recently been dismantled. It always amazed me how much work was needed after a suspect had been charged.

Although we had confessions from Hughes and Campbell we had to get all the paperwork in perfect order. It was what Cornock expected, it was what Assistant Chief Constable Neary expected, as well as the CPS lawyers and the barristers who would present the case. Lydia was sitting by a desk, as formally attired as I was.

'Morning, boss,' Lydia said. 'Big day today.'

'Certainly is.'

I drifted over to my office deciding to kill time before the court appearance by watching the interview with Judy Campbell again. I clicked through to my computer and found the footage and Lydia must have heard my voice and the preliminary exchanges with Campbell because she came through into my room and sat down. We watched in silence as Campbell's initial antagonistic attitude turned to aggression and then anger and eventually defeat. Challenged about her fingerprints in Carey's house left her open-mouthed. By the end she was sobbing.

'It's amazing how two people can feed off each other and turn themselves into something they couldn't be on their own,' Lydia said.

I stood up and grabbed my coat before turning to Lydia. 'Let's go.'

Queen Street bustled with shoppers, mostly masked, and we took a right passed the Sherman Theatre and then over Boulevard de Nantes towards the Crown Court building. A couple of gardeners were attending to the winter maintenance routine at Gorsedd Gardens. The coffee stall that served fantastic espresso was shuttered and closed.

A crowd of journalists and three television crews were gathered outside the entrance, shivering in the cold. They gave us a preliminary interested look, trying to decide if we were worthy of their attention and interest. They ignored us and got back to gossiping.

In the porch I pushed open the double doors into the warmth of the hallway. Once we were through security we found court room one but there was no sign of the Crown prosecution lawyers so we threaded our way through the passageways to the rooms reserved for police.

Inside, the Crown prosecutor waved at me to join him. As I approached I overhead him and the prosecuting barrister talking about cars. He'd recently bought a BMW 5 Series and the barrister boasted about his Mercedes SUV. It made me think I should have worked harder at school.

'This was a most difficult case for you,' said the barrister. He had a loud rich voice. 'I think you've done exceptionally well.'

'Thank you.'

The conversation didn't have the edge of lawyers preparing for a trial. There wasn't going to be any cross-examination, nobody was going to challenge me or the evidence we had assembled. The early guilty pleas Hughes and Campbell had entered had given them maximum credit for the sentencing exercise the judge was going to undertake that morning.

'There's a lot of press outside,' Lydia said.

The Crown prosecutor nodded. 'They've been hounding us for details about the case, requesting interviews with senior officers.'

'It wouldn't surprise me,' I added. 'There are lots of victims. More than enough material for some juicy headlines.'

'I understand Superintendent Cornock was quite rude to a couple of them.'

The barrister announced. 'We'd better get to court. We don't want to keep the judge waiting.'

We retraced our steps and the lawyers led the way into the main court building, its air-conditioning system humming quietly in the background. The barrister adjusted his wig and hauled his gown onto his shoulders, exchanging small talk with his colleagues representing Judy Campbell and Jack Hughes.

Choreography was important. The judge entered. We got to our feet and once the judge was seated, we all sat down. Then Campbell and Hughes were brought up from the cells underneath the court. It took most of the morning for the prosecuting barrister to outline the case referring to all the evidence assembled.

The judge nodded and occasionally interrupted. She had read all the papers in advance in any event. Judge Patricks had shared with me at one of our regular meetings complimentary comments about the judge – suggesting she'd be suitably tough. He'd even proposed, half-jokingly, that he be appointed the presiding judge. He had a golden tan when I'd seen him – a month's holiday in the Seychelles had done wonders for his recuperation.

The journalists filling the press section scribbled frantically and there was even a court reporter drawing a likeness of Campbell and Hughes sitting alongside the security guards in the dock.

As the judge nodded for the defending barristers to address her in mitigation, I noticed Margaret Fabrien slipping into the court and sitting down in one of the benches at the rear. By the time Hughes' barrister had finished we had heard all about the appalling assaults he had endured and the mental torture and anguish he had suffered. It almost made me want to reach for a handkerchief and dab away a tear of sympathy. Campbell's lawyer didn't do as good a job.

She came across as unsympathetic and uncompromising, although Campbell's character references painted a glowing picture of her as an engaged aunt to several nieces and a valued member of the staff at her place of work.

I read the time. The judge would probably take time to ponder the sentences over lunch. But as Campbell's lawyer sat down the judge turned to the dock issuing an instruction. 'Stand up.'

Both security guards stood up in tandem with Hughes and Campbell. The judge wasted no time.

'There is only one sentence I can pass and that is life imprisonment for both of you. I have considered carefully the salient factors I need to consider in imposing a minimum term. In doing so I have listened to the eloquent mitigation provided by your learned counsel. However, I cannot ignore the cold-blooded, heartless nature of your crimes. I impose a minimum term of twenty-five years for each of you.'

The judge waved a hand towards the dock. 'Take them down.'

Then she stood up and we did the same. Once the judge had left, conversation erupted around us.

The prosecuting barrister dragged off his wig and thanked me and Lydia again. The Crown prosecutor nodded his agreement. I left the court room and a journalist I knew whispered conspiratorially, 'Can you give me the inside track on the story, John?'

'You'll have to talk to the PR department.'

Lydia joined me as I was scanning the crowded hallway looking for Margaret and, eventually, I saw her talking to Superintendent Cornock. I joined them.

'Congratulations, John.' Margaret sounded positive. 'It is a very good result. And you were right all along.'

'But you were right too – about two killers, I mean.'

Cornock cut in. 'That was an excellent result. And the Justice for All website has been taken down and Larkham is going to be more circumspect in the future – apparently

ACC Neary spoke to her.'

A reprimand from the ACC would be enough to justify a long holiday on an isolated Scottish island so I didn't envy Larkham.

Margaret left to catch her train back to London, although she was going to detour to the National Museum first. Cornock drifted away to talk to the Crown prosecutor. Wyn came over to join Lydia and me.

'Great result, boss,' Wyn said.

'You both did well.'

They beamed.

I read the time. 'Let me buy you both lunch.'

We left the Crown Court building. It wasn't raining nor too cold.

My mobile buzzed with a message from Superintendent Cornock telling me he had some new case to discuss. I didn't reply; it could wait, so I switched my phone off and joined Lydia and Wyn and we walked into town.

Printed in Dunstable, United Kingdom